Saving

Book 4

Chloe Chadwick

Meg M. Robinson

Also By The Author

Dedication

To my family, who has been nothing but supportive of me and helps me to keep pushing myself.

Chapter 1

The January air was crisp, bordering on biting, as Chloe followed Sheriff Adams out to his cruiser, running to catch up with him. She was the newest deputy in the Salus Sheriff's Department, which brought the number of deputies up to a grand total of two. Since Salus wasn't a crime-ridden island, that was more than enough, or had been before Chloe had arrived. Once she'd stepped foot on the island a few months ago, things had gotten a little crazy. Murders, plots, forced amnesia…Life in a town populated by supernatural people was never dull.

She looked at Wesley as she buckled in. He was a bear of a man. Quite literally, actually, since he was a grizzly shifter. His build matched, as he was several inches above six feet and well-muscled, almost stocky. His short black hair was covered by his sheriff's hat, but his pale gray eyes and neatly trimmed beard were visible. She smiled, just looking at him. He was handsome, extremely handsome, but in a rugged way that she appreciated. Which was a good thing, since she'd started dating him just a few weeks before. The boss thing made it tricky, but it was working so far.

"What's the call?" she asked him as he pulled out of the parking lot.

"Drunk shifter causing trouble at On the Rocks," he told her, referring to the single bar on the island. "He's had a few too many and is threatening customers."

Drunk already? It was barely past five. Not really unheard of, but still not a great sign. "Who and what is he?" she asked, knowing that shifters could range from the harmless—deer or birds, for example—to the extremely dangerous. Such as Wesley's grizzly bear, or the saber-tooth cat that one of the councilors could turn into.

His lips quirked upward. "Name's Patrick, and he's a lion."

"Well...crap." Definitely on the danger scale, though she felt some excitement, too. She was still meeting different supernaturals, and this would be her first lion. Still, it would be better all-around if he didn't shift. "A bear can take a lion...right?" she asked with a frown as she pulled to mind his animal form. He was large, but lions had to be called king of the jungle for a reason.

"Generally, yeah, but I'm hoping we don't see a single patch of fur in the bar." He flicked a glance at her. "That's going to be your job."

Anticipation and nervousness tangled in her belly. Her powers as an aether elemental weren't often involve in their calls, so while not a first, it was still new enough to give her jitters. "I've never tried that with a pissed off shifter."

"No, but you did manage it, several times, with me. You can do this, Chloe."

She blew out a breath and hoped he was right. Then again, dating or not, if she failed and he got mauled by a lion, she'd never hear the end of it.

Why did she like dating a man who ribbed her, again? Oh, right. Because she gave as good as she got, it was fun, and it was never mean or serious.

When they reached the bar, they jumped out of the car and moved quickly to the front door. Unlike him, she wasn't dressed in the tan uniform—she'd refused—but wore a pair of black jeans, a heather gray shirt, and a thick, dark gray coat.

Where he was dark and rugged, she was bright and feminine. Her blonde hair was light and a mass of curls she'd fought into a ponytail that morning. Her skin was tanned, which only enhanced the blue of her teal eyes, which she considered her best feature. She was almost a foot shorter than him at five seven, with a slimmer, though still athletic, build. Which meant she could keep up with his longer stride with only a little effort.

To Chloe's surprise, there wasn't a crowd outside, though there were a number of cars in the parking lot. The building was soundproofed, so they didn't hear a peep until they opened the door. A roar spilled out, along with an anxious murmur of noise and an angry yell from the bartender, Anastasia.

"The sheriff's on his way, Patrick! You better knock this shit off!"

It took Chloe's eyes a moment to adjust to the darker interior, but she still saw the barstool go flying at Anastasia's head. Fortunately, as a vampire, Ana's reflexes were good enough for her to dodge the stool, though it took out a shelf of bottles behind her. Ana bared her fangs, close to losing her temper on the lion. "Dammit, Patrick! This isn't funny!"

The lion in question was an inch or two under six feet with a solid build. His skin was darkly tanned, which made his light brown hair seem paler than it likely was. It was impossible for her to tell what color his eyes normally were, as they were currently the orange-brown of his lion. A sure sign his beast was close to the surface.

He definitely wasn't going to let them cuff him peacefully.

"Keep him human," Wesley murmured to Chloe before he started toward Patrick. "Hey!" he called, keeping his voice even. "What's the problem here?"

Unwilling to see Wesley slashed by a drunk lion, Chloe focused on her power. As an aether elemental, she had the ability to not only sense magic, but to control it to an extent.

She searched through the magical signatures of the room—every one of the two dozen people in the building were supernatural in some way—until she located what had to be Patrick. Magically, shifters felt like their animals would if physically touched, so Patrick felt like anger and coarse fur against her skin. She dimly heard Wesley talking to the inebriated shifter but kept her focus on the magic. Even the sight of the bar faded, her awareness replaced by all the power in the room.

She reached out to gently sip at Patrick's power, trying to keep it from building to the point where he would spontaneously shift. Strong emotions could trigger all sorts of things in supernaturals, as she knew from firsthand experience. And, since she was still getting used to using her power on the fly, she wanted to be ready without acting too soon and setting him off.

Patrick wasn't content to simply yell at the sheriff and let out another roar as he lunged. His power surged as he tried to shift mid-leap, and Chloe stopped sipping and yanked hard. It was effective, but not as effective as she'd hoped. He remained in human form but was able to grow claws. Frantically, she pulled harder, but couldn't tell if she managed it before those claws sliced into Wesley. Nor could she take the time or focus to check, not without losing some of her control over Patrick's power and risking even more injury. Wesley might be one of the toughest people on the island, and healers were fantastic at their job, but some things could be fatal before a healer could be reached.

She grit her teeth, hating that she had to stand there, feeling useless even though she knew she was making it easier for Wesley. But the fight—which lasted less than a minute—felt like it took hours. Fortunately, Wesley got Patrick facedown on the floor, arms cuffed behind him, before Chloe reached the point where she was overloaded with power. Since all the cuffs carried by members of the sheriff's department were enchanted to prevent magic use, the moment the cuffs were on, she released her grip on Patrick's magic. Her own power resisted, wanting more, but she shut it down and breathed a sigh of relief. Fortunately, she'd been able to stop before all that power within her needed to be expelled, whether she wanted it to or not.

"Did he get you?" she asked, approaching and finally taking a good look around the room. Most of the customers were at the far side of the room. Two were injured, one sporting a bloody nose and lip, while the other was holding her head. Probably more flying furniture, Chloe guessed.

"Not bad," Wesley told her as he got to his feet and hauled Patrick upright. The sleeve of his left arm was ripped and there was some blood, but it didn't look like enough to worry about. She worried anyway. "Check to make sure no one's seriously hurt while I get him in the cruiser." Patrick snarled and squirmed, but Wesley had a good grip on him and managed to get him out of the bar.

She blew out a breath and turned back to the crowd. "Is anyone seriously hurt?" she called, pitching her voice to carry over the angry murmurs. They dulled for a moment before she saw shaking heads. Relieved, she pulled out a notepad and voice recorder, then started taking statements. Wesley joined her after a few minutes and they split the remaining customers.

All in all, only the two she saw had sustained any injuries, though Patrick had shoved half a dozen more and pissed off the entire bar. Not to mention all the property damage he'd caused. The liquor bottles he'd broken had probably cost a month's pay alone, so Anastasia was all too happy to press charges. "I've chalked his attitude up to bad days in the past, but for him to actually attack people? It's not okay," she told Chloe, angry enough her eyes were black. Literally black, not just dilated enough to appear black. Chloe caught herself staring for just a moment before she shook herself and resumed making notes. One day she'd adjust to the various eye changes supernaturals went through.

There wasn't much more to say. Ana was going to close the bar for the rest of the night to clean up and asked them to tell Patrick he was banned from On the Rocks until he straightened up his act. That was not only understandable, but probably wise, so Chloe promised to pass it on.

Once everyone had been spoken to, and the two injured parties were driven to the hospital by friends, they left. To Chloe's relief, Patrick had passed out while they'd been inside, and was pleasantly quiet as they drove back to the sheriff's office.

"How bad did he get you?" she asked, looking Wesley over as well as she could. His clothes were rumpled from the fight, but other than the one cut, she didn't see any injuries.

He grinned at her. "Worried about me, Boo-Boo?"

"I don't want a new boss before I finish getting you trained, Yogi," she shot back, though she had to keep a smile off her face.

"Nah, won't happen. No one else is crazy enough to take my job. But I'm really okay. Little scratch, but it's not deep." Before she could insist he show her, he lifted his left arm and turned it, so she could see the two relatively small slashes in the fabric. There were two cuts to the skin beneath, but even from the passenger seat she could see they really weren't too bad. His shifter healing would probably take care of that in an hour. "You did good, by the way. Told you that you had it."

"It's different when I don't know exactly when it's coming," she admitted before twisting to look at the unconscious lion. "He do this often?"

"Not like this, no," Wesley answered with a shake of his head. "He'll get drunk now and again, but he usually doesn't escalate to violence. He's going to be pissed when we tell him he's not allowed back in On the Rocks, but it might do him some good."

"Especially since there aren't any other bars on the island."

"Mmhmm. And drinking alone in your house isn't the same."

"Think it'll do any good?"

He glanced at Patrick in the rearview mirror, sighed. "Can only hope, but I wouldn't put money on it."

Back at the office, Wesley woke Patrick up then ushered him inside and into a cell before he'd truly regained consciousness. To Chloe's surprise and relief, he passed out again almost instantly after hitting the cot. Not that she was able to focus on him much, since a half-grown gray wolf had noticed her entrance and rushed her with enough force that he almost knocked her down.

"Oh, I know," Chloe murmured, dropping to one knee so she could rub her hands through his fur. "I need to get you trained so you can come with me, don't I?" she crooned. He wasn't a pet, and certainly hadn't been a planned addition to her home, but weeks ago her familiar—a crow named Mavros—had found the pup injured in the woods, and he'd adopted her as much as she'd adopted him. And since she'd taken on the role of deputy, Wesley was insistent Lykos be trained for police work. A bear's nose was superior to any canine's, but as Wesley had pointed out, he couldn't always be with her. Lykos would also be an added layer of protection, which she definitely needed. In the months since she'd been on Salus, she'd been in three separate altercations where she'd literally been fighting for her life. It seemed to happen every couple of weeks, almost like clockwork.

It was starting to piss her off.

"You really do," Wesley agreed, giving Lykos a scratch behind one ear before he walked to his desk. "Why don't you get started on that while I take care of the report?"

Chloe arched a brow. "You're willingly taking on

paperwork and letting me off the hook? Who are you and what have you done with Wesley?"

"But see, this will save me paperwork in the long run. You get him trained up, you're less likely to get hurt. The less you get hurt, the fewer forms I have to fill out."

"Gee, you're such a thoughtful guy." But it made sense, and working with Lykos was infinitely more fun than paperwork. Sure, the wolf was young, and wanted to play more than work, but he was smart, too. He had sit, lay, down, and fetch down pat. Stay, on the other hand, was a lot more trouble, and they needed to get the basic commands figured out before they added in the training specific for a K-9 animal.

He also had a great deal more energy than Chloe did, so when Wesley told her to head on home, she was all too happy to listen.

"I'd ask if you're sure, but this guy is exhausting." She checked her watch. "And it gives me time to run home and freshen up before I head to Phillip's for dinner."

Wesley leaned back in his chair. "How's that going? Does it feel real yet?"

Chloe walked over to his desk and leaned against the edge, right by his keyboard. "Not really. I mean, yes, it's good that I've got family. I don't feel alone anymore. But to go from having literally no family after Granny died to having a half-brother and cousins? One of which is my best friend? It's…weird." Which was putting it mildly. Her mother had died when she was a baby and she'd never known her father. Other than her grandmother, she'd had no known family, and she'd lost her grandmother a few months before. A month ago, her best friend, Lexi, had confessed to being her cousin, and weeks ago, the vet she'd taken Lykos to had admitted that he was her half-brother. It had been a lot of revelations.

"Just weird? I thought you loved having Lexi as a cousin.

I mean, yeah, she can be exhausting, but she's all heart."

"No, it's good, too," she admitted, "it's just a lot of adjustment. I haven't exactly gotten a lot of time to process."

"You do like to get involved in all the trouble on the island," he drawled.

"Hey!" she said indignantly, bumping her knee against his leg. "You know it's not my fault."

"Maybe not your fault, but you still end up in the middle of everything. You're a magnet for trouble."

"And yet you still made me your deputy."

He shrugged. "You are handy to have around, though. And it makes it easier to keep an eye on you."

"Just so long as dating me isn't for the same reason," she grumbled, folding her arms over her chest.

For a long moment he just arched a brow and considered her. Then, moving more quickly than a man his size should be able to, he grabbed her. She let out a soft sound of surprise when he yanked her into his lap and kissed her hard. When surprise gave way to need, he gentled the kiss. When she went soft against his chest, he deepened it. Only when she was breathless did he finally end it with one final, light press of his lips against hers. "Never," he told her, voice quiet but firm, "think I'm dating you for any reason other than I want to be with you. I can't always figure out why since you're going to make my hair go gray, but I do."

"I don't know," she told him, realizing her voice was soft and breathy, but not caring. "If doubting gets me kissed like that, I might have to wonder a dozen times a day."

His chest rumbled against hers as he chuckled. "Pain in my ass," he said affectionately. "Go have dinner with your brother. I need to cool off and finish my paperwork."

She grinned. "Maybe you'll get lucky and Patrick will wake up," she teased as she slid off his lap and walked back to her desk, slipping on her coat and hat before slinging her messenger bag over her shoulder.

"Hopefully that won't happen until tomorrow," he said, sending a dark look toward the cell. "And remember, tomorrow's your day off. Barring an emergency, you're not allowed in the office."

"Such a strict boss." But she had forgotten. She'd been too focused on learning to do her job properly. "Maybe I'll hang out with Lexi and we'll get into some trouble together." His answering groan had her laughing as she opened the door for Lykos and followed him outside.

Chapter 2

After stopping briefly by her house, she drove to Phillip's. It was no surprise to Chloe when she saw Mavros perched on the edge of her brother's roof. He occasionally spent the day doing whatever crows did rather than hanging out with her, but he rarely missed an opportunity for food. And, since he was emotionally linked to her, he knew where she was going to be.

She grinned as she got out of the car and let Lykos jump out after her. "Freeloader," she called to the crow, who didn't take offense, but flew down to his favorite perch on her shoulder. He butted his head against her cheek before dropping from her shoulder to land on Lykos's back. The wolf let out a happy yip and spun in a circle, nearly dislodging Mavros. Since it was a game they played often, the crow simply spread his wings for balance and did his best to stay on the wolf's back.

Chloe only shook her head, amused at their antics, and walked to the front door. The moment she reached for the doorbell she hesitated. Brother or not, she had only spoken to Phillip a handful of times. It would have been different if they'd grown up together. Maybe it would be different if she'd even known he existed for the first twenty-seven years of her life. But no, he'd been kept from her, just as the identity of the father they shared had been. It was still being kept from her because, she was told, it would be 'dangerous' for her to know who he was. As far as she was concerned that was total bullshit, but her brother hadn't spoken a word, and the only contact she'd ever had with her father had been in dreams. Literally, she'd met him while she was sleeping, as he had said it was the only safe way they could communicate.

She forced down the anger that tried to build, but it had also dispelled her nerves and allowed her to ring the doorbell. Sensing her shift in mood, Mavros abandoned playtime with his friend to settle on her shoulder once more. Though Lykos had no such connection, he raced over and leaned against her legs. Buoyed by their support, she smiled and stroked her fingers over the crow's chest before she ruffled the fur between the wolf's ears.

Phillip opened the door, a smile on his face. Something in her own expression made it falter slightly. "Is everything okay?"

Chloe pasted a smile on her face. "Long day."

"Ah. Yes, I imagine police work could be very trying," he said with a nod as he motioned for her to come inside.

"Paperwork is a bitch." Once she stepped inside, Lykos briefly abandoned her to greet Phillip. She couldn't blame him. Her brother had been the one to heal the wolf when she'd found him with two broken legs. And she did like her brother, even if she didn't know him well. The fact that Phillip hunkered down to rub the wolf's belly contributed to that. She couldn't trust a person who didn't like animals. Especially her animals.

"That is one thing we both have in common," he said, the smile returning. "Would you like a glass of wine or a beer?"

"Beer. I'm not feeling domesticated enough for wine at the moment."

He laughed and nodded. "Beer it is, and I think I'll join

you." He disappeared into the kitchen, raising his voice to carry out to her. "You've got good timing. Dinner will be ready in about five minutes. Just enough time for you to vent about work if you want."

She settled on the couch, Lykos curling up on her feet. Mavros settled on a perch that hadn't been here the last time Chloe visited. It was a branch, stripped of bark, and attached to a heavy base. Part of her softened, knowing Phillip had picked it up just for her familiar. "Not really anything specific to vent about. Had to arrest a drunk shifter at the bar and deal with paperwork, but just…" She shrugged. "Long day," she repeated.

"Was the shifter that much of a problem?" he asked, offering her one of the beers before he sat down.

"Not really. I kept him from shifting—mostly—and Wesley did all the hard work. I'm just…" She sighed and took a sip of her beer. "I'm trying to find my normal. It's not easy."

"No, I don't imagine it is," he murmured. "You've been through a lot the past few months. I hope I haven't made it worse."

Habit almost had her assuring him that no, he hadn't, but she wasn't going to lie to him. Especially not in this. "A little," she admitted. His face went carefully blank so she continued. "Having a brother? That's not a bad thing. I'm honestly thrilled to have a brother. But it's something else new, something else I have to adjust to. And knowing that you know who our dad is, but won't tell me?" She smiled, but without humor. "I don't know if you've noticed, but I'm kind of a nosy person. And there's entirely too much about my own family that I'm ignorant on, and it's almost unbearable."

Phillip sighed and ran his hand through his hair. "If it weren't dangerous for you to know, I'd happily tell you, Chloe. But I just found you. I don't want to lose you, especially not this soon."

"And why is it so much more dangerous for me to know than you? And before you say telepathy, both our minds can be read."

"First, I've had a lot of experience blocking mind reading, so no, both our minds can't be read," he told her gently. "Second, there's less reason for my mind to be read than yours. I think you were told that they're looking for someone fitting a description, right?" When she nodded, he said, "Well, they're looking for a woman. I'm not only a man, but I'm new in town, and it's not known that we're family. So my mind is relatively safe."

"Those are both fair points," she admitted reluctantly. "I don't have to like it that you're right, though, so don't gloat."

"I wouldn't dream of it," he told her sincerely, though one corner of his mouth tipped up slightly. "I know this is hard for you. I can't imagine how I'd feel if I were in your situation. But I promise, he's trying to take care of the threat against you. He wants to know you, but he'd rather never meet you than be the cause of your death."

She'd gotten the same vibe off him, and he had been helping her when he could. Always in dreams, but help was help. She sighed. "He seems like a good guy, even if he's always cryptic," she said, unable to keep the wistful note out of her voice.

"He is. But you know, I'm not a bad guy either."

She laughed. "I know you're not. But that's about all I know about you."

"Yes, I suppose we haven't had that much time to really get to know one another." Something buzzed in the other the other room. "We can remedy that over dinner, though," he promised as he got up to pull food out of the oven.

She stood, and though Lykos cracked an eye open, he opted to remain where he was. Mavros let out a soft caw but he, too, stayed put. "Why a veterinarian?"

"Well, I can heal, obviously," he said as he began transferring food from a casserole dish to plates. "Most healers tend to go for helping humans, but I've always liked animals, sometimes more than people. I've also always been able to sense what they were feeling." He smiled. "Since it led you to me, I think it was the right decision. What about you? Why a private investigator?"

"Part of it is that I'm nosy," she admitted as she sat at the table. "I like knowing things. More than that, I like figuring them out. I never figured on moving into law enforcement, though."

"Why did you?" he asked, carrying the plates to the table.

It was some sort of chicken casserole, with cheese, peppers, and what looked like tortillas. She took a testing bite and found it had a pleasant heat to it and an even better flavor. "This is good," she told him. "And it was a combination of things. First being that there isn't really all that much call for private investigators on Salus. Second, I do still need a job, and Wesley offered one." She paused a moment, then decided to give him the last, and possibly most important reason. "I also ended up getting involved in so much here on Salus that it seemed stupid not to make it official. If nothing else, it means I have more resources available, and a better knowledge and understanding of the island and the people on it. Plus, I'll be getting paid for being involved."

"I had heard you'd gotten into some trouble, but he didn't go into too much depth."

"Well, it wasn't pretty. A man was murdered the night after I got into town and his body was found behind my house. Then my grandmother's best friend was killed. Some of the town thought I was responsible. Turned out the vampire councilor, Kyra, had been...I don't know...mind controlled into killing them, and then attacking me."

The shock and anger on his face eased a little of her

resentment. "A vampire attacked you? Don't take this the wrong way, but how did you survive?"

"Mavros," she said, smiling toward the crow, just barely visible from where she sat. "He distracted her at a critical moment. Then…well, I'm not sure what happened after," she admitted. "There was a light that seemed to hurt her and knocked her out until help could arrive."

He didn't say anything about the light, just looked toward the living room, where the crow remained on the perch. "I'm glad he did. I love that crow a little more now."

"Oh, until that point, I'd thought he was stalking me. That he was either a shifter or a spy for a witch or something," she told him, grinning at the memory.

Phillip chuckled. "A familiar-to-be was a much better option. What else? Or was it just that and the amnesia cases?"

"Man. The amnesia…Salus isn't having good luck with councilors," she muttered, shaking her head. "I still can't believe Daphne was involved," she said, remembering how she'd completely misjudged the elemental councilor. "But no, there was one other thing. Someone stole Hypnos's Opium Horn and used it to put the entire island to sleep." There was more, but it involved Lexi. Her cousin had earned Chloe's loyalty and trust. While Chloe hoped Phillip would do the same, he wasn't there yet.

"Ah, and you being an aether elemental helped keep you awake?" he guessed.

"Yep. I woke Wesley and that asshole Diego, and we managed to get everyone else woken up." Thinking of that meant she had to think of the man she'd killed. The only time she'd taken a life. It was something that still weighed heavily on her, and it must have shown.

"That sounds like a good thing, so why do you look so sad?" Phillip asked slowly.

She gave him a sorrowful smile. "Because I killed

someone. He was trying to kill me, so it was self-defense, and an accident to boot, but…" She trailed off and shrugged helplessly. "I still killed someone, Phillip."

"Oh, Chloe. I'm so sorry." He rose and moved around the table, pulling her out of her chair so he could wrap her in a hug. It was the first time he'd done so, and she felt tears prick her eyes as she held onto him. "Taking a life is never easy," he murmured. "I have no doubt it was your only option. And if it was a choice between you and someone who would do something so…heinous…then I'm glad it was him."

She pressed her face against his shoulder, savoring the contact, even as part of her wished it was their father. "Thanks, Phillip. I'm mostly okay with it. It just hits me, now and again."

"I get it. But it also says something about you, that you'd do that to yourself for the residents of Salus. Most of whom I'm sure you've never met."

She hadn't thought about it quite like that, and it helped. She'd taken that on so they didn't die or lose all hope. And when she put it into that perspective, she was more okay with it. Slowly, she drew back and smiled. "Thanks," she told him again, relieved no tears had fallen.

"I know we're not close. We can't be since we don't know each other well, but I am here, anytime you need anything," he promised as he retook his seat.

"I think I knew that, even before I knew you were my brother. I did leave Lykos with you."

"You did, though I might have refused if I'd known what you were attempting."

She rolled her eyes. "You and Wesley are both so overprotective."

He arched a brow. "Your boss is overprotective?"

Sensing a chance to rib him a little, she kept her expression neutral. "Well, yeah. I mean, most guys are protective of women they're dating."

To her delight, he didn't just roll with it, but sputtered. "Dating? You're dating your boss?"

She grinned impishly and nodded. "I am. But hey, he has saved my life," she pointed out.

"You're dating him because he saved your life?" he asked, his voice increasing in volume.

Laughing, delighted with his reaction, she shook her head. "No, that's not why I'm dating him. I'm dating him because I like him, a lot. Saving my life is just a reason why I can trust him."

That settled him a little. "Being able to trust him is good," he said slowly. "I take it you've never been married?"

"Nope. Had a couple boyfriends, of course, but no one serious enough to tie myself to. What about you?"

"I was engaged once, but it didn't work out."

His voice was so flat she didn't pry, though she was definitely curious. There was a story behind that, but she wasn't yet comfortable enough with him to poke at open wounds. "I'm sorry. Sometimes people suck."

"That they do."

They kept the rest of the conversation to tamer subjects. Education, places they'd lived, even favorite colors. Surprisingly, they both preferred blue. After dinner was done, they moved to the living room and continued the conversation. Since Chloe didn't have to work the next day, she stayed later than she'd intended. By that point, Lykos was out cold, and Phillip had to carry him to her car. Even Mavros was content to ride on her shoulder, dozing.

"We'll do this again sometime soon, right?" Phillip asked before she joined Lykos in the car.

Unable to resist teasing him, she said, "Maybe we could have dinner with Wesley. You two should get to know each other soon, I think."

A wicked gleam shone in his eyes. "I'd love to get to know

him. I've never gotten to play the overprotective big brother before."

She groaned. "On one hand, that sounds absolutely embarrassing. On the other, seeing you try to interrogate a six-foot-four bear shifter could be hilarious."

"Guess you'll just have to take the chance to find out, won't you?" he asked cheerfully.

"Ass," she said, but she was smiling.

"Ahh, I'm already fitting into the role then. Good. Now drive safe."

"I will," she promised, sliding into the car and heading home. She was almost to her house when she realized she'd let go of some of her anger at him for keeping the identity of their father a secret.

Chapter 3

C hloe slept in, which for her meant she got an extra half hour, but it left her feeling well-rested, physically and mentally. Lounging in bed wasn't an option, though, not with Lykos tugging at the covers and whining.

"Why can't one of you have thumbs?" she grumbled good-naturedly as she slid out of bed. She was followed downstairs by both crow and wolf, and the moment she opened the back door, they shot outside. Leaving the door cracked for them, she put coffee on and went upstairs to grab a quick shower and change. When she came back down, they were playing outside, so she enjoyed her first cup of coffee before getting them breakfast.

They decided to stay at the house while she ran out to see some friends, but only after they'd gotten love lavished on them both. It was something all three of them enjoyed, which meant she was smiling as she drove to the diner.

Joel's wasn't quite empty, but it was definitely past the breakfast rush, which Chloe was grateful for. She was more grateful to see Lexi—her best friend and cousin—behind the counter. "Hey, Lex," she called as she slid onto an empty seat near the end. It wasn't exactly her usual spot, but she did like being off to the side so she could have a chance for conversation with Lexi.

"Morning!" Lexi replied cheerfully. But then, the brunette was almost always happy. Happy and pretty, both inside and out. She was a few inches taller than Chloe, with a willowy build. Bright blue eyes seemed to actually sparkle, her mood was always so light. Her dark hair was pulled back into a ponytail at work, which suited her 'uniform' of jeans and a polo shirt, but Chloe knew Lexi much preferred to dress in fun clothes—especially if they were snug, cute, and maybe a little revealing. "You want your usual?" she asked as she immediately started to make Chloe's caramel coffee.

"Yup. Fed the critters, but I couldn't deal with a bagel for breakfast again," she admitted.

Lexi grinned and set the coffee down before scribbling down Chloe's usual breakfast order to give to the cook. "How can a woman as smart as you not be able to cook more than grilled cheese?"

"I've tried, believe me. And Granny tried to teach me. I follow the directions, but things just end up going a little...wonky."

"And by wonky you mean...?" Lexi prompted.

"Generally? Completely inedible," Chloe admitted. "Sometimes just extremely unappealing."

Lexi was obviously fighting against laughter as she shook her head. "That's sad, Chloe. Just...sad."

Since she agreed, Chloe could only sigh. "Yeah, yeah. I know."

"Maybe I should teach you to cook."

"That won't happen anytime soon and wouldn't do any good, trust me. But if you want to talk about bettering ourselves, maybe you should come to the gym with me," she suggested. She missed running with someone, but the offer wasn't just about wanting a workout or running partner. Lexi was a very social, very likable person who was single, and not really by choice. Oh, she dated, but it never worked out. However, a few weeks ago, she'd seen the way her cousin had looked at Garrett, the owner of the gym. She'd also seen how Garrett had looked at Lexi. Playing matchmaker wasn't normal for her, but it couldn't hurt to just ensure those two got a little more time to see if they clicked, right? She wasn't really shoving them together, and if there wasn't any heat there, no harm done…she hoped.

"The gym?" Lexi asked, wrinkling her nose adorably. "You want me to get sweaty?"

"You do realize a lot of guys go to the gym to work out, right?" Chloe responded, grinning when Lexi's expression turned thoughtful. She definitely knew her best friend.

"They do, don't they?" Lexi murmured. "I suppose I could maybe give it a try. Once." She paused, then wrinkled her nose again. "But not today. I'm working a double. What about tomorrow? I've only got the morning shift, so I won't be exhausted before we even make it to the gym."

"Tomorrow works. Gives me time to take care of a few things I've been putting off." And she was pleased enough that, after she'd eaten, she added a big tip before she left. Lexi came across as nothing but a horny party girl to people who didn't know her, but she was so much more than that. She was an amazing woman and even better friend. One who would do anything to help the people she cared about. She was smart, funny, and fiercely protective of her friends and family. But it was even more than that.

To almost everyone on Salus, she was a waitress and psychic who was a medium. Chloe was one of the few who was aware that her cousin was actually a witch—though she could indeed speak to the dead—and she was also the protector of Pandora's Box. While it was normally safe enough, Chloe knew it was something that constantly dwelled in the back of Lexi's mind. So, if Chloe could lighten that load a little by playing matchmaker, she was happy to do it.

But for now, she wanted to spend some time with

another good friend, and one who also had a lot on his plate. She pulled in front of the bookstore, happy to see it was quiet for now. Happier still when she found only Zane inside, dealing with something on the computer. His dark hair was mussed, and he looked a little frazzled. He was tall, with a lanky build, but he fit the definition of an adorable geek. He was also one of the smartest people on the island, possibly due to the fact that he'd read most of the books that had passed through his store.

"There's the newest elemental councilor," she said brightly as she walked up to the counter.

He groaned and dropped his head to the counter, nudging his glasses askew. "Don't remind me."

"Can it really be that bad?" she asked, ruffling his hair affectionately.

He shifted his head so he could look up at her. "You know, better than anyone, the track record of councilors on this island lately. Not to mention...I'm not a politician. I'm just a guy who likes books."

"Which makes you well-educated, and not being a politician means you know what people like you and I need," she pointed out. "It might not be easy, but I think you can do this." She smiled and softened her voice. "Zane, you know this is an elected position. You weren't the only elemental up for the job, but from what I hear, you really did win by a landslide."

"Well, yeah, but—"

"But nothing," she interrupted with a shake of her head. "You're well-liked and people trust you to make the right call for all the elementals on the island. You're not going to let us get screwed over, whether as a group or individually. And if there's a problem—and we both know there will be— you'll be a help in figuring it out."

He lifted his head, giving her an uncertain look. "You really believe that?"

She smiled. "Come on, you know I wouldn't bullshit you. Yes, I really believe that. Will you be perfect? Of course not. No one is. But I know you're not going to try to kill me like Kyra did, or wipe memories like Daphne, so you're already so far ahead of your predecessor it isn't funny. Besides, you have to believe it at least a little or you would have refused the position."

Smiling weakly, he straightened. "Good point. Okay, I'll do my best."

"Great. Now, what do you know about the new vampire councilor?"

"Natalia?" He tried to straighten his hair and shrugged. "Not much, really. Nice enough woman, I guess, especially for a lawyer."

"A lawyer? Well, great," she said, wrinkling her nose. She wasn't a huge fan of lawyers. They were a necessary evil, but they also tended to confuse things, often unnecessarily. "I wish Francois hadn't backed out."

He chuckled. "All he wants to do is cook. I heard that he said he backed out because he thinks the best way to take care of the island is to cook for them."

"I can't argue with that." She fondly remembered the food at Banquet, the restaurant Francois owned. It was the nicest restaurant on the island and served several types of cuisine. "He could've won easily by bribing people with his chocolate cake, though," she said on a sigh.

"Ah, but if he'd won, he wouldn't have as much time to bake that cake," he pointed out, frustration replaced by amusement.

"Good point. Okay, no, I love Natalia the lawyer now. She saved the taste buds of Salus."

"I'm sure she'll be very relieved. Did you need anything, though? A book, more practice with anything?"

She smiled fondly at him. He was the one who'd taught her to use her powers, though his element was air where hers was aether. His manifested in an entirely different way than hers, but he'd known the theory behind aether powers, which had been more than good enough to get her started. "I'm good with the practicing for now. All the catastrophes have given me more practice than I need for a bit, especially with absorbing magic. Books though? Always. This time…do you have any language dictionaries?"

He blinked in surprise. "Are you trying to learn a language or translate one? Because dictionaries aren't the best way to learn new languages. They could help with filling in some blanks, but there's more to a language than just knowing the words. There's—"

Knowing he could easily slide into lecture mode, she cut him off. "Translate, for now. Granny had a lot of stuff, and not all of it is in English."

"Ahh. Yeah, I can help you with that." He moved out from behind the counter and toward the row of shelves dedicated to linguistics. "What languages do you need?"

"I'm not exactly sure," she admitted. "One I'm pretty sure is Latin. Another looks like it might be Italian?"

He searched for a moment and pulled two books off the shelf and offered them to her. "If it turns out not to be Italian, just bring it back and we'll find the right language."

"Thanks." They chatted for a while, about his concerns regarding his new position, his relationship with the grumpy mechanic, Cole, and magic. When customers started to wander in, she paid and gave Zane a quick hug before she headed home. Now that she had the dictionaries, she was eager to put them to good use. She had a very important book to translate.

More than a month ago, just after Chloe had discovered

that Lexi was her cousin, she'd found the last—and most important—piece of her inheritance. A book, hidden by magic, that was a combination journal of magical experiences and book of spells. Her Granny's grimoire. Since Chloe had only recently learned that spells were magic literally anyone could do—with the right words and spell components—it was a treasure trove of information. Not to mention an insight into her grandmother that she'd never gotten when she was alive.

Not that she was bitter or anything.

The problem was that Granny had been somewhere around fifteen hundred years old when she'd died. Which meant the grimoire dated back almost that long, before English had even existed. And while she could somehow read and speak Ancient Greek—despite having never learned it—the rest of the languages were just jumbled letters to her. Hence the dictionaries.

She returned home, greeted enthusiastically by both Mavros and Lykos. It was one of the many benefits of living with a crow and wolf. They always welcomed her home like she'd been gone for years, even if it had only been minutes. There was little that could make a person feel more loved than the uninhibited affection an animal could give them. Deciding the grimoire could wait a few, she dropped down to one knee on the cold grass and greeted them happily, accepting the sloppy kisses from Lykos and headbutts from Mavros. "Did you guys miss me or are your bowls empty?" she teased as she rubbed hands briskly over fur before more gingerly giving feathers a stroke.

"You!" Mavros told her sternly, before he added, "And food." Then he promptly stuck his head under his wing to preen his feathers.

Chloe laughed and shook her head. "Well, we can't have you two starving." She gave Lykos one last quick hug before she stood, careful not to knock Mavros from her shoulder, and went inside. After getting them both something to eat—and grabbing a quick snack for herself—she went upstairs, dropping her messenger bag in a chair and freeing her hair from the confining ponytail. She retrieved the grimoire from its hiding place, found a pen and mostly empty notebook, and went back downstairs. It was cold out, and she wasn't going anywhere, so she started a fire before she curled up on the couch to work.

She started with the parts she could read and was immediately enthralled. Though Granny had been very, well, grandmotherly as far back as Chloe could remember, in her youth she'd apparently been a little more of a free spirit, at least when it came to magic and her powers. She'd experimented, pushed her boundaries, and just had fun with it. She'd even written her own spells, which baffled Chloe. Then again, she'd never even performed a spell, so she didn't have a real understanding of how complicated making a new one was. Maybe it wasn't as difficult as it sounded, but for now, she was impressed.

In the beginning, the spells were simple or meant for fun. It was shocking to see a spell for changing hair color in the grimoire, as the Granny she'd known hadn't been bothered about such things. The types of spells had just started to change when the language did. Though it was tempting to break out the Latin dictionary, she flipped forward until she saw English again. These spells were more sophisticated—and complicated. The instructions for doing aether wards were here, but she was familiar with that, now. There were other spells for wards, though the notes said the aether ward was the strongest, and these should be used to supplement the aether wards. Layered wards made each one stronger, it seemed, which made sense. Sort of. Reading on, she found spells to heal and identify magics, and she tore off small slips of paper from the notebook to mark those.

Then she found a section of Greek in the middle of the

English and her brows lifted. It was another ward, this one a spell meant to be placed on an object rather than a place. Granny did admit in her notes that it hadn't been thoroughly tested, but that she was confident it would work to block or lessen most god powers. A larger strip of paper was torn to mark the page, but she read through the spell several times. Not that she hoped to ever need it, but she'd met three gods in the few months she'd known they were real. It never hurt to be prepared.

Once she'd skimmed through everything she could read, without anything else popping out at her, she returned to the Latin section and started to translate. It was far from a quick process, as she had to look up each word, and it didn't translate exactly. A few things didn't really make sense, and she had to wonder if Granny had used a dialect different than the one in the dictionary. Lots of changes could happen in a language over a couple thousand years of existence. Not to mention local dialects confusing the issue.

Nearly two hours later, she called it. Her neck was stiff and her brain was going mushy. When she closed the books, she realized Lykos had curled up in front of the now smoldering fire and was dozing. Mavros was perched on the back of a nearby chair, watching her.

"Don't suppose you can translate Latin?" she joked.

He cawed softly and shook his head.

"Yeah, me either." It was still early, but she didn't want to go out into the cold again. Nor was she quite ready to simply curl up in front of the TV, or even with a novel. Instead, she went upstairs, to the storage room, where all of Granny's things were kept. After hiding the grimoire and notebook, she sat cross-legged in front of one of the smaller chests, no more than a foot long and ten inches high. Opening it, she found jewelry and other trinkets. In the past she'd avoided going through what she'd mentally deemed Granny's treasure chests, but she was curious. And, as the grimoire had proven, there was no telling what she would find.

She started to take things out of the chest, one at a time, and set them on the floor beside her. It really was a random assortment of objects. A cuff bracelet was set beside a pretty, pearlescent shell and a rock that looked completely ordinary but for a pale line that bisected it. Other pieces of jewelry—made out of leather, gold, and silver so old it was black—joined the bracelet, as did a number of other natural objects. Quite a few of them were pretty enough, but almost as many were baffling. Why would Granny have kept a small piece of white coral? Or a rough square of faded green fabric? Unfortunately, there were no notes to explain the meaning behind any of the objects. And there had to be meaning for her to keep these seemingly insignificant items.

A couple of things she liked enough to want to wear or display, but it felt wrong somehow. What if the ring she liked was a memento of someone Granny had loved who had died? Or if that gorgeous green and purple stone had some sort of negative magic tied to it?

After placing the last object on the floor with the others, she peered sadly into the chest. Nope, no secret note at the bottom, and nothing on the underside of the lid. She sighed and started to carefully grab a handful of items to replace them when she noticed something odd about the chest. It looked off. She lifted it and studied it from several angles before deciding that yes, the exterior dimensions definitely didn't match the interior. Then she laughed when she figured it out. "A false bottom, Granny? Really?" It was so clichéd it amused the hell out of her.

She tried to wedge her nail in the seams, hoping to pry it up. Or down, if it opened beneath the chest. It took several minutes—and one broken nail—before she managed to lift the thin strip of wood. Gently she pulled it free, hoping there would be some sort of note explaining things. Granny had left her a secret letter before, after all. Two of them, actually. So she was mildly disappointed when all she saw was a necklace. It had a thin silver chain and a small pendant that held some kind of yellow stone. It was kind of pretty, but also kind of boring. The rest of the jewelry in the chest had been more interesting.

Drawing it out of the small compartment, she realized there was a faded note beneath it. The handwriting wasn't familiar, and it said only 'For Protection'. Protection from what, she wondered, as she cradled the pendant in her palm and poked at it with her magic. No magic, which was odd. How could a necklace with no magic offer any protection?

"More secrets," she sighed. She wasn't about to wear the necklace, but neither could she bring herself to put it back in the chest. She did put everything else back, but she took the necklace to her bedroom and set it on her dresser.

Deciding she'd had enough serious for one day, she ran a bath, grabbed a novel, and spent the next few hours relaxing amidst scented bubbles. And firmly pushing thoughts of secrets out of her mind.

Chapter 4

hloe was running in darkness. Her feet slapped against frigid, unforgiving stone as she chased the figure in front of her. Only the faintest light let her see the shadow of the person she followed, though she couldn't tell where it was coming from. Rock and earth surrounded her, and neither were known for their luminescent qualities, but she couldn't stop to puzzle that out. If she stopped, the world would lose so much.

She was done losing.

The figure rounded a bend in the tunnels, and when she made the same turn, she stumbled to a stop and stared down the straight, empty passageway. She couldn't see any side tunnels, but her quarry was gone. Confused more than anything, she walked forward cautiously, searching the ground as much as the walls, but she didn't find any tunnels or pits where someone might have disappeared.

After a minute of searching, she heard footsteps behind her. Rapid steps, heading in her direction. Worse, she felt the chill against the back of her neck that she had come to realize meant vampire magic. The side of her throat ached dully in an unpleasant reminder of her run-in with Kyra. Unwilling to come face to face with the vampire again, she broke into a run, no longer caring where her original target had gone to.

Chloe had only made it a dozen steps when her feet stopped abruptly, though her body continued forward. She threw her hands up, scraping them harshly against the uneven stone beneath her. Hissing at the pain, she looked down, but could see nothing holding her feet in place. She kicked and tugged, but they remained where they were, as though held in place by the rock.

The footsteps grew closer.

She shoved herself upright and twisted, trying to get a glimpse of the vampire she could feel approaching. Her hand slapped against her hip, but the holster she'd grown so accustomed to wearing was empty.

Her heart stopped for two terrifyingly long seconds when she heard the unmistakable sound of someone now coming at her from the other direction. Her quarry? Was she about to be caught between two people? Two enemies?

Dread and a cold sensation washed over her, but her focus was so intent on the approaching sounds that she didn't recognize it for elemental magic until water rushed in from the darkness. It swirled around her feet, icy enough to make her shiver, and rapidly began to climb. But it wasn't filling the tunnel, it was creeping up her legs, surrounding her in a thick layer of liquid.

"No, no, no, no," she chanted quietly as she fought to free her feet, to latch onto the magic, to do *something*. But her power was useless. Every time she reached for the magic controlling the water, it slipped through her grasp more easily than normal water would.

It continued to slither up her body, rapidly covering her legs, her torso, then making its way up her neck. As it began to cover her face, she saw the first figure come into view.

Hiro. But no, he wasn't here, couldn't be here. He was imprisoned in Tartarus. Zeus had sent him there personally. She'd seen it.

"Did you really think we were gone? Did you think you

were safe?" a familiar voice whispered in her ear, just before the water fully enveloped her.

Kyra. But Chloe had thought the vampire gone as well. She'd died in a jail cell right in front of Chloe and several others. She couldn't be here anymore than Hiro could.

Fear made her body try to breathe rapidly, but the presence of the water over her face forced her to hold her breath, causing her panic to increase.

"You will never be safe." This voice was distorted by the water, but Chloe's eyes widened as she saw Daphne, the former elemental councilor, step beside Hiro, a smug smirk on her lips.

Her body's desperate need for air forced Chloe to inhale, despite every attempt not to, and her throat and lungs burned as water filled them. The sensation had her thrashing, twisting, desperate to escape her watery prison.

But her torment wasn't over. Two more people joined the three who already delighted in her misery. Diego, her cheating ex, approached, a satisfied smirk on his lips, a smug Peyton—the woman he'd cheated on her with—held tight against his side. They watched, supremely pleased, as she convulsed and drowned in a cave, surrounded by dry stone.

As her body began to fail her and the world turned black around the edges, Diego leaned in to whisper to her. "You will always be alone."

It took Chloe more than an hour to recover from the nightmare. She'd woken trembling and covered in sweat, though she felt frozen from the inside out. Sensing her fear, Mavros had immediately settled on her shoulder and tried to comfort her, while Lykos had crawled in her lap, alternating between uneasy whining and wet kisses.

When neither animal could truly comfort her—though she appreciated their effort—she debated calling someone but couldn't bring herself to do it. She was a twenty-seven year old woman. Calling someone because she'd had a bad dream should be beyond her. Instead, she drew away from wolf and crow and turned the shower on, simply standing under the hot water until it had thawed the ice in her belly.

She didn't understand why she was dreaming of those particular people now. Yes, Diego and Peyton were still on Salus, but for the most part, they avoided each other. The others? Kyra was dead, Hiro may as well be dead, and Daphne was in prison. They were gone and couldn't hurt her—or anyone else—ever again. So why was her subconscious dragging them into her dreams, much less all in the same place? Yes, there were connections between all of them, but most likely, she decided, it was just because she had issues with all of them. Which made her wonder why Hiro's allies hadn't been there. Why the man she'd been forced to kill hadn't joined in the torture.

By the time she'd dried off, had dealt with her hair and gotten dressed, she had decided she wasn't going to dwell on it. Nightmares happened. Yes, they sucked, and yes, she'd had prophetic nightmares in the past, but there was no way this was foretelling the future. It was simply impossible. So she was going to push it out of her mind and do what she could to have a good day. After all, she had an interesting job, family, friends, and a sexy guy she was dating. Why shouldn't she have a good day?

Despite that, she didn't feel like dealing with people right away, worried the nightmare showed on her face, so had toast, yogurt, and coffee for breakfast after feeding her critters. Sure, it didn't compare to the bacon omelet she could have had at the diner, or the caramel coffee, but it filled her belly.

When it came time for her to head to work, both Mavros

and Lykos insisted on accompanying her, which she appreciated. Besides, Lykos really did need the training. He seemed smart for a wolf—at least if she went by dogs as a standard—but he wasn't quite as intelligent or understanding as Mavros. But that, she admitted, could possibly be his age and the fact that he couldn't speak or send emotions to her like the crow could.

Once again, she wondered why she couldn't have the ability to communicate with animals.

To no one's surprise, Wesley was there when she walked into the office. He hadn't beaten her by much, though, judging by the fact that he was just putting on coffee. She was pleased he'd begun using the coffee pot she'd gotten him for Christmas, though it hadn't really improved the end product. His coffee was still insanely bad. Fortunately, he had a lot of other qualities to make up for that lack.

"Morning," he said when he saw her, giving her a lazy smile that had her own lips curving. Then he crouched down as Lykos bounded toward him, expecting attention, which Wes happily gave.

"Morning," she told him, settling at her desk. The cell was still occupied, which surprised her. "Patrick's still here?"

"Mmhmm. We'll release him when he wakes up."

She frowned and glanced to the sleeping lion. "Release him? Seriously? No punishment after all that property damage and the injuries?"

"I didn't say that," he said as he rose to his feet. "He'll get a fine and mandatory counseling. Some community service, too. Pretty standard for most crimes on Salus."

"Oh." She considered, but that was about what he would have gotten if this had happened in a human city. And the counseling might actually help. She nodded. "That's okay, then."

He strode to her desk and cocked his head as he studied her. "You look tired."

"Gee, thanks. That's just what every woman wants to hear," she said dryly.

He grinned and rested a hip against her desk. "That's me. I'm nothing but flowers, chocolate, and sweet nothings."

She rolled her eyes but was amused. No, he wasn't the romantic sort, but she was okay with that. Romance could hide any number of shortcomings, as Diego had proved. Wesley was exactly who and what he seemed to be, and he had his own way of being sweet.

"Seriously though, you look tired."

"Didn't sleep well," she admitted.

"Everything okay?"

"Yeah, just had a nightmare."

The question had been asked sincerely, but without any real worry. Now concern had his brows bunching slightly and his mouth thinning. "Anything I should know about?"

Knowing exactly why he asked, she smiled faintly and shook her head. "No, nothing like that. It definitely wasn't a prophecy."

"Are you sure?"

Her smile turned wry. "Considering it featured Hiro, Kyra, and Daphne? Pretty sure."

"You want to talk about it?"

"Not really. I'd like to just put it out of my mind, but thanks."

A groan had them both turning toward the cell and the man stirring inside. "Ah, our guest is awake."

"All you. I've got a canine deputy to train," she told him, grinning. "Besides, you're the boss. That means you get the fun jobs."

Leaning down, he brushed his lips lightly across hers. "Remind me to fire you later," he told her before going to deal with Patrick.

She laughed softly and checked her email, half-listening as Wesley told the lion what had been decided as his sentence. When Patrick started ranting, she tuned them both out and left her desk to start working with Lykos. How awesome was it that she was getting paid to play with her wolf? True, Lykos's attention span was about the same as a goldfish's, but she was making progress every time she worked with him. She wasn't quite sure how she was going to manage to teach him to track scents or detain suspects, but Wesley had promised to help her when it reached that point.

The sound of the cell door opening had her glancing over. Patrick looked annoyed, but Wesley had him clearly under control, so she stayed where she was. She kept an eye on them, though, just in case she needed to step in. Patrick, it seemed, had learned his lesson, at least for now, and left without needing to be escorted.

"I'm going to drop him back at his car then I'll be back," Wesley told her.

"I'll hold down the fort," she promised.

By the time he returned, Lykos was absolutely done training. For the last five minutes, any attempt at giving him a command had resulted in him licking her face or trying to chase an uncooperative Mavros.

"That looks productive," Wesley told her as he crossed to his desk, not even trying to hide his smile.

"He's like a little kid," she complained, but she gave the wolf an affectionate ruffle before she went back to her own desk.

The rest of the day was quiet. There was a single call, a woman named Marie, who swore her house had been broken into. Wesley decided to send Chloe to deal with it alone. She was suspicious when he looked like he was fighting amusement, but went anyway, eager for the experience and to meet another inhabitant of the island.

Marie was adamant that she'd locked her door before she went to bed, but it was wide open when she'd gotten up and a chair in her kitchen was knocked over. Chloe had searched for evidence of a break-in and found none. She took prints and promised to look into it, though she couldn't find any sign of a crime. Marie even had to admit nothing was missing or out of place but for the chair, but she was insistent that Chloe launch a full investigation and recruit any witch necessary to find out who'd broken in.

When Chloe was finally able to escape—which took over an hour—and head back to the office, she found Wesley, grinning hugely at her.

"So? How did it go?"

She narrowed her eyes and stalked over to his desk. "How did you expect it to go?"

"I'm guessing she demanded you use every resource we had to track down the person who broke into her house, because she's absolutely positive she was robbed or someone's messing with her, even though the only sign that anything's off is a door being open or something being moved."

"And how would you know that?"

"Because she's telekinetic and likes her nights out a little too much. Every month or so she goes out, gets blackout drunk, and when she gets home, can't work the key. She opens the door with her powers and doesn't remembering doing it the next morning. Sometimes she stumbles into things."

"Then why in the hell don't you just tell her that?" she asked, throwing her arms up in exasperation.

He snorted out a laugh and grinned again. "You think I haven't? She doesn't believe me, or anyone else. She insists she can handle her liquor and would never get so drunk that she forgets anything." Shrugging, he admitted, "Arguing wastes so much time, I usually just promise to look into it and then go back to whatever I was doing."

Oh, she really, really wanted to hurt him now. "And you

couldn't have told me this before I went out there and wasted an hour?"

"Nope," he answered, completely unapologetic. "It's part of the job. Cops don't just deal with serious crimes or life-threatening situations, it's also talking to the delusional or crazy people. Sometimes it's talking to the lonely person who makes up things just to have someone to talk to. Occasionally it's helping a kid out with something that's minor to us, but deathly serious to them, like a missing baseball or bicycle. You have to deal with it sometime, and this one was harmless and predictable."

Chloe couldn't say all her irritation faded, but a good chunk of it did. He was right, she just hadn't thought about that part of the job. "Still could've warned me," she grumbled.

"I'd say I was sorry, but honestly, I'm just happy it wasn't me this time." But he did give her a smile that tried to be apologetic.

"Jackass," she said, but with no malice.

"Yep," he agreed, "but I'm a jackass who's going to let you go an hour early since that's how long you spent with her."

"And a jackass who better watch out next time we spar."

He chuckled. "I look forward to it."

Chapter 5

It didn't surprise Chloe when she arrived at the gym before Lexi. She knew her cousin wasn't truly interested in working out and had only agreed to potentially meet a guy. She didn't judge Lexi for that. Being alone wasn't easy, and Lexi had been alone for too long. For all that it came off like Lexi was just interested in a hookup, Chloe knew she was looking for romance, for love. Which was why she hoped her meddling would be worth it.

Chloe waited just outside the front door, dressed in her usual workout gear of black cotton pants and a blue tank top, though she had added a coat until they got inside. When Lexi pulled up and got out of her car, Chloe called out, "Hurry up! It's cold!"

Lexi must have agreed, because she jogged to Chloe, eagerly hurrying inside. "Yoga pants may make my ass look good, but they're not warm," she complained as she shed her coat.

Chloe grinned. Lexi was definitely dressed more to look good than to work out. Oh, the clothes were suitable enough for exercise, but the snug purple and black yoga pants and matching purple tank top were definitely meant to draw male eyes to her. And she was wearing makeup. Not gobs of it, and not quite the same she'd wear on a date, but it was still noticeable if she paid attention. "You'll be warm soon enough. Exercise is good at that."

"Can't believe I agreed to work out," Lexi muttered, wrinkling her nose. "Tell me you're going to go easy on me?"

Chloe cheerfully shot down that idea. "What fun would that be? Besides, some guys like the hot and sweaty look." She grinned, a teasing gleam in her eyes. "It gives them…ideas."

Lexi groaned, but gamely followed Chloe as they checked in then stowed their things in Chloe's locker. Despite her words, Chloe wasn't going to try to leave Lexi sore and panting. Not only would that likely not help with her matchmaking plans, but she did enjoy having someone to work out with, or even just run with. If she made Lexi miserable, she wouldn't be likely to join Chloe again. Love and friendship could only go so far.

They made their way to the indoor track and spent a few minutes stretching—and in Lexi's case, checking out the men who were already running. To Chloe's disappointment, there was no sign of the handsome werewolf who owned the place. Still, they were just getting started and he had to be around here somewhere. She'd stall if she had to. There were massages and a juice bar, so there were options to keep Lexi around until Garrett showed his face.

"So, I heard a rumor the other day," Lexi said when they stepped onto the track and started with an easy jog to warm their muscles.

Chloe gave a short, low laugh. "You work in a diner, which means you hear rumors every single day, so you're going to have to be more specific."

Lexi grinned. "True. People do like telling me things. But this one involves you."

Chloe groaned. "Great. What now? Tell me it's not that I'm a murderer again. I really hated that one."

The grin dimmed with sympathy. "I know you did, and

no one believes that, now. They know better."

She sighed but nodded. "Yeah, I know. But what *are* they saying now?"

"Not they. Him. I don't think it's something that's widespread." And that sly amusement returned. "Not yet, anyway."

Chloe gave her a suspicious, sidelong look. "You going to tell me what you heard, or draw this out until we're done running?"

"I could, because driving you crazy is one of life's little joys, but I think it'll be more fun telling you. Because I heard that a certain deputy has been seen at a certain sheriff's house on a number of occasions in the last few weeks. And that the sheriff's car has been parked in front of her house more than once, too."

Her shoulders wanted to hunch, but Chloe refused to give in to the urge. She also wasn't sure why she hadn't told Lexi that she was dating Wesley. It wasn't like she was ashamed of Wesley or anything. He was handsome, strong, smart, and an all-around great guy. Superstition, maybe? Her relationship with Diego had been public knowledge from the beginning, since he'd asked her out after a town meeting. She knew that had nothing to do with the relationship ending, since it had crashed and burned because she'd caught him cheating. Literally. You couldn't get much more positive of infidelity than seeing your boyfriend with a bitchy redhead riding him.

She knew Wesley wasn't like that. Was he perfect? Hell no, but that was what she liked about him. She enjoyed their banter, more than she thought she would. He also had a temper, made horrible coffee, and was occasionally a little too by the book for her. But he was also protective, randomly sweet, and honest. And Diego? He'd seemed just a little too perfect, which should have been a tip off. Well, too perfect until he'd been jealous of her friendship with

Wesley. A friendship which had, at the time, been just that. Yes, she'd been attracted to Wesley, but she couldn't help who she found handsome. However, she'd never acted on it, would never have acted on it, if she hadn't found Diego with Peyton. But the kicker? Diego been sleeping with Peyton since before he ever asked Chloe on their first date.

She'd been the other woman and hated that he'd done that to her.

"I can't tell if that's confirmation or not," Lexi said, making Chloe realize she'd been lost in her head for a full lap.

"Sorry. No, it's true. I won't say it's serious because we've been taking it slow, but we are dating."

"Yes!" Lexi pumped her fist triumphantly. "That is some of the best news I've had in forever. I can't believe you kept it from me, you bitch," she said with a grin, bumping her shoulder into Chloe's, just hard enough to jolt Chloe a step to the side.

"I know, and I'm sorry. I haven't told anyone. I haven't even told…" She trailed off, grimacing internally. Lexi didn't know about her brother, either, though that wasn't by choice. She'd promised both Phillip and her dad not to tell anyone but Wesley. For her safety, apparently. It sounded like bullshit to her, but they'd convinced her to hold off. That didn't stop the secret from twisting in her gut. "I don't know. Maybe I didn't want to jinx it?"

"Won't happen. *Can't* happen," Lexi said firmly. "I mean, okay. Diego turned out to be a grade A dipshit, but Wesley? He's solid. I'm just surprised it took this long for you two to get together." She glanced at Chloe, arched a brow. "How long has this been going on, anyway?"

Now Chloe did hunch her shoulders a little. "Since just before Christmas?"

"Seriously?" Lexi's voice went up half an octave. "You've been holding on me that long? I don't know if we can be friends anymore," she pouted, her eyes narrowed.

"I told you, I felt like telling anyone would jinx it! Besides, it's not serious."

"What does 'not serious' mean, exactly?"

Chloe shrugged. "We're just taking it slow. Especially since we started dating not long after I dumped Diego."

"Yeah, but you caught Diego cheating."

"True, but I don't want a rebound guy. Hell, when I showed up on Salus, I wasn't looking for any kind of guy. Still not sure how I ended up where I am."

"That's easy. You're an awesome woman. So don't overthink it. If you want to take things slow with Wesley, then take things slow. There's nothing wrong with that."

"For a horny as hell waitress, you've got some good advice," Chloe told her with a smile.

"Ah, but I'm horny as hell because I actually do listen to my own advice. Most of the time. Quality always trumps quantity."

They ran in silence for several minutes after that until Chloe finally spotted Garrett. He was an inch or so over six feet, with a muscular build that said he used the gym he owned. His hair was short and light, his skin tanned, but not darkly. Though she was firmly stuck on Wesley, she could admit he had beautiful green eyes. Even the tattoos that covered his arms added to his appeal.

And he was the main reason why she'd invited Lexi to join her. Last month, when she'd ended up having drinks with Lexi and Garrett, there had been a spark between her best friend and the owner of the gym. A spark she hoped to fan into a fire.

Grinning to herself, she didn't follow the track when they reached the next curve, but went straight, slowing after she left the track, pleased when Lexi stayed at her side.

"Hey, Garrett," Chloe said with a smile, more pleased when she saw Lexi flash a megawatt smile.

"Hey there," Lexi told him, her voice lower and more seductive than it had been when she was talking to Chloe. It wasn't quite a sex-kitten voice, nothing that overt, but Lexi definitely thought the buff wolf shifter was worth the extra effort.

"Hi, ladies. Having a good run?" he asked, smiling at them both, though Chloe noticed his gaze lingered on Lexi longer than it did her. She cheered quietly in her head but kept a pleasant smile on her face.

"I'm loving it," Lexi answered without hesitation. Chloe managed to hide her laugh, though it was difficult. Lexi had definitely not been loving the run, but she wasn't about to bust her cousin. Normally it might be fun to tease Lexi a little, but not when she was hoping to convince those two to give each other a try.

With that in mind, she kept the friendly smile on her lips rather than the grin that wanted to form. "Always. I'm hoping to convince Lexi to become my running partner," she told him, arching a brow and grinning at Lexi.

"Oh? Are we going to be seeing you around here more often, then?" Garrett asked, gaze fixed on the brunette. It might be wishful thinking, but Chloe thought he looked wolfish, in the best of ways.

"I think you just might," Lexi said with a smile. "I never knew it could be so enjoyable. But it could just be the company."

"It very well could be. The right company can make anything enjoyable."

"Anything?" she asked flirtatiously.

He grinned, and Chloe was delighted to see he had dimples. Lexi deserved a hot guy with dimples. "If it's really the right company, absolutely."

Lexi laughed softly and eased a little closer to him, her hand settling on her hip. "I think I need to test this theory of yours."

Since it didn't seem that either of them even remembered she existed, Chloe slowly backed up to give them some alone time. The fact that they didn't realize she'd left told her she made the right decision. Grinning, she left the track and grabbed her things out of her locker. She didn't feel the least bit of guilt for ditching Lexi. Her cousin likely wouldn't notice Chloe was gone for a while, and she had driven so it wasn't like she'd need a ride home. Part of her regretted not finishing her workout, but she didn't want to be a distraction or excuse for either of them. And she could always make it up tomorrow.

Since her phone was silent until after she'd gotten home, showered, eaten, and had curled up with a book, it was further proof she'd chosen right. And even then, she only received a text.

> *Lexi: Where'd you go?*

Chloe grinned and set her book aside to reply.

> *Chloe: Took you long enough to realize I was gone.*
>
> *Lexi: …How long ago did you leave?*
>
> *Chloe: Right after you started flirting, so about an hour ago. I'm home.*
>
> *Lexi: Oh. Oops. Well I have a date tomorrow night!*
>
> *Chloe: That's great! I thought you'd hit it off with Garrett.*
>
> *Lexi: Did you set this all up?*
>
> *Chloe: I plead the fifth.*
>
> *Lexi: lol. Thank you.*
>
> *Chloe: For what? I didn't admit to anything. But I hope it's a fantastic date.*
>
> *Lexi: Me too! Good night.*
>
> *Chloe: Night!*

She was smiling as she started to set her phone aside, but before she put it down, she thought about her own love life. Yes, they were taking things slow, but slow didn't mean avoiding each other or not moving forward in their relationship. Instead of going back to her book, she texted

Wesley, asking if he wanted to meet up for sparring the next night. Not only would it be a workout on its own, but she just wanted to spend some time with him. He responded quickly, telling her to be at his place at six thirty.

"Good," Mavros told her from where he'd settled on the back of the couch.

Surprised, she looked at him. "You can read?"

He let out a caw that somehow sounded indignant. "Yes!"

"Sorry," she told him, genuinely apologetic at the unintended insult. "That was kind of rude. I'm just not used to animals who are as smart as people. Like, reading smart." And while she knew Mavros was smart, he was in a class of his own in her head. He was the only crow she'd ever interacted with, so she didn't have any kind of comparison. "Besides, you never told me you could read."

He spread his wings in what she'd come to think of as an avian shrug.

Lifting a hand, she stroked the back of her finger over the feathers of his neck. "So, you approve of Wesley, huh?"

"Yes. Good for you."

"He kind of is, isn't he?" she asked, looking to where Lykos was curled in front of the fire, snoring quietly. It amazed her how she'd come to the island totally alone, but now had a circle of people she cared about, and who cared about her. Getting to this point might have sucked, and wasn't all puppies and roses now, but it was worth it. It had to be, or what was all the suffering for?

Though she'd never been one to believe in fate, she was starting to think it might have had a hand in her life. Some might say her life was nothing more than cause and effect, with some coincidence tossed in, but coincidence was something else she'd never believed in. Fate made more sense, especially since she now knew the Fates were real people, not just fairy tales.

One of these days, she might even thank the Fates for

what they'd given her. For now, she let herself get lost in the book while thoughts of Wesley and her family danced in the back of her head.

Chapter 6

Work the next day was fairly quiet. Most of Chloe's time was spent working with Lykos, though Wesley helped with that some, too. He didn't need Lykos to track scents—his nose was more sensitive than any canine's—and a grizzly was more formidable than a single wolf any day of the week, but it was a good idea for Lykos to be able to work with them both. And Wesley was the one with scent-tracking experience.

Unfortunately, they could only work with Lykos in short bursts with his attention span the same as a toddler's. But most of her remaining time still went to his training, just in the form of searching websites for information and watching videos of police dog training. While she liked dogs, she'd never had one growing up, which meant she'd never trained one before, even as a pet who needed to learn sit and stay. She didn't think she was doing too bad a job at it, though. Lykos was learning.

She left a little after five, going home to change and grab something to eat. Wesley was still at the office when she left, opting to wait until Jack—a vampire who was the only other deputy—made it in. It really was a good system. Jack didn't work every night, of course, but it did leave Wesley and Chloe free to focus on the daytime, unless emergencies popped up.

When it came time for her to leave for Wesley's, she wasn't surprised when both Mavros and Lykos joined her. They loved her and wanted to be around her most of the time. Fortunately, they were both extremely fond of Wesley as well. Lykos, especially, since Wesley often ended up wrestling around with the wolf. It was kind of adorable to see the big, too serious sheriff rolling around with the young wolf.

The sun was just below the horizon when she pulled up in front of Wesley's cabin. Lykos raced out of the car and onto the wide porch, letting out a bark and scratching at the front door to let Wes know he was there. Mavros, as usual, was slightly more dignified, settling on her shoulder.

Chloe was in good spirits as she started for the porch, though she knew she was going to end up exhausted. She always did, but despite that, these training sessions were something she looked forward to. Not only was it time spent with Wesley, but she was getting better at protecting herself. A very good thing considering the trouble she tended to get into. Through no fault of her own, of course. Not that it really mattered whose fault it was when it still involved her getting her ass beaten and needing a healer.

A few feet from the porch steps, she paused, cocking her head as she frowned. The hair at the back of her neck rose, but this sensation had nothing to do with the presence of magic. She wished it did. Magic she could identify, could combat. This was worse. It felt like she was being watched. She turned slowly, scanning the nearby area, but trees surrounded the cabin, and with the sky just past twilight, she couldn't see into the woods to spot anyone watching her. Still, the feeling was an eerie one. It most definitely wasn't Wesley watching her, that much she knew, but who was? And even more importantly, why? She knew there were people on the island who weren't her biggest fans, but was there anyone who disliked her so much they would spy on her?

Determined to find out, she thought quickly. Though whoever was out there wasn't actively using magic, maybe they had magic on them she could sense. She'd just started to gather her power so she could send it outward when the door opened behind her. Lykos let out a happy yip and she looked back toward him to see Wesley crouching down to greet the wolf.

He grinned at her as he straightened. "You going to stand out there all day, or are we going to spar?"

The feeling of being watch had disappeared the moment the door had opened, so she brushed it off. No reason to worry Wesley when it was probably nothing. She smiled and joined him on the porch, pleased when he brushed a kiss over her lips. Though their relationship was new, she liked the casual touches. Not just the kisses, but when he touched her back or brushed a hand down her arm. It made her feel like she mattered, like he couldn't do anything but touch her.

And it helped reinforce that she wasn't alone anymore.

"We're definitely going to spar. I owe you for sticking me with Marie, remember?"

He laughed and motioned for her to come in. "Consider that a rite of passage. Even Jack's dealt with her. But if it gives you inspiration to work hard, I'll send you to her every time she calls."

Her eyes narrowed. "You wouldn't."

"Oh, I absolutely would," he promised with a wide grin.

With Chloe grumbling, they went through the house and into the back yard. Mavros left her shoulder to find a spot in a tree, while Lykos curled up on the deck, gaze fixed on Chloe and Wesley.

The air was rapidly cooling with the sun down, and she shivered a little, but neither Chloe nor Wesley hesitated to shuck their coats and get to it. They'd warm up as soon as they started sparring, and coats would only hinder their movements.

They'd developed a routine over the last month. They started off slow, letting their muscles warm until they were less likely to hurt themselves—and until the cold didn't bother her quite so much. It didn't affect him the same way, as shifters tended to run a few degrees hotter than everyone else. After loosening up, they ramped it up. It wasn't a constant fight, as Wesley stopped her frequently to correct her form or teach her a new move. Though he teased her at times, the corrections were never condescending, and he never lost patience with her. She appreciated it, since she knew she was still very much a novice. Not that it would have been a fair fight even if they were equally skilled. He stood half a foot taller than her and had at least eighty pounds on her, all of it muscle. But she was making him work harder than she had in the beginning, which thrilled her.

Another habit they'd developed was starting to fight harder when they began to get tired. No stopping for tips, no going slow to practice a move, just Chloe doing her absolute best to knock him on his ass while he tried to do the same to her without actually hurting her. At first, she'd thought it was counterproductive, as a tired body was one that didn't cooperate fully, but he'd pointed out that she wouldn't always be coming to a fight well-rested.

And this time, she had extra incentive to push herself. As they studied one another, each waiting for the other to make the first move, she remembered the wasted hour spent at Marie's house. Then, giving him a dangerous smile, she stepped forward and swung a fist at him. After that, she stopped thinking and started reacting, letting her body do what she'd been training it to do. They traded blows and kicks, with him pulling his punches and her throwing them as hard as she could. At this point, it wasn't necessary for her to hold back. She was getting better, yes, but he'd literally been doing this longer than she'd been alive. Almost four times as long, actually.

Her muscles were starting to protest the exertion when he used a new tactic on her. He stepped in and placed one foot behind hers before knocking her off balance. She felt herself falling backward and instinctively grabbed for him to halt the descent, her fingers gripping his shirt tightly. Just inches from the ground, his arms came around her, stopping her from impacting the cold, hard dirt. The position left their faces only inches apart, her body held against his.

Neither moved as they stared at one another, their breathing fast and heavy. His eyes had gone the yellow of his bear, though this time she knew it was with passion, not rage. Her own eyes were sure to have changed as well, when a desire to learn to protect herself had turned to simple desire. For him. For what she'd been denying them both for far too long.

Chloe was reluctant to break the moment and lose the intimacy of it, so altered it instead, prolonged it. Her head lifted and she covered his mouth with her own. His answering groan told her he felt the tension in that instant, too. The second their lips connected, he dove, devouring her with a hot, hungry kiss that she felt right down to her toes. But though his mouth was demanding, the arms around her were gentle. As they kissed, he slowly straightened, his arms tightening to pull her firmly to him so his heart pounded against hers. Her fingers slowly released their grip on his shirt so her hands could slide up until her arms circled his neck.

"Stay the night," he whispered against her lips before kissing her once more. "Say you'll stay."

She'd told him she wanted to take things slow, but right now all she wanted was to feel his body against her, inside her. To show him with every part of her how she felt about him. The moment they'd met she'd been attracted to his body, and as the weeks had passed, the attraction had evolved, expanded, into a genuine liking for the mind inside the handsome shell. A liking she'd pushed back and ignored while she'd been with Diego. Only once that relationship was over had she realized just how much she enjoyed being around Wesley. How happy and safe he made her feel. How complete. Deputy might be her title, but he felt more like her partner than her boss. She looked forward to seeing him, even arguing with him. She liked just watching him, the expressions on his serious face, the way his muscles flexed when he moved. And she found herself thinking about him entirely too much.

She hadn't wanted a man when she arrived in Salus. Hadn't wanted to care about anyone. But if what she felt for Wesley wasn't the start of love, she had no clue what love was.

"Yes," she answered in a murmur, helpless to resist any longer.

He groaned and held her more tightly. She felt nothing but pure feminine delight when he bent, slid an arm behind her knees, and scooped her up. Unable to help herself, she skimmed her lips along his throat and smiled when he growled and carried her to the cabin. Knowing what was coming, anticipating it, she scraped her teeth over his pulse while one hand yanked her hair from its ponytail. It would be wild after the confinement, but that's how she felt right now. Wild and free.

When he left the door open long enough for Lykos and Mavros to come inside, she was sure she'd made the right choice. But then he lost patience, carrying her quickly to his bedroom and shutting the door firmly before either animal could join them. He didn't want to risk an interruption, and neither did she.

Despite his obvious need, he laid her gently on the bed

but immediately rested his body over hers, mouth finding hers once more. She kicked off her shoes, letting them thud to the floor. Her hands slipped beneath his shirt, feeling the warm, hard muscle beneath. She'd seen his body before when he'd shifted, and she wanted to touch every inch of that impressive form. To see if she could make him tremble for her.

Fingers skimmed over his belly and chest, until he leaned back and yanked his shirt over his head with a quick, impatient movement. Seeing that broad chest, she wanted more and her hands dropped to the waistband of the sweatpants he wore. "Be sure," he warned her, his voice a low growl, further proving just how much he wanted this. And how close he was to losing control.

"I've never been more sure of anything," she told him, and realized it was pure truth. Her thumbs hooked the band of both pants and boxers and pushed them lower, until he took over when she could no longer reach.

Completely nude and unashamed, he trailed a finger down her throat and between her breasts. When she said nothing to dissuade him, but arched to follow his touch, he pulled her shirt off with a great deal more finesse than he'd dealt with his own. He unzipped her sports bra and made a small sound at his first sight of her. Bending his head, he touched her with nothing more than his lips and tongue, teasing her breasts until he drew a soft moan from her.

That sound, small though it was, seemed to push him past patient to needy. He drew back until he could tug her pants down, and she lifted her hips to help him. When she was as bare as he was, he settled his hips between her legs. She could feel him pressed against her, hard and hot, and rocked unconsciously against that rigid flesh, breath catching at the sweet friction. But he wasn't going to be rushed. He kissed her again, hard enough that she knew she'd feel the kiss long after it ended. His rough fingers moved lightly over her skin, the heat from them seeming to scorch her in the best of ways.

Each kiss, each caress built the need for him until it was unbearable. Though they'd only been together a few weeks, it seemed that she'd been waiting for this since the moment she first saw him, something inside her recognizing him. Friend, partner, lover. Mate.

"Wesley," she whimpered, which seemed to be that last push he needed to stop teasing her and give in to what had been building for months. He shifted his hips and slid inside her, inch by inch, until they were fully joined. She whispered his name again, relishing the way he felt against her, within her. How could she ever feel alone again when he could inspire these sensations, these emotions?

Lifting his head to look down at her, he stroked his fingers over her cheek, murmuring her name in return. Then, he began to move and heat coiled throughout her body. Nothing had ever felt like this, as if liquid joy were flowing through her veins.

Moving together as the moon bathed them in pale light, Chloe forgot about all the troubles she'd had the last few months. She forgot about how lonely she'd felt, how much she'd wanted to forget Salus ever existed and go back to the 'real' world. In that moment, he truly was the only thing that existed for her.

It was perfect. But while she loved watching his face as he thrust into her, she needed just a little more. Wanted that extra bit of contact, of connection. Her fingers slid through his short hair to cup the back of his head, drawing him down for another kiss. That heightened everything else, so the pleasure multiplied until it was almost too much. Then, it shattered, leaving her arching helplessly beneath him, clinging to him as she let out a soft cry which was muffled by his lips.

When she reached that peak, he couldn't hold back any

longer, groaning as he dropped his head to rest his brow against hers. He thrust once more, burying himself inside her as he let go and joined her.

It was several minutes later when Chloe registered that he was heavy. She shifted beneath him, not truly minding his weight, aside from the fact that it restricted her breathing. Sensing her discomfort, he carefully withdrew, slid an arm around her, and rolled them until they lay on their sides, his brow once more against hers.

Neither said a word for a while, content to enjoy the intimacy and afterglow as they recovered. He ran a hand over her hair and smiled a lazy, satisfied smile. "You have the craziest hair of anyone I've ever met," he told her in a quiet voice.

She gave him a sleepy laugh in return. "Believe me, I know."

"I like it." Oddly enough, he sounded like he meant it.

That anyone could like her hair made her grin and she pushed at his shoulder until he rolled onto his back. Scooting closer, she rested her head on his shoulder and draped an arm over him. But though he radiated heat, not all of her was pressed to that warmth and she shivered. She reached down, groping for the covers, but realized they were lying on top of them.

"Why is it so cold in here?" she complained, but without a lot of force behind it. She just felt too good to truly get riled up about anything.

He groaned playfully. "You have to be difficult, don't you?" But he solved the problem by hauling her on top of him, shoving the covers back, then rolling them onto the exposed sheet. Once he'd tugged the covers up around them, he settled beside her once more.

"You wouldn't know what to do with me if I was easy going. I'd be too boring for you," she murmured.

"True," he agreed easily, rubbing a hand lazily over her

back.

She sighed, pleased she'd decided not to force them to wait any longer. Her only regret was that she'd wasted so much time with a man who didn't appreciate her like Wesley did. But, refusing to live in the past any longer, she closed her eyes and slipped into sleep with a smile on her lips.

Chapter 7

Chloe woke to the scent of Wesley on the sheets. It brought back the memory of the night before, which had her lips curving into a lazy, satisfied smile. She stretched an arm toward him, but found the space beside her not only empty, but cold. A sleepy pout slid over her face as she cracked an eye open. Nope, no sexy sheriff. Pity. She would have liked to start the day the same way she ended the last one.

Yawning, she stretched before opening her eyes fully. After a quick trip to the bathroom to freshen up, she found one of his tee-shirts and slipped it on, along with a pair of boxers. She went to look for him, but didn't find him in the kitchen or living room. Nor did she find Lykos or Mavros. Frowning, she called for them, but heard nothing but silence.

Though it had snowed while she slept, she still opened the back door and stepped out onto the deck. "Wesley? Mavros?" Nothing. She focused on her familiar, shocked when she didn't feel him in the back of her mind like she normally did. Nor did she feel Lykos. Unease crept up her spine and she went back into the house, finding her clothes and pulling them on. When she holstered her gun at her hip, she felt a little better, but something was definitely wrong. After grabbing her phone, she tried calling Wesley, but it went immediately to voicemail. The text she sent went unanswered, too. The calls to the sheriff's office, Lexi, and her brother were the same.

Ten minutes later, she hadn't found any sign of the bear, wolf, or crow anywhere around the cabin. She got in her car and sped toward the town. There wasn't another car on the road, but she'd slept in, well past when people were normally heading to work. A sense of déjà vu had her half-expecting to see bodies when she got to Salus, but fortunately it all looked normal, until she passed the diner. She slammed on the brakes, frowned, then reversed the car until she could look in the front window. Cars were parked outside, but she didn't see a single person inside either the vehicles or Joel's.

Putting the car into park right there in the street, she jumped out and ran inside. "Lexi? Joel?" she called as she made her way behind the counter and into the kitchen. No one. The fact that she didn't find any bodies was small relief. What added to her unease were the plates and cups, still filled with food and drink, left on the counter and tables.

Chloe checked the buildings around the diner, but they were all the same. Not a single person, not a single body. She didn't even see or hear any animals, not even birds singing. No one answered when she tried calling, so she decided to check everywhere she could think of.

Sheriff's office? Empty.

Veterinarian office? Empty.

Bookstore? Empty.

School, council building, gym? Empty, empty, empty.

When she went to the ferry, she found it at the pier, but though there were cars on it, no one was on board.

"What the hell is going on?" she murmured to herself, the chill she'd been feeling settling deep in her bones. Even when she'd seen Salus caught in the grip of a persistent, magical sleep she hadn't felt this unnerved. Or this alone.

She drove to the far end of the island and everywhere in

between, searching with all her senses for some sign of someone. Nothing. No people, no magic. Even the wards had disappeared. Still, she looked. It felt like she searched for hours, and the forced solitude was starting to get to her. Though she knew it was all in her head, she started hearing voices. Each was spoken in a low voice, ominous and without any sense of whether it was male or female, young or old.

"You're alone, Chloe."

"You've always been alone."

"Everyone you're close to dies."

"What made you think you could have friends, could have family?"

"You're cursed."

"Stop it. Just stop it," she whispered to herself as she found herself in the parking area near the Oak. Out of all the places on the island, it was the place she felt most comfortable, other than when she was with Wesley or her family. Given to Salus by Zeus when the community had formed, it not only radiated magic, it acted as an anchor to support the wards that hid the island from humanity.

It had also been the site of several life-changing moments for her. With the voices crowding her thoughts, she got out of the car, unable to focus enough to either shut the car off or close the door. She ran to the Oak and collapsed against it, nearly sobbing when it felt...dead. There wasn't a trace of magic in the tree. What was meant to be a slice of solace on a literal island of sorrow had instead added to the depth of her grief.

"Why?" she whispered, turning and sliding down until her butt hit the dirt. "Where are they? What did you do with them?" she asked, confusing the voices in her head with an actual entity. While the voices continued, they didn't answer her.

"You will always be alone, Chloe."

"Cursed."

"They will always leave."

"You did this."

"I will take everyone you care about."

That last voice was deeper, harsher, but beyond that it sounded less…ethereal. Instead of being in her head, it was like it was hissed into her ear. She curled into a ball as her eyes darted left, right, searching for the source, but she saw no one, felt no one.

The other voices continued, no longer speaking one at a time, but layering over one another, growing in volume until they were thunderous. And they all said the same thing, over and over.

"Alone."

"Hey, come on, honey. Wake up. Wake up for me."

Strong arms were around her, holding her against a solid chest as she trembled. She smelled the familiar scent of Wesley, but couldn't stop shaking, couldn't slow her breathing.

"Chloe, it's just a dream. Wake up," Wesley repeated, pressing a kiss to her forehead.

"I'm awake," she whispered, and was shocked by the weak sound of her own voice. She cleared her throat, tried again. "I'm awake." God, she hoped she was awake this time.

His arms only tightened around her, pulling her so she was half sprawled over his chest. "Good. That's good."

His voice was rough, unsteady, which worried her. He was the steadiest person she knew. Tilting her head back, she looked up at him. "Didn't mean to wake you."

"I'd rather you wake me up than suffer through a nightmare. At least I assume it was a nightmare?"

"Yeah," she murmured, pressing her face against his

neck. The smell of him, the feel of him soothed her and warmed the ice in her veins.

"Want to tell me about it?"

She'd rather let the dream slip away but had a feeling it would stick to her like glue, just like the one from a few nights ago. Maybe getting it out while she lay in her lover's arms in the darkness would purge it from her. "I woke up and you weren't here. No one was, not even Mavros or Lykos. Everyone's phones went straight to voicemail, including yours." She started to close her eyes, but it brought images back to the front of her mind. No, it was better to stare into the dark, or into Wesley's face. "It was like when Nick and the others put the island to sleep, but somehow worse. Instead of bodies, there were just empty buildings." She blew out a breath, rested her head on his shoulder. "I don't know why that was worse...No, I do," she corrected almost immediately. "I think—I know—being alone is my worst fear. I realized that after Granny died, when I thought I didn't have anyone anymore."

"But you're not. You've got me, Lexi, Phillip, not to mention your friends."

She smiled a little, as even while comforting her his voice was a little gruff. "I know. But I searched for hours, I think, and started hearing voices. All telling me I was alone, would always be alone. That I was cursed." Her brow furrowed. "Then there was another voice. It was different. Scarier. It said it would take everyone I cared about."

"Not going to happen," he growled softly. "I'm not going anywhere, and Lexi? Well, from what you tell me, she's actually some super powerful witch. Phillip? I don't know what his deal is, but he seems like he can handle himself. And I know Zane comes off as just a nerd, but I wouldn't underestimate him, either. He's too smart to be an easy target."

"I know you're right, but you know fears aren't exactly

rational."

"No, they aren't," he agreed. "Do you think you can go back to sleep?"

Just the thought of sliding into unconsciousness made her shudder. "I'd rather not. I know not all of my dreams are bad, especially since I've only spoken to my father in dreams, but two nightmares in such a short time?" She shook her head. "No, I don't want sleep right now."

"I bet I could exhaust you so you could sleep without nightmares," he said, and though there was a growl in his voice, this time it was a sound that sent heat settling low in her belly.

"Oh? And how are you going to do that?" she asked as her lips began to curve.

He shifted, settling her more fully atop him, until her knees fell on either side of his hips. "You're a smart girl," he murmured, sliding a hand into her mass of curls, drawing her head down toward him. "I think you can figure it out," he added, before he kissed her, lingering, savoring her.

With a sigh, she sank into the kiss, happily figuring out what his method would be. An hour later, still draped over him, she drifted into a sweet, dreamless sleep.

When she woke next, the sun was up and she wasn't alone. Wesley's body was pressed securely against her back, his big hand splayed over her hip. At some point he must have woken and gotten up to open the door, because she felt another, smaller body curled up against her shins. A quick glance told her it was Lykos. It didn't take long for her to spot Mavros perched on the headboard above her head.

She wasn't alone. She'd never be alone again.

Smiling, she snuggled into Wesley, which roused him

enough that his arm tightened around her. "Morning," she murmured to him, shivering when he nuzzled the back of her neck.

"Morning," he replied, his voice rough and growly from sleep. She loved the way it sounded.

"You're being a bad sheriff," she teased. "Shouldn't we be at work?"

"I am. I'm protecting and serving right now. See how protected you are?" he asked, giving her another squeeze.

She laughed and shook her head. "We should both be at work."

He groaned and buried his face in her hair. "Fine." But he nipped at her shoulder before he slid out of bed and into the bathroom.

The movement had Lykos lifting his head and yawning hugely. Unable to resist the cuteness, she reached down to pet him before she also slid out of bed. It was only after they had showered that she realized she had a problem. Since she hadn't intended to stay the night, she only had the clothes she'd worn the day before.

"I'm going to have to swing by my house on the way in," she told him while she watched him get dressed. It was quite a treat, getting to actually study him in the light. She like describing him as a bear of a man, but with his shirt off, he somehow looked bigger. Thick, muscled arms, wide shoulders, and a broad chest with a light dusting of dark hair were an extremely appealing combination. A combination that made her wish they didn't have to go to work.

"You've got time. Especially if we grab breakfast at the diner."

"That works. Want to just meet me there? Lexi knows my usual."

"Sure."

They parted ways at their cars with a kiss, but while Mavros was on her shoulder and ready to go, Lykos refused to get in her car. Instead, he stuck by Wesley and whined until they figured out what he wanted and gave in.

"Furry little traitor," she muttered as he jumped into the cruiser, though she was more amused than hurt.

At home, she changed in record time. On impulse, she put on the bracelet her dad had given her for Christmas. It was pretty, if not really suitable for a cop, but she didn't think Wesley would mind. Hammered gold had been fashioned into a wide cuff. In the center of it was some sort of blue-green cut stone. She couldn't identify it but didn't really care. It matched her eyes—their eyes—which made her feel connected to him. The only connection she really had. For now, she hoped.

Pleased to be in clean clothes, and feeling a little better with the bracelet on, she drove to the diner, parking beside Wesley's cruiser. Inside, she saw him sitting at a booth with Lexi setting two coffees on the table in front of him. She also saw the knowing grin Lexi flashed her when Chloe walked inside.

"Morning, Mavros," Lexi called, softening the smile for the crow perched on Chloe's shoulder. The impish expression returned when she leaned a hip against the side of the booth, careful not to step on Lykos, who was curled up calmly at Wesley's feet. "Hey there, Trouble."

"Would you quit calling me that? I haven't gotten into trouble in weeks," Chloe pointed out as she slid into the booth opposite Wesley.

"I don't know, looks like you got into some trouble last night. Or one of you did, anyway," she teased.

"Lexi? I love you, but it is way too early." So early that Chloe didn't waste any time in picking up her coffee and sipping, not caring that it scorched her tongue.

"Have to agree with Trouble," Wesley drawled, smiling when Chloe shot him a dirty look.

Lexi huffed. "Fine, then I won't tell you how my date

went last night."

Chloe didn't believe that for a minute. Lexi looked like she was about to burst with the news. "Okay," she said, as though she wasn't almost as eager to hear how it had gone.

But Lexi knew her best friend too well and grinned, nudging Chloe to scoot over. Chloe obliged and Lexi's voice dropped to an excited whisper. "It went fantastic!"

"Who'd you go on a date with?" Wesley asked, and it sounded like he actually cared. Not to the extent Chloe did, but everyone cared about Lexi.

"Garrett. The guy who owns the gym," Chloe answered before she smiled at Lexi. "That's great. I'm glad it wasn't a dud."

"So freaking far from being a dud," Lexi agreed with a nod. "He wanted to do the dinner and a movie thing, so I was a little skeptical. I mean, sure, he's hot, but dinner and a movie is so…clichéd. But I had a really good time. Even though he was a complete gentleman," she complained with a deep sigh.

Wesley arched a brow. "Don't women want men to be gentlemen on dates?" he asked, a little confused.

"I mean, I guess, but only to a point," she explained with a shrug. "We don't want guys groping us or anything, but if a guy's too much of a gentleman, it can be boring. Or it can seem like he isn't interested. Which is dumb, because why go on a date if you're not interested in someone? But he straddled that line, you know? Didn't grope, but he was absolutely interested."

"So, there's going to be a second date, then?" Chloe asked, pleased her matchmaking attempt seemed to be working out so far.

"Definitely. Though I'm not going to let him get away with the safe date this time." Lexi paused at a bell, glanced toward the kitchen. "Oh! Your breakfast is ready. Be right back!" She hopped up and made her way to the food, bouncing with each step.

Wesley smirked. "If you're hoping for a gentleman with me, I think you're going to be disappointed."

Chloe grinned and shook her head. "No, gentlemen are the safe option. I want a guy who treats me well, sure, but you don't have to be a gentleman for that." She considered a moment, laughed. "And believe it or not, you being an ass sometimes counts. It's hard to be focused on something stressing me out when you're busy harassing me."

He looked pleased and surprised. "Good to know."

Lexi returned, setting their plates down. "I'd stay and chat, but a couple of people just came in," she told them apologetically before going to serve her new customers.

Wesley shook his head slightly. "I don't understand why you need coffee every morning when you could just spend five minutes with her. It feels like a caffeine buzz anytime I'm around her too long."

"Ahh, but the more time you spend around her, the more used to it you get. Lessens the effect. So you're going to have to deal with me bitching about your coffee. At least until you learn to make it correctly."

"But then what would you bitch about?" he asked.

She laughed. "I'm sure I could find something. I hate to break it to you, Yogi, but you're not perfect."

"Sure I am. It's just under the surface."

"How far under the surface?"

He shrugged. "No idea, but it's in there."

Amused, the nightmare temporarily forgotten, she just grinned and ate her breakfast. By the time they'd finished, the diner was packed, so they left the check and tip on the table and sent Lexi a wave before heading to the office.

Given how things had been going, Chloe expected a quiet day, largely spent training Lykos. She was wrong.

Chapter 8

The workday started off normal enough. Paperwork, working with Lykos, a few minor calls that could be handled over the phone.

Around noon, Chloe decided both she and Lykos had done enough for the moment and rose, stretching out muscles that had grown stiff from sitting on the floor. "I'm thinking pizza for lunch," she told Wesley, who was still busy with paperwork.

"Sounds good to me. Pepperoni, mushrooms, and bell peppers?" he suggested, glancing up at her.

She wrinkled her nose. "You're lucky you're cute. Peppers on half," she countered.

"You don't like bell peppers?" He shook his head slowly, a sad look on his face. "I don't know if this relationship will work."

She grinned wickedly. "I don't know. I think I make up for it in other ways."

"True," he agreed, returning the grin. "Peppers on half works."

She ruffled Lykos's head. "Stay here with Wes," she told him as she grabbed her bag.

Before she could take a step toward the door, every desk phone in the office rang. The only reason that would happen

69

is if someone dialed 911. In the weeks since she'd been a deputy, she'd heard it happen once, and it had been a kid calling on accident. Magic meant there were solutions to most things that would be considered emergencies in the human world, solutions most people could handle on their own without calling for help.

The amusement fled both of them. More used to dealing with emergencies, Wesley picked up the phone first. "Sheriff Adams." He paused to listen for a few seconds then shoved back from his desk as the feel of fur permeated the office. "Be right there." He slammed the phone down and ran for the door, grabbing his hat out of habit on the way.

She raced after Wesley with Lykos hot on her heels. Mavros followed but took to the skies as she headed for the cruiser. She let Lykos in the back then jumped in the passenger seat even as Wesley started the engine. "What's wrong?"

"Fire at the Oak," he answered as he sped out of the parking lot, fast enough she heard the tires chirp against the asphalt.

She stopped breathing for a second. No, not the Oak. While she couldn't say she only had good memories of the tree, she loved it. Then her mind flashed to the nightmare. The Oak hadn't been burned in it, but it had been void of all magic. Had that been a glimpse of the future? "What? How bad?"

"Bad enough. The tree's still standing for now, but it and multiple trees around it are burning. They've already called the fire department, but said it was getting worse."

"Shit," she whispered. While she knew from firsthand experience that firefighters on Salus didn't use trucks and hoses, if the fire got too bad, she wasn't sure they would be able to handle it without outside help. Unfortunately, she didn't know if they had a typical fire engine on the island so others could help douse the flames. "How many fire and water elementals do we have on the island?"

"Enough." His voice dropped to a level she was sure he didn't intend her to hear when he added, "I hope."

They weren't the only car speeding toward the center of the island where the Oak grew, and she hoped the cars in front of them were all intending to combat the fire. She saw several flashing red lights to go along with their blue, which gave her hope. Flashing red could mean fire engines and another resource to prevent the huge tree from being destroyed.

They had to park farther back than she usually did, unable to see the Oak—or fire—with all the trees and cars in their way. The wind was blowing the smoke toward them, further obscuring their vision and burning their eyes, but neither hesitated to hurry toward the precious tree. It was the anchor for the wards, which meant that if the Oak was destroyed, the wards that kept them hidden would disappear as well. And if humans were suddenly able to see an island where there had previously only been water, things could get really bad, really fast.

"Oh, god," she breathed when she caught her first glimpse of the blaze. The upper branches on one side of the Oak were fully aflame, as was part of the trunk. Dozens of trees on that side were also burning, and it was easy enough to see how quickly this fire could spread to the entire forest. Even worse, this forest spread across the entire island, and had a multitude of homes within its borders.

She felt the tingle of magic even before she could make out the figures of the elementals and witches working to subdue the blaze. Two of them she recognized—Diego Sanchez, her ex, and Howard, the fire elemental who had thought she'd been responsible for putting the island to sleep a few months back. Right now, she didn't care how she felt about them, or vice versa. They needed to get this fire out, now. She'd even deal with Daphne and Hiro if it meant saving the Oak.

Chloe knew she couldn't do anything directly to help. Her powers didn't lie in controlling the elements, only magic. She could, however, give a boost to those who could interact with the fire, keep them going long enough to make a difference.

"Chloe!" Wesley called as she broke into a run toward the line of those trying to protect the Oak.

"I have to help!" she answered without stopping. When she reached them, she quickly checked to see who felt like they were faltering. Howard was one of them. She laid a hand on his shoulder, but it didn't seem like he noticed, too intent on trying to pull the fire away from the flammable wood and into himself. She pushed power from herself and into him, giving him extra magic to work with. Immediately he began to pull harder, faster on the flames.

One by one she went through the line of people doing their best to put out the flames, boosting the weakest first, then those who still had more power left. There was only a moment of hesitation when she reached Diego, but she didn't care if he cheated on her with every woman on the island if he helped put this fire out.

Wesley was keeping busy while she pumped power into the firefighters. Dozens of other people had responded, and he was organizing them to get water from nearby houses to douse trees that hadn't yet been touched by the flames. If magic couldn't stop the fire, there was always a chance they could prevent it from spreading with non-magical methods. Humans did it, so they could, too.

Mavros watched from the sky, and Chloe worried the smoke would get to him, but she couldn't do anything to help him at the moment. To her relief, Lykos had stayed in the car, even though she saw that she hadn't bothered to shut the door when she got out.

With so many people the scene quickly turned to chaos.

She had expected, with so many people working to contain it, that it would be a relatively quick process, yet after an hour, the fire still burned. The Oak—which had been everyone's priority—had been extinguished, but if they didn't get the rest of the fire, the Oak could still be at risk.

"Is this normal?" she asked Howard in a half-yell so he could hear her over the roar of the flames and the sound of so many people.

To his credit, Howard had also put aside their previous animosity and looked simply concerned and drained. "Only with magical fires," he admitted.

Since she had essentially exhausted her magic—including the power she stored in a bracelet tailor-made for that purpose—she decided to investigate. She stepped back, away from the crowds and fire and toward the cars packed into every available space. With so many people using magic constantly, it would take her a minute to sift through them to see if there were any magical anomalies—specifically someone working to keep the fire going—and she didn't want to get in the way or get trampled.

Closing her eyes, she breathed slow and deep as she focused on the magical signatures in the area. Some were easy to discard, as she recognized them. One by one she identified then dismissed magic, regretting that she hadn't done this first, before she tired herself. Now it would take a lot longer to manage, if it was possible at all.

Arms came around her from behind, gripping so tightly it was hard for her to suck in a breath. When a hand covered her mouth an instant later, her eyes flew open, but all she could see was the fire and insanity in front of her. She tried to scream as she was dragged backwards, toward the trees that had yet to burn. Whoever was holding her was strong, and when her power ebbed, so did her physical strength, so struggling didn't free her, only made her attacker grip more firmly. To make matters worse, her arms were pinned to her sides, limiting how she could fight back.

She heard Lykos barking madly before she saw him, running as fast as he could toward her. His alert triggered Mavros, who let out a loud caw and dove, not toward Chloe, but the crowd.

A curse was muttered behind her, and though it sounded male, she couldn't identify the voice from a single word. He moved faster toward the woods where she'd be completely out of sight, and she fought with everything she could. Twisting, kicking, trying to shove her elbow into any part of him she could reach.

At the ruckus from both wolf and crow, a few people started turning, started paying attention to something other than the flames. Lexi was one of them.

"Hey! Let her go!" she yelled as she ran toward Chloe. Another man, one Chloe recognized as a regular at the diner, followed close on her heels.

Lykos reached her first, snarling and snapping at whoever was behind Chloe. A half-grown wolf didn't seem to be much threat to the man, and Chloe's temper peaked when he took the time to kick the pup. Lykos yelped sharply as he was knocked back several feet, with enough force to have him rolling several times across the ground. Even injured, he wasn't about to give up, and both love and rage rose in Chloe as Lykos got unsteadily to his feet to resume protecting her.

A roar echoed through the trees, and even without being able to see the source, she *knew* it was Wesley.

With so many people now paying attention, and with a pissed off bear shifter on the way, the man decided to cut his losses. He let go of her, then turned and darted into the trees as she stumbled at the abrupt release. She spun, hoping to catch sight of the man, but saw nothing but dark clothes and what she thought was dark hair. Mavros wasn't going to let him just get away and flew into the trees after him.

Part of her wanted, desperately, to follow, to investigate

like her familiar was, but they had more immediate problems. The fire was still burning, and her wolf was hurt. Mavros was smart, and he was quick. She had to trust that he would get what information he could, because she needed to make sure Lykos was okay.

She closed the distance between them and dropped to the ground by the wolf, who half-sat, half-fell beside her, giving his tail a half-hearted thump.

"Oh, baby. I'm so sorry. Are you okay?" she crooned as she ran her hands gently over his furred body. He flinched away from her when her fingers found a spot on his ribs and anger surged once more toward her attempted abductor.

Before the rage could take hold, Lexi and Wesley reached her. Even with all the magic swirling around her she could feel Wesley's bear, and a quick glance up at them showed his eyes were yellow. "Did he hurt you?" he growled, at the same time Lexi asked, "Who was that?"

"He pissed me off is what he did. He kicked Lykos!" That, to her, was more of an outrage than trying to take her. "And I have no fucking idea who he was. He was behind me the whole time."

"I think he was using a disguise spell, too," Lexi admitted. "I couldn't get a good look at his face, but his coloring seemed to shift."

That was a problem for later. If she focused on it now, she'd lose sight of the other issues. "We'll find him. Mavros is on his tail. Is Phillip here? Lykos is hurt."

"Oh, shit," Lexi breathed, sympathy for the wolf flashing over her features. "I think so. I'll go get him!"

She raced off and Wesley knelt beside Chloe and Lykos. Though he laid a gentle hand on Lykos's head, stroked with obvious affection, his gaze was on Chloe. "Are you really okay?"

"I am," she assured him. "All he did was grab me and pull me toward the trees. He honestly didn't hurt me. I'm more worried about Lykos." Her gaze flicked to the fire, pleased to see they'd made progress in the short time since she'd been grabbed. An insane thought occurred to her. What if the fire had been set to lure her out? It wasn't likely, but it was something she'd need to talk to Wesley about. Later, after the fire was extinguished and Lykos dealt with. When they weren't surrounded by what felt like half the town.

"Why don't you heal him?" Wesley asked quietly, though no one was close enough to overhear.

"I don't really know how," she admitted. "Sure, I've healed you and Lexi, but both times it was an accident, so I'm not sure how I did it. I don't want to make it worse, so I'll let Phillip do it." She managed a weak smile. "Besides, aren't I supposed to be keeping that a secret?"

"Yes, but I know how much he means to you." He glanced down at the wolf, who was still despite his pain. When Lykos realized Wesley was looking at him, he gave another small tail wag, even as he whined softly. "Hell, I've grown fond of him, too. It's not easy to know he's in pain."

"No, it isn't."

Phillip ran up, Lexi a few feet behind him. "What happened?" he asked, dropping to Lykos's other side.

"Some asshole tried to kidnap her and kicked Lykos when he tried to protect her," Wesley answered.

Concern for Chloe and the wolf was obvious, but Phillip rested his hands on Lykos, who licked his chin. Warm, soothing magic tickled at Chloe's senses as her brother repaired whatever damage the kick had done. When he finished, Lykos leapt up to lavish kisses on Phillip, who only laughed and gently pushed the wolf down before rubbing him briskly. "That's enough of that," he said, but he was smiling. Until he looked at Chloe once more and his expression went cold with the same rage showing on Wesley's face. "Did you drive here alone?"

Chloe shook her head. "No, I rode with Wesley."

"Good." He glanced between her and Wesley, ignoring Lexi for the moment. "Let me know when you leave. I think the three of us need to chat."

"I take it there's something I need to know?" Wesley asked with a scowl.

"Yes. Later."

"And what about me? That is my best friend you're talking about," Lexi said dryly, crossing her arms over her chest.

Phillip glanced to her, then gave Chloe a questioning look.

"I trust her as much as I trust you or Wesley," Chloe answered without hesitation.

He sighed. "Okay, Lexi can come, too."

"Good. Now, let's get this fire put out so we can leave and you guys can let the rest of us in on the secrets," Lexi said, turning away to return to those still working on the blaze.

"I'm going to pay for that," Chloe muttered, having seen the hurt in Lexi's eyes. She regretted that and would do her best to make it up to her cousin. "Okay, Lykos. Back in the car," she said, pointing toward the cruiser. To her delight, that command seemed to be one that had stuck and he raced back to it and jumped in. Sitting in the driver's seat, of course, and looking very proud of himself.

Wesley helped her to her feet. "How drained are you?"

Almost completely, but she wasn't going to worry him more than he already was. "I'm fine. It looks like they're getting it under control in any case."

"Don't overdo it," Phillip warned her as both he and Wesley fell into step on either side of her.

"Yes, Dad," she said with a roll of her eyes.

He shook his head, voice serious. "No, I mean it. You've never seen an aether when they fully drain their powers. You'll think you've got the flu on top of mono for a couple of days, unless someone can top you up."

"Shit. Really?"

"I wouldn't lie about something like that," he promised.

"I'll be careful." But she wasn't about to let the Oak burn. To her relief, though, they'd gotten the fire on the trees surrounding the massive Oak out. Some of its branches were scorched, but it didn't look as bad as she'd expected, for as long and hot as the fire had burned. Maybe it had some added protections, since it had been given by Zeus? Still, she gave a little more power to some of the elementals, who were looking even more exhausted than she was. A few thanked her, but most of them were running on fumes and barely seemed to realize anything existed but for the fire.

It took another ten minutes until the last of the flames disappeared, pulled into the bodies of fire elementals, or doused by the water elementals and witches. Another half hour was spent searching for any stray embers that could flare up, but none were found. Then the volunteers who had no influence over fire got to work. They helped those who had fought the fire to sit or lay down, brought them food, water, or healers as needed. Some started driving the exhausted workers home, as rest was the best thing now for most of them.

Mavros returned a few minutes later, landing on her shoulder as he admitted defeat. He'd lost the man who had tried to take her, and hadn't found any sign of him, though he'd searched long after his last glimpse. She reassured him that she was okay and appreciated the attempt before he joined Lykos in the car.

For a minute she watched them through the windshield and couldn't help the guilt stirring in her gut. The day had been hard on her animals. She knew it wasn't her fault, but she was the cause. Tonight, she would lavish love and praise on them. Not just because of the guilt, but because if it hadn't been for them alerting the people nearby, she might have actually been taken.

But she couldn't dwell on that, not right now.

The sun was just starting to descend below the horizon when people started leaving. It was total chaos, with people stopping to ask what the cause of the fire had been or waiting to be able to extract their vehicles from the mess the parking area and nearby roads had become.

The councilors—aside from Natalia, the vampire councilor—were among the last to leave. Chloe was too drained to be either angry or amused when Diego refused to meet her gaze. Instead, she focused on the other councilors.

Diego was the witch councilor, and she knew Colin—the shifter councilor—fairly well. They'd worked together some to rescue Pandora's Box, and again when the former elemental councilor, Daphne, had stolen memories from several residents of the island. He was a stocky, attractive guy who could turn into a freaking saber-tooth cat.

Erick was another councilor she knew, though not one she liked. A psychic, he'd been elected to be omni councilor—the one position that could be any type of supernatural. And, though he was extremely handsome, he gave her a weird vibe. She wasn't sure why, as he'd been instrumental in rescuing Lexi from Daphne. Something she'd forever be grateful for.

Then there was Zane, her personal favorite of the councilors, and the only one she'd personally voted for. Even with his misgivings about being a councilor, he took the job seriously and she'd seen him helping out earlier.

"Do we know what the hell happened here?" Colin asked.

"Not yet," Wesley admitted. "One of the fire elementals said it almost had to be magical to cause them so much trouble."

"Shit!" Chloe's outburst had all four councilors and Wesley staring at her.

"That was inappropriate, Miss Chadwick," Diego said

stiffly, which earned him a dirty look from Wesley.

Chloe just smiled sweetly, unwilling to let him get under her skin. "Perhaps it was, but I just remembered I'd heard the same thing and was trying to check when someone tried to *kidnap* me, so I got distracted."

"Can you get anything now?" Zane asked.

She shook her head. "Probably not. It was iffy when the fire was still burning, since there was so much other magic around. Without the fire burning? There's no one actively trying to keep the place going, and it would be hell trying to pick a single signature out of everyone else's. And that's if it existed in the first place."

"Will you check anyway?" Colin asked.

"Sure." She wouldn't mind getting away from Diego in any case. Stepping away from the group, she walked onto the charred ground near the Oak. It was still warm, but not uncomfortably so. Kneeling, she placed one hand on the earth, the other on the tree. Closing her eyes, she once again began to sift through the various magics around her, knowing that nothing would happen to her this time. Not with those closest to her on alert.

The Oak felt like it always did, which relieved her. The wards were intact. She pushed past the nearby sensations from Wesley and the councilors. She ignored the feel of Mavros and Lykos in her mind. Then came the hard part. Fire magic, regardless of the source, all felt similar to her. So while she felt quite a bit of it, it was impossible for her to narrow down which—if any—had caused the fire rather than ended it.

When she admitted defeat several minutes later, she rose, leaving her hand on the Oak for a moment longer, letting its magic relax and energize her. Only then did she turned back to the waiting group. "There was just too much fire magic done here today," she told them. "I can't tell any of them apart at this point. They've all sort of melded together."

Colin grunted softly and nodded. "It was a long shot. You'll keep us updated though, and continue investigating?" he asked, addressing both her and Wesley, which she appreciated.

"We will," Wesley assured him.

"Thanks."

The councilors left, though Zane lingered to check on Chloe. After she promised him she was fine and gave him a hug, he left, too, leaving only Wesley, Lexi, Phillip, and herself.

"Back to the office?" she asked.

"Mmhmm. Sounds like you've got a story to tell," Wesley said, his voice holding a hint of the annoyance he felt at being kept in the dark.

"You got me in trouble," she muttered to Phillip as the four of them headed for their cars.

Phillip just grinned. "Just consider me the annoying big brother."

Though she glared at him, she liked the sound of that.

Chapter 9

C hloe felt like she was leading a parade as she walked into the office, with two men, a woman, a wolf, and a crow all trailing behind her. Ignoring them for a moment, she put on a fresh pot of coffee. She was drained but couldn't bring herself to drink leftover coffee, especially not since Wesley had made it. She hoped that Lexi and Wesley would give her time to get some caffeine in her before they got started, but Lexi dashed that hope the second she walked into the office.

"Okay. What the hell is going on?"

Sighing and needing something to give her a little boost for this conversation, Chloe opted for a can of Coke while she waited for the coffee. "You guys want the long or short version?"

"Why don't you start with the short version then fill in details as needed?" Wesley suggested as he sat behind his desk.

Though she was sure Phillip would fill them in if she asked, that felt like the coward's way out. And she'd been the one keeping secrets, even if she hadn't wanted to. Even if it was under the advice of her father and brother. She owed it to Wesley and Lexi to be the one to fill them in. "Okay." She leaned against the edge of Wesley's desk, opened the soda, and took a quick drink. "To start, Lexi's my cousin on my mom's side. Phillip? He's my brother. We have the same dad. So half-brother, really, but I don't care about that. He's my brother."

Phillip didn't really look surprised to hear about Lexi, but her cousin's eyes widened almost comically. "Your what?" she asked, her voice an octave higher than normal. "You didn't tell me you'd found out who your father was!" She sounded shocked and hurt.

"Because I haven't," Chloe quickly assured her. "Phillip knows who he is, and I've met him—sort of—but I have no idea who he is. Both he and my brother—" and she shot an annoyed look to Phillip, "—feel that my knowing his name is too dangerous."

"Dangerous in what way?" Wesley asked, his eyes narrowing. "I know you wanted to keep your relationship secret, but you didn't mention you being in danger."

"No, no, no," Lexi interrupted, waving her hands in a motion for them to stop. "Yes, that's important, but we'll get back to it. What do you mean you've met your dad but don't know who he is? How is that possible?"

Chloe gave a slow shrug. "Because I've only met him when I'm dreaming. He somehow joins me in my dreams and we have conversations. I know what he looks like, I've talked to him, but he won't tell me anything about him. Hell, he didn't even tell me he was my dad. I figured that out on my own."

"Why didn't you tell me?" Lexi asked quietly, obviously upset.

"I wanted to," Chloe assured her, crossing to her friend, but Lexi stepped away from the hug. Right now, she wished she hadn't let her brother and dad convince her to keep this a secret from the two most important people to her. "They—my dad and Phillip—told me that if I knew, it could be dangerous. If I let other people know, it could be dangerous. I might have risked it for myself, but I didn't want to put you in the line of fire. I couldn't."

"You knew," Lexi said accusingly to Wesley.

"Chloe wasn't sure Phillip really was her brother. I did the DNA test to confirm it. That's the only reason I know," he promised Lexi, his voice gentling.

Lexi harrumphed but turned back to Chloe, arms folding over her chest, eyes narrowed. "So what's this danger, then?"

Chloe motioned to Phillip, who had remained suspiciously quiet up to this point. "He probably knows better than I do, because they haven't told me much on that. Just that someone's looking for me but doesn't know my name."

"You both know that her mother and grandmother were murdered, I assume?" Phillip asked. When they both answered in the affirmative, he went on. "Our father has enemies. Around the time Chloe's mom was killed—a little before, I think—he got word that someone was hunting for his daughter. We believe both Lydia and Cynthia were killed in an attempt to get to Chloe. We also believe some of the…trouble…that's occurred since she arrived on Salus is related to that."

"How does that make it dangerous for her to know who her dad is? Or for us to know any of this?" Lexi asked, the hurt turning to concern and confusion. "It's not like she's going to go around telling his name to everyone."

Phillip smiled faintly, but she saw the strain in his eyes. "Our dad is a smart guy. He thinks whoever is after Chloe wants to be certain she is her father's daughter. And since mind reading is a relatively easy thing, if she knew who her father was, they could pluck the information from her mind. Even if it's someone who can only read surface thoughts, it's a shockingly easy thing to get someone to think about something. And before you ask why it isn't equally dangerous for me to know, I have centuries of practice protecting mine from such intrusions."

"Why would anyone want to hurt Chloe, though?" Wesley asked. "I know you said you don't know who's looking for her, but if it's an enemy of your dad, why not go after him? Especially if this has been going on literally since she was born?"

Phillip looked pained. "That's difficult to explain without revealing his identity. And even that would only be a guess without knowing who's targeting her. A good guess, I think, but still just a guess."

"And I know I can trust you two, but this really does need to stay within this room," Chloe said, making sure her voice held no doubt whatsoever. "As much as I hate it, we can't even tell Zane right now. Not until we know more."

"Of course," Lexi said, finally releasing enough of her anger to give Chloe a quick, hard hug. "And I'm happy you found your brother, even if you didn't tell me. You're a bitch for that, you know," she said, pulling back just enough to look at Chloe.

"I know. But if it makes you feel any better, you're not just my best friend, but you were the first family I found on Salus. Phillip gets second best," she promised, flashing her brother a quick smile of apology. He only smiled back, understanding.

"That helps. A little. I still might not forgive you, except I owe you for the other night."

"What'd she do the other night?" Phillip asked curiously.

"None of your business," Lexi said, regaining her cheer enough to flash him a grin.

"Can we get back to the fact that someone tried to kidnap Chloe with about a hundred people around?" Wesley asked, his bear peeking out, though his eyes remained the gray of storm clouds.

"I had a thought about that," Chloe admitted slowly. "I mean, it's probably crazy, or maybe a little egotistical…"

"If you're thinking someone set that fire to get you out there, possibly to try to take you in the middle of the confusion, I had the same thought," Phillip admitted.

She nodded. "I was," she confirmed.

"Wouldn't it be easier to take her when she's alone?" Lexi asked, frowning.

"Possibly, but we don't know who's behind all this or what powers they might have," Phillip pointed out. "If she's alone, there aren't other people to distract from a single man—or small group—sneaking up on her, especially if magic is involved. Or it could be they'd stand out if they were alone. Maybe their magical signature is unique or strong, and the presence of so many other people is needed to mask it."

"It still makes more sense, to me at least, to try to grab me when I'm alone. I mean, look at what happened today. Lykos and Mavros made a fuss and attracted attention. Because they did that, he failed," Chloe retorted. "Hell, he didn't just fail, he almost got caught. If he hadn't bailed, I have no doubt he would have gotten mauled."

"I'd try to track him, but there were so many people out there, not to mention the smoke, that finding a single scent would be difficult. Just like Chloe trying to pick a single person's magic out of all of them," Wesley said, slumping back in his chair, a fierce, angry look on his face.

"If he was using some sort of disguise magic, it's likely his scent would have been disguised as well," Lexi pointed out. "At least if he wasn't being lazy about it."

"Not to mention that Mavros chased him and lost him. It's hard to outrun a crow," Chloe added.

Said crow chimed in then, from where he sat on the back of Chloe's chair. "Disappeared," he agreed.

"So, how do we keep me from getting kidnapped when we don't know who's coming for me, why exactly they want me, or anything else that could keep me safe?" Chloe asked bitterly. "I can't really just hide somewhere, and my dad said that leaving the island wouldn't help, either. Apparently, it would make me a sitting duck. But I refuse to live in fear or constantly keep looking over my shoulder. That's no way to live."

"We'll figure it out," Wesley said firmly as he rose to his feet and crossed over to her. "I know you won't like it, but you avoid being alone when possible, are careful when you absolutely have to be alone, and when we find this guy? You don't hold back." She started to speak but he shook his head, put a hand lightly over her mouth, and kept going. "You don't hold back," he repeated, emphasizing each word. His voice dropped, giving an illusion of privacy, but she had a feeling both Lexi and Phillip could still hear him. "I know you still feel bad about killing Ernst, and if I had my choice, you'd never need to use your gun again, but if you let that make you hesitate, when it's a choice between your life or the life of someone who wants you dead? I'm going to kick your ass before I hand it over to Lexi and Phillip to kick, too." Mavros let out an indignant call. "Lexi, Phillip, and Mavros," he qualified as he removed his hand.

Chloe glared up at him. "Fine. But I'm not going to hide behind you three, either. I do that, and it's just as likely you'll get hurt as I'll get taken."

"No one's asking you to hide behind us," Phillip interjected. "But having backup is just smart. It's harder to get past two people than one, and none of us are weak. And trying to do this alone is stupid."

"Listen to them, Chloe," Lexi asked softly. "None of us want to lose you any more than you want to lose us. Let us help you."

"I'm not going to be stupid," Chloe insisted. "I don't *want* to get kidnapped, I just don't want to live my life in fear. That's no kind of life!" She took a breath, then another, to calm herself. "I'll be careful. I promise. For one, I'll stop leaving Mavros and Lykos at home sometimes. And

Mavros?" The crow cawed and flew to her shoulder. "If something does happen to me, if I do get taken, you get to one of them as soon as possible, okay?" He let out a distressed sound now and leaned against the side of her head. "You guys know he can always tell where I am, so it's not like you'll be hunting for a needle in a haystack," she told the others.

"I also want you to let me—or one of us—know if you see anything suspicious. Anything at all," Wesley insisted. "I don't care how small or silly it seems, you let us know."

"I can do that." She wasn't dumb, and she'd been honest with them. She didn't want to get kidnapped—the idea terrified her—even if it was a certain way to discover who was after her. And she was desperate to figure out who was behind all this. Most of all, she wanted to be allowed to simply live her life, without worrying about world-ending plots or grudges that went back decades. She wanted to get to know her brother, have fun with her cousin, and explore her relationship with Wesley.

She really wanted to explore her relationship with Wesley.

Sighing, she wrapped her arms around Wesley, leaned into him, amused when Mavros moved to Wesley's shoulder. Lexi smiled at the simple act, while Phillip looked like he wanted to punch Wesley. It was such a big brotherly reaction that Chloe wanted to laugh. Instead, she pressed her face against Wesley's chest to hide her grin.

After a moment, she stepped back. "I promise I'll be careful and let you guys know if I'm worried about anything."

"You'd better. I know embarrassing stories about your childhood," Lexi warned with a sly smile. "Lydia and I talked over the years, you know. And she is still hanging around if I need more ammunition."

Chloe blinked at her in surprise. That wasn't something she'd thought she needed to worry about. Now she was wondering exactly what stories Granny had passed on. There were more than a few that she wouldn't want anyone knowing. She'd been kind of an awkward kid, physically and socially. Not a complete dork, but it was close. "You wouldn't."

"Oh, I absolutely would," Lexi said cheerfully. "Just keep that in mind before you decide that it won't hurt to just check that one dark corner before you call someone," she added as she turned and walked toward the door. "Talk to you later!"

Chloe groaned and shook her head. "I can't believe Granny betrayed me like that."

Phillip chuckled. "Think of it this way. If we'd grown up normally, it would've been me with all the embarrassing stories about you."

She narrowed her eyes at him. "Aren't you supposed to be endearing yourself to me? Or at least being the loving older brother?"

He walked over, kissed her forehead. "I am the loving older brother. Sometimes that means being a jerk to keep you safe."

"Gee, thanks."

"Because of that, I won't argue if you want to have dinner or just hang out a couple times a week until we figure this out."

"Now that I can go for." And to harass both him and Wesley, she smiled sweetly. "Maybe the three of us could have dinner. You know, so you two can get to know each other, too. My boyfriend and brother should be on good terms, don't you think?"

Wesley grimaced, but said, "I can do that."

Phillip looked equally as displeased for several seconds before he grinned. "Just wait until he gets to meet Dad. He is going to be the definition of an overprotective father."

Wesley sighed. "I can't wait."

Chapter 10

To appease everyone, including herself, Wesley stayed at her place that night. After the near miss, she was all too happy to spend the night loving him until they fell asleep, limbs tangled together.

The next morning, he made her breakfast—except for the coffee, of course—before she followed him to the office. As promised, both wolf and crow went with them. They weren't even going to let her be alone in the car, despite being directly behind the sheriff.

They wrote up the report on the fire at the Oak, and Chloe was pleased when she heard earth elementals and witches had already been out to the tree and repaired the damage. Though she'd felt the wards, knew they were intact, the witches had checked them as well and reported back that they were still functional and strong.

While she couldn't say work was quiet that day, the only calls they received were people inquiring about the fire. Primarily wondering how it had started and why it had taken so long to put out. They spent the entire day answering questions, and the calls were still coming in when Jack arrived to take the night shift. He confirmed he'd gotten several calls the previous night, so wasn't surprised. Chloe felt bad about leaving him to continue fielding them alone, but he assured them both that he had it and to enjoy their evening.

That night was spent at Wesley's. They sparred, ate, and shared a shower long after the water had gone cold.

Bears had amazing stamina.

She didn't so much fall asleep that night as pass out from exhausted bliss, with him pressed against her back.

The next few days passed in much the same way. She was only ever alone in the bathroom, as both Mavros and Lykos went with her anytime she was in the car. Half the time her car was followed by someone else's. Lexi's, when they went to the gym. Wesley's, when they left work.

Four days after the attack, the calls about the fire had slowed down. They only received three, which apparently meant the rest of the island was free to go back to their normal habits. Including the ones that involved having to call the cops.

A familiar—a wolf, in fact—had consistently been caught digging in a neighbor's backyard. Given that familiars had human intelligence and understanding, this meant it wasn't done out of ignorance, but spite. Especially since the familiar's witch and the elemental neighbor had a not so friendly rivalry. Wesley left to deal with that, but only after making Chloe promise to stay in the office until he got back, with the door locked.

She really hoped they found whoever it was who was hunting her soon, because she was starting to feel more than a little smothered. Too much longer and she'd crack.

When he returned an hour later, he looked both irritated and amused. Apparently, those neighbors regularly found little ways to annoy each other. It was harmless, but occasionally frustrating for all parties involved. The last time he'd been called, the elemental had frozen all the witch's pipes, leaving him without water. Before that, the witch had used magic to lock the elemental in the house. Even the windows had been sealed.

It was like the Hatfield and McCoys, except with less shooting and a grudge that lasted centuries instead of decades. And neither could remember exactly what had inspired the feud, or so they claimed.

When noon rolled around, she was shocked when Wesley didn't protest Chloe going to the diner to get them lunch. He did insist she take Mavros with her, but the crow wasn't keen on leaving her in any case. Through their bond, she knew he was feeling like he'd let her down by losing her attacker. No amount of soothing could convince him that it wasn't his fault.

Joel's was packed, but that wasn't unusual during lunchtime. There weren't any stools available, so Chloe stood at the end of the counter to wait until Lexi was free to take her order. She glanced around to judge the general mood after the blaze at the Oak and stiffened when she saw Diego and Peyton in a booth. It wasn't just that Diego had been cheating on her with Peyton, though that was bad enough. He'd also been sleeping with Peyton since well before he'd started dating Chloe. Before he'd even met her, actually, and she couldn't figure out why. He hadn't hidden their relationship, had been seen in public with her on multiple occasions, so it wasn't a simple case of wanting a woman on the side. Instead, it was his relationship with Peyton that had been kept secret. The part of her that yearned to figure things out wanted to check into it. The part of her who wanted to move past being cheated on told her to let it go, that they deserved one another and weren't worth her time.

The latter part won out. Most of the time. Especially since she was with a man who didn't play games like that.

Unfortunately, just as she noticed the couple, Peyton noticed her. She smirked and said something to Diego, which had him looking in Chloe's direction. Rather than join in with Peyton's amusement, he looked at Chloe coldly, as though she'd been the cheater, then turned back to Peyton and took her hand.

"Ignore them. They're both a waste of your time," Lexi said as she walked up to Chloe, smiling at both her and Mavros.

"I was just thinking the same thing. I just wish I knew why he did it."

"I don't think the answer would actually help you," Lexi said sympathetically. "Besides, you're with a much better man now."

Chloe smiled. "I really am. And speaking of that man, can I get lunch for the two of us, to go?"

"Sure. You want your usuals?"

"Yeah, that works. Thanks."

Lexi scribbled the order on her pad, gave it to the cook. She couldn't come back to talk to Chloe until she brought the takeout boxes over. There were the two expected big ones, and a small one she knew would include something for Mavros and Lykos. "Why don't I come by tonight? We can have a girl's night. Trash the cheating ex, gossip about the new guy, and drink way too much wine?" Lexi offered.

Chloe grinned as she passed over her card to pay. "That sounds great. I get off at five."

"Same here, so I'll be over around five thirty. I'll bring the wine, you get the pizza?"

"That works for me." And while it was another way of ensuring she wasn't alone, girl's night shouldn't feel quite as confining. "I look forward to it," Chloe assured Lexi as she left the diner, refusing to give have last look at Diego and Peyton.

The rest of her day was a little easier. She loved her nights with Wesley, but there was definitely something to be said about just hanging out with another woman. Wesley was just happy she wouldn't be alone in her house all night. And a little disappointed she wouldn't be in his bed again.

Truthfully, so was she. It was shockingly at how quickly she'd become accustomed to having him beside her while she slept. How much she liked it.

There was only one other call that day, which both Chloe and Wesley responded to. A man had reported the theft of his prized guitar. Nothing else was missing, which struck Chloe as odd, but Wesley proved just how well he knew the island and its residents when they quickly traced it to a teenage boy a few houses down. The boy, Jacob, was a music enthusiast who had just wanted to borrow the guitar for a little while but had gotten caught up in playing the exceptional instrument. When the guitar's owner heard, he'd declined to press charges, and had actually invited Jacob over to play now and again.

When five rolled around, Chloe kissed Wesley goodbye, which he turned into a lengthy affair. Not that she could complain about that. In fact, she was still smiling as she pulled up in front of her house and let the animals out. Though neither had complained about spending most of their day in the office, they raced around the yard, stretching their legs and wings.

For a minute she just watched them, delighting in their play. Mavros would swoop down, just enough to tease Lykos, who would race after him, leaping into the air but always missing the crow. Though she'd been skeptical when she'd decided to bring the pup home, she had to admit they got along wonderfully. Lykos chased Mavros regularly, but it was always done playfully, and he always stopped short of doing anything that could hurt the more delicate creature. Which was good because, while she loved the wolf and couldn't say she favored fur or feathers, it was Mavros she was mystically connected to. Hurting him would be like hurting herself.

When they ran around the back she decided to head

inside and out of the cold. She'd just slid her key into the lock when she heard a soft sound about the same time she felt a small prick on the side of her neck. Confused, she started to lift her arm to rub at the spot, but the limb wouldn't cooperate. In fact, none of her muscles would work. They felt so heavy and sensation quickly retreated from them until all she could feel was their unnatural weight. It reminded her, just for an instant, of when Hiro had paralyzed her with magic in his attempt to get Pandora's Box, but this wasn't magic. No, that prick had to be from a needle, or maybe some kind of tranq dart, which was more terrifying. Magic she could defend against, could fight against. Something mundane injected into her body? She had no way to protect herself from that.

Which meant when she felt arms wrap around her, lifting her roughly, she had no way to struggle, no way to call for help. Mavros and Lykos were just around back, but she couldn't even reach out to her familiar. For the first time since her powers had been unlocked, she realized she didn't feel a single of trace of magic, not even her own. It terrified her more than she would have thought possible.

Helpless, she saw her house moving away, felt herself carried further from it. She was set down, shocked when her body remained vertical once she had been released. Something coarse and dark was shoved over her head without any care, blocking out any other sights which could help her. Blocking out the sight of whoever was taking her.

She felt herself being lifted again, then dropped onto something hard and unforgiving. Another needle was shoved into her neck, another substance pumped into her veins, and the world started to feel fuzzy around the edges. She heard a single bark that sounded like it came from far away, but she couldn't know if that was a true representation of the distance, or a result of whatever drug was working through her body. Immediately after she heard another sound. Her blurry mind thought it might be a trunk closing, but she had no way of checking.

Her body rolled to one side as whatever she was in started to move rapidly. Desperately she scrambled to reach her power, even the tiniest scrap of it. To contact Mavros, to do something, anything, to free herself. But whatever had been injected into her did too good a job and her mind grew as heavy as her limbs, until it was hard to think. Everything felt weightless and heavy at the same time, confusing her further.

Her last thought before she slid into the black was that Wesley had been right to worry.

Chloe drifted back to consciousness. Her arms and legs were numb, and her mind wasn't much better. It felt like there was a wall wrapped around her brain, preventing her from connecting two thoughts together. She was upright, which further confused her. She never fell asleep sitting up as it always gave her a crick in the neck. Lifting her head, an act which took entirely too long and too much effort, she managed to open her eyes, which felt heavier than lead. What she saw left her even more baffled.

She was in some sort of large, rectangular room, the walls, floor, and ceiling made of some pale, roughly-shaped stone. It was completely empty but for a chair set in front of her and a trio of torches which provided only dim, flickering light. There were no windows, no doors that she could see. Curious about where she was, she started to twist, to see what was behind her, when she realized she could only move a few inches. Looking down, it took her groggy brain several long moments to realize she was chained to the chair. The metal links bound her ankles, wrists, and waist, which was what had halted her movement.

She tugged at the restraints, but they held firm. Her body wasn't as responsive as she would like, so she decided to save what little energy she had and try when she had more control of her limbs. Instead, she moved as much as she was able to, turning her head until she could just make out the edge of a door out of the corner of her vision.

Straightening, she slumped back in her chair and frowned. Where the hell was she? More importantly, why was she here? Someone had clearly brought her here, but who? She started to call out, but the memory of being taken from her front yard rushed to the front of her mind and she clamped her mouth shut. There was no way she was going to alert her captor to the fact that she was awake one second sooner than necessary. If she'd learned anything from movies, it was that the torture would begin the moment they knew she was awake.

She pulled at the chains, knowing she couldn't break them, but hoping she could shift them enough to slip free. When that didn't work, she glared at the chains and changed tactics. Closing her eyes, she searched for magic. When she realized her powers were still blocked, she felt her body try to go into panic mode. She fought it down, knowing it wouldn't help, and she'd been in a lot worse situations than this before. Okay, not really, but she was going to tell herself that until she was out of here. Keeping her eyes closed, she took several deep breaths and focused on something else, anything else to keep her calm.

Lexi. She was going to Chloe's house. She'd find Mavros and Lykos alone and realize Chloe was missing. Then she'd get in touch with Wesley and Phillip. Lexi and Phillip were strong witches and Wesley had the whole bear nose thing going on. They'd also have Mavros to act as a homing beacon to find her. Which meant she probably hadn't been here long, or they'd already have found her. Between the five of them, they'd be able to handle whatever asshole had decided to kidnap her. Six, if she could get free and find out what had happened to her powers.

Her powers. She groaned softly as she realized she'd become more dependent on them than she'd realized. Sensing magic had become as vital and commonplace to her as sight or hearing. And to think, when she'd first learned she was an elemental, part of her had wanted to ignore it all. To go back to being an ordinary human.

The door behind her slammed against the wall and her eyes flew open. Shoulders tensed, but she fought not to show any sign of the anxiety she felt. Anxiety that was quickly pushing toward terror. She waited as the quiet sound of soft-soled shoes on stone approached, then looked up as a figure came into view. Her eyes widened, then quickly narrowed. All traces of fear fled, replaced by annoyance and an odd sense of vindication.

Erick Jensen.

She'd known something was off with him, but she couldn't have predicted he'd go this far.

He said nothing until he sat on the chair across from her, flicking a speck of lint off the thigh of his perfectly pressed slacks. Then, he smiled, what she thought of as a politician's smile. Or it would be, if it weren't for the frigid hatred in his pale blue eyes. "Isn't this where you express surprise to see me, followed immediately by a flurry of questions, such as where you are, why you're here, etcetera, etcetera?" he asked, disdain thick in every syllable.

Chloe cocked her head and arched a brow. "I actually can't say I'm really all that surprised that it's you. As for the rest?" She shrugged, as much as the chains would allow. "You'll either refuse to tell me or start bragging about it in a few minutes. Either way, me asking wouldn't make a difference."

"You're not surprised?" he asked, hatred shifting to confusion. It lasted only for a moment before his gaze sharpened on her. "Why not?" he asked, tone suspicious and somehow triumphant.

"Seriously?" she asked incredulously. "You've been creepy since the day I met you. Hell, Erick, the reason I never called you after our date was because you gave me bad vibes. It only got worse from there."

He rejected that explanation immediately with a sharp shake of his head. "No. That's not it. You know who I am, don't you?" he accused.

The question made her pause and frown at him. How could she not know who he was? He was a fucking town councilor. Everyone knew who he was. So why the question? The easy explanation for it would be that he'd gone off his rocker—which he obviously had—but she thought there was more to it than that. "You're Erick Jensen, one of the councilors on Salus," she answered slowly.

"If you've figured out who I am, you know who your father is, don't you?" he went on as though she hadn't spoken.

"What the hell does one have to do with the other?" she blurted out, forgetting in her surprise that she was being held hostage by this man.

He stood and leaned forward, gripping her shoulders firmly. "Who is your father?" he demanded, his breath hot against her face.

For the first time, she found herself intimidated by him. It wasn't a feeling she was comfortable with. Before he'd just seemed like some weird jackass, but now? He was being unpredictable, and she didn't like that. "I don't know," she answered honestly.

"Liar! Who is your father?" he repeated, fingers tightening painfully, making her wince as they ground on bone.

"I don't know! I've never met him, and my grandmother wouldn't even talk about him when I asked," she insisted.

"You lie," he hissed. "There's no way you could know who I am without knowing who your father is."

"You introduced yourself to me when we met, that's how I know your name!" she shouted as she tried to pull away from him. There wasn't anywhere for her to go, and his grip was bruising now. "If you've got another name, I've never heard it, and even if I had, I wouldn't admit it."

He straightened and, though he released her, her shoulder throbbed from the sharp press of his fingers. "We'll see if you're still spouting that same lie after a couple more hours down here by yourself." His steps were sharper, more rapid as he left her. When the door shut behind him, the torches abruptly winked out, leaving her in absolute darkness.

Chloe's breath quickened. She'd never been particularly afraid of the dark or claustrophobic, but being trapped in a solid black room by a man who hated her was enough to have her heart rate spiking. It didn't help that she'd latched onto something he said. A couple *more* hours. If she'd already been down here that long, then where were Wesley and her family? Why hadn't they found her yet?

Her stomach rolled as possibilities filled the darkness.

Chapter 11

C hloe tried to stay calm. She even tried to sleep, but the discomfort from the chains and her anxiety regarding her situation kept her awake. It was impossible to tell how long she'd been there, but it certainly felt like hours since Erick had left, if not longer. At this point, she wouldn't be surprised if it was days.

Eventually, she almost began to wish Erick would come back. She'd prefer Wesley, Lexi, or Phillip, but the dark solitude was starting to get to her.

Desperately she tried to access her powers, but something was still preventing it. She didn't know if one of the injections had been a long-lasting drug, or if there was something about the room she was in, or maybe the chains around her, that blocked her powers. The cuffs the sheriff's department used could do that, so why couldn't these chains or the stones around her be the same? Which added another layer of terror. If it was the chains blocking her, could they also be blocking her connection to Mavros? She didn't truly understand how that bond worked, but maybe that was why no one had found her yet?

Though not as immediate a concern, she was also worried about Erick's interest in the identity of her dad. Was he the one her dad and Phillip were worried about? The one who'd been looking for her? But if that was the case, how could a psychic whose only power—as far as she knew—was clairvoyance hide from a witch? More, how had he managed to kill two apparently powerful aether elementals while making it look like an accident?

When she finally accepted that sleep wasn't going to give her a reprieve from her current situation, she began to sing. Softly, at first, then at the top of her lungs. Classic rock, modern pop, anything that came to mind. At least until the lack of anything to drink dried her throat too much to sing.

Everything either ached or was painfully numb. Her throat was raw and the inside of her mouth was unbelievably parched. When the door opened behind her and the torches instantly lit, she almost let out a sob of relief. She had to squint against the sudden light, though she knew the flames were far from bright.

"Ready to tell me the truth, yet?" Erick asked as he settled in his chair once more, looking almost calm. Almost. There was still a wildness in his eyes she couldn't miss. A wildness that warned her she should choose her words very carefully.

"I have told you the truth," she croaked slowly and softly. Her tender throat wouldn't allow much more than that.

He looked disgusted, though it could have been as much for her answer as the voice it was given in. "I find it very hard to believe that your father hasn't contacted you. I find it harder still to believe Lydia never once told you anything about him."

"You should," she told him wearily. "Anytime I mentioned my dad she changed the subject. If I pressed, she got angry. As for why my dad hasn't been in my life…" She shrugged, the movement small, due as much to exhaustion as the chains. "It sounds like you know him, so maybe you can tell me. I've always wanted to know about him."

The smile he gave her had her stomach flipping and her pulse quickening. He leaned forward and rested a hand on her knee. It didn't do anything, just lie there for now, unmoving, but somehow it was threatening. A reminder that she was bound and he *could* hurt her at any time. "You may think you know me, but you don't. So I'm going to let you in on a little secret that will help with that," he said, giving her knee a light squeeze, though she didn't mistake it for friendly. "One thing I can do, without fail, is identify a liar. You are most definitely lying to me." His hand tightened again, stopping just before the point of pain. "I would suggest you start telling me the truth, or I'm going to have to...persuade you." As he said persuade, his fingers curled, digging in, harder than she would have thought possible. Somehow, she felt it, even with her legs asleep, and winced at the sharp, stinging pain. A cry wanted to tear out of her throat, but she choked it back, refusing to give him the satisfaction. If it was the only way she could fight back—for now—then she would bite her tongue off before letting him hear her scream.

Chloe knew she had to be careful in what she told him. While she definitely wanted out of here, and to avoid being hurt, she wouldn't risk her dad, especially not before she'd ever actually met him. She also wasn't going to risk her brother, and she was afraid he might suffer the same fate as her if Erick knew she wasn't her father's only child. And though she wasn't entirely sure he was being honest about his ability to tell truth from lie, she didn't want to anger him more than necessary. She'd told him the truth, despite what he believed, but maybe she'd expand on it. Be more open, even if she wasn't about to tell him the whole truth.

When his hand relaxed, she drew in a slow breath, calming herself. "Erick," she began tiredly, "I've never been in the same room as my father. I've never talked to him on the phone or over a video call. I've never texted or emailed him. I don't even know what his name is. Or why he wasn't around when I was growing up. I can't tell you what I don't know."

Truth or not, her answer still infuriated him. His hand tightened on her knee before he released her abruptly. Before she could sigh in relief, he backhanded her. The blow was hard enough to snap her head to one side and cut the inside of her already sensitive mouth. The blood was almost a balm, providing some moisture to parched tissues. When it was followed by another hard hit, she couldn't quite hold back the soft cry of pain.

He grabbed hold of her face, squeezing her cheeks and chin firmly as he forced her gaze back to his. "Apparently you didn't get the message. You're going to stay here, and you're going to suffer, until you tell me the name of your father."

She tried to speak, but he dropped his hand to her throat, squeezing just hard enough to cut off her air supply. "No more lies. I'll leave you to think about things a little longer. But next time? You'd better be ready to give me the name." As she tried to suck in a breath, he leaned in so their cheeks touched, and dropped his voice to a low whisper. "A few slaps is mild, Chloe. Remember that, before you decide to hold out on me next time. History has invented all kinds of methods of torture."

He let her gasp for a minute longer, until the world started going gray around the edges, before he released her and left, leaving her panting in darkness once more.

It took time for the adrenaline to fade, for the ache his hands had caused to lessen. It took even longer, but Chloe did start to doze. She thought it was more likely that she was randomly slipping in and out of consciousness. Not a great sign, she knew, but it was a reprieve from the darkness and her thoughts. History had indeed invented quite a few ways of torturing people, and she didn't want to experience any of those methods. Especially since she really didn't have a name to give Erick. Nor was she sure why he was pushing so hard to get the name. If this was all because of something her dad had done—or Erick believed he had done—why was he keeping her alive? Using Phillip's theory, he'd already killed Granny, her mom, and several others, so why not her? Unless what he had in mind for her father's daughter was worse than a quick death.

It was tempting to give him a fake name, something to get him to release her, or at least give her something to drink. If he was telling the truth about his ability to sense lies, it would likely only make things worse. Because he was right, what he'd done so far was minor as far as torture went. As long as she got out of here soon, nothing he'd done would cause permanent damage, after all.

The torches lit and she weakly lifted her head, not yet ready to deal with Erick, but happy there was some light again. To her shock, it wasn't Erick who came into her field of view. It was Wesley.

She was so relieved she wanted to cry but was too dehydrated for tears. Instead, she gave him a smile, though she knew it was weak, and whispered his name.

She'd known they would find her. She'd known *he* would find her.

"Chloe," he murmured, eyes yellow with rage as he knelt in front of her and cupped her face. The touch, though gentle, landed on a bruise caused by Erick's backhand, and she winced. "Are you all right?" he asked, his voice a low, urgent growl.

"Will be. Just need water and healing," she told him, slowly turning her face from his hand, lessening the throbbing in her face.

"You'll get them. We've got to be quick though." His

105

hand dropped and he started working on the chains.

"What took you so long, Yogi?" she asked, some of the anxiety slipping out of her.

Then he gave her a confused look. It only lasted for a second, but she saw it. He didn't understand why she'd called him Yogi. That didn't make sense. She'd started calling him that only days after she'd met him. Hell, she'd given him a stuffed Yogi for Christmas last month. So why the confusion?

She remembered the fire at the Oak, the kidnapping attempt. Lexi had said the man who'd tried to take her had been using disguise magic. Which meant this was not her sweet, surly bear. No way would Wesley forget their nicknames for each other.

Though tired and light-headed, Chloe managed to work out that stating that fact was probably not wise. Better to see if she could use it. She only hoped her brain wasn't too sluggish to manage it. But god, she'd love a gallon of water, an entire pizza—maybe two—and at least twelve hours sleep.

"There are a lot of hidden places on Salus," he told her as the chains around her legs loosened. Sensation rushed back into her limbs, the pins and needles more painful and intense than she'd ever felt. She had to bite her lip to hold in the cry and felt the skin split beneath her teeth. "We've been searching for you for two days."

Her eyes widened. "Two days?" If he was telling the truth, it explained the dehydration. Yes, it had felt like days, but she thought that was just a trick of solitude and fear.

He nodded sharply and got the other two chains undone. "Half the island's been hunting for you. Do you know who did this to you?"

Deciding to play along, at least for now, she nodded as she tried to move her arms and legs, but it was taking a minute for her to regain control of them. Two days in a chair had taken its toll. "It was Erick."

'Wesley' did a good job of feigning shock. "Erick? Councilor Erick?" When she nodded, he asked, "Why?"

"He wanted to know the name of my dad." She started to go on, to remind him of how he knew that, but he interrupted.

"Your dad? Do you know why?"

"Not a clue."

This time it was a sound from outside the room that stopped her from continuing. He pulled her out of the chair and, though the sudden pressure on her legs made her whimper, he wrapped his arms around her and pulled her toward the wall, just out of sight of the door.

They watched the door for a moment before he looked back to her and dropped his voice. "There are men all over this place. I'm good, but I can't fight them all at once. You've got to help me." He stared into her eyes and she could see the malice in them, hidden under the thinnest veneer of concern. "Who's your dad? Maybe it'll help me figure out what's going on."

"I don't know. I've never known. I told you that."

"Chloe, we don't have time for you to hold back because you promised to keep this a secret or something. Who is your dad?"

She was out of the chains, but there was no way she could run, not yet, nor could she feel her magic. There weren't a lot of options, and certainly no good ones. She couldn't very well tell him she knew he wasn't Wesley, but neither could she give him what she didn't have. Resigned, she sighed and shook her head. "I really don't know. I've never been told, I've never seen it written down, and I have no idea where to even look for the information."

"Tell me!" he insisted, no longer whispering.

"I can't tell you what I don't know," she answered, tension beginning to coil within her as she braced for more slaps. Or the torture Erick had promised.

He roared, but it didn't sound like Wesley anymore. After a moment, the sight of Wesley faded as well, melting away until it was Erick standing in front of her. He released her as though she were offensive to him and stepped back, making her have to lean against the wall to remain upright when her legs buckled. "I warned you! I gave you multiple opportunities to avoid this," he snarled before agony hit every nerve in her body. Her mouth opened in a scream, but her vocal cords couldn't produce the sound. Her body bowed and twitched against the pain, which felt like it would never end.

When it did finally stop, she struggled to catch her breath and opened eyes which had slammed shut against the onslaught. The sight that greeted her made her mind stutter. She was in the chair, the chains still around her. But how? She'd been free and against the wall a moment ago. How had she gotten back into the chair so quickly?

Unless she'd never actually left the chair. She looked up at Erick, who was standing this time, rather than sitting. There was a flash of satisfaction, no doubt at her confusion, before rage and frustration replaced it. He swung at her, this time with a closed fist. She almost didn't feel it, not after the intensity of whatever he'd done to her when she'd thought she was free. Almost. But then he kept hitting her, over and over.

She could see his face through one eye, and she saw something other than the expected. His hair and eyes were darker, and his features had shifted. There were enough similarities that this face looked like a relative of his normal one, but it was most definitely a different face.

Before she could fully process that, the world blissfully went black.

Chapter 12

When she woke again, she was alone and in the dark once more. She wasn't entirely sure she'd be able to see even if the torches had been lit. Her entire face felt puffy and throbbed in time with her heartbeat. It was difficult to tell with the absolute absence of light, but she was pretty certain one eye was swollen shut.

She took stock of what injuries she could, wishing for the thousandth time that her hands weren't bound. Gently probing at her mouth with her tongue, she winced. Her cheeks and lips had been cut, almost shredded, but it seemed like he'd kept his attacks strictly to her face. She wasn't sure why. Movement of the small muscles told her blood had dried on her skin as well, adding an uncomfortable itchiness to the pain.

It took several minutes before she realized she could feel something new, something the pain had been masking. No, she realized, not new, just something that had been suppressed. Her powers! They weren't as strong as they normally were, but she could feel magic around her. Even better, she could feel Mavros. The connection was weak, a single string compared to the thick rope it normally was, but he was there.

Chloe closed her eyes, fighting to keep her breathing slow

and steady. Being able to contact Mavros wouldn't do any good if she hyperventilated and passed out. When she had calmed herself, she reached out, straining not to lose that thin magical strand connecting them. When she felt his surprise, then his elation, she almost laughed with pure relief. She had to be careful here. Communicating like this wasn't like speaking. It wasn't even how books portrayed telepathic communication. This was less words and more emotions, but concepts could be transmitted.

She pictured the room she was in, frustrated she couldn't tell him more about her location. She also did her best to convey that it was Erick who had taken her but wasn't sure how well it translated. The confusion about her location would be clear enough, but not the thought regarding Erick.

She tried again, but the connection was still tenuous, and before she could manage to reach him, she felt it thin too much to get to him. It left her alone once more, but it also left her with hope. Mavros knew she was still alive, and he'd relay that to the others. Even better, though the exchange had been brief, it might have been just enough to let him get a fix on where she was. She wasn't entirely sure how that worked, as it seemed to be one-sided. She could sense Lykos, but that was a different kind of connection. If it weren't for his enchanted tag, she wouldn't be able to sense him any more than he could sense her.

All she had to do now was avoid pissing Erick off too badly before the calvary arrived.

Chloe slid in and out of consciousness, with no idea of how much time had passed. Each time she woke, she felt a little weaker, and her stomach had gone beyond simply growling to cramping with emptiness. The dried blood on her face itched like crazy, but her attempts to rub it off on her shoulder had been only partially successful. Each time she'd tried, she'd only aggravated the bruises on her face and cuts on the inside of her mouth.

The torches flared and she felt little more than resignation that she was about to endure another visit from Erick. The man was absolutely insane. Even if her dad had done something completely heinous, what purpose was served in torturing her for his name? More, why was he still pushing her for a name she obviously didn't have?

He'd gone for a different tactic this time, though. When he sat down, through her one open eye she saw he held a clear insulated bottle. His face was calm, and his voice was as smooth and charming as she'd ever heard it. "Good morning, Chloe. I imagine you're feeling a little worse for the wear after your stay here."

"I can't imagine why," she said, the sarcastic note overshadowed by the raspy sound of her voice, but she couldn't help it.

"Yes, no food or drink for a few days can certainly take its toll on the body," he went on companionably. "I've certainly treated you harshly, but I'm here to remedy that." He lifted the bottle, wiggled it in the air. "I've got some water here that would no doubt feel and taste amazing right now. Would you like some?"

"What's in it?" she asked, unable to keep the blunt question from slipping out. She was equally unable to stop staring at the water. Part of her mind told her to just take it, drink the water. Whatever was in it couldn't be worse than her current situation. And he didn't have any reason to drug her now. She was already his captive.

"Just ice." He feigned a sudden understanding and nodded. "Ahh, I see. You think I might have put something in it. A poison, perhaps. I think I can reassure you on that." He opened the bottle, drank, then held it toward her without

111

replacing the lid. "You can have as much as you like, though you should probably drink slowly," he offered, holding it near her mouth.

Chloe wanted that water more than she wanted her next breath. She couldn't recall ever craving anything more and couldn't take her gaze off the spectacularly clear liquid, the chilled cubes floating in it. But she also couldn't risk it. If she gave in now, it would make it harder to resist in the future. But oh, she wanted it. She turned her head away from the thermos and the temptation it presented. Maybe it would be easier if she couldn't see it. "No."

He arched a brow and kept his arm extended. "No? You're rejecting my olive branch?"

She could smell the water and had to fight her body's instincts to give in. A few sips, that's all it would take. Closing her good eye, she shook her head. "I'm rejecting your manipulation."

"You do realize that if you don't accept my kindness, I'll have to go back to less pleasant methods of persuading you?"

"Doesn't matter. Can't tell you what I don't know."

"Bullshit!" he yelled, flinging the bottle so it hit the stone and clattered to the floor with a plastic thud. Water poured out, darkening the stone, and she almost whimpered at the waste. "There's no way you haven't spoken to him, he wouldn't allow it!"

So much for not pissing him off. "It sounds like you know. Why don't you tell me who he is?" she asked, glancing back to him.

He punched her. Not in the face this time, which was both relief and punishment, as he shoved his fist into her already aching belly. She doubled over as much as the chains allowed, her breath exploding out of her. Before she could recover from that, he did it again. It was probably a blessing that she hadn't drank any of the water, because it felt like she would have thrown up if she had anything in her stomach.

"So you can just say whatever you think I want to know?" he asked with a sneer as he straightened. "I'm not quite that gullible. No, I want the truth, not a ruse meant to placate me. You—" He cut off and his head whipped toward the door. Snarling murderously, he looked back down at her. "Don't think this means you're safe," he warned her before he ran toward the door.

Oddly, this time the torches didn't go out. She barely noticed, as she was trying to catch her breath and prevent herself from dry heaving. The reason for his quick departure was a more important puzzle in any case. Not that she wasn't relieved, but it was weird. What could make him leave like that? Her brain was simply too fuzzy for her to focus enough to even consider possibilities.

A few minutes later she heard the sound of running, and it was getting closer. Tensing in anticipation of yet another unpleasant experience, she twisted as much as she could. With the one eye closed because of swelling, she couldn't quite get the door in her line of sight. It wasn't necessary, though, as the footsteps didn't stop at the doorway.

"She's here!"

Just as she identified the voice as belonging to her brother, he ran into her field of vision. He knelt in front of her, took in her battered face. Pure rage showed first on his features before it shifted to sympathy. "Oh, Chloe," he murmured, as more footsteps grew closer.

Wesley ran into the room, closely followed by Lykos and Mavros. "Chloe!" He ran over to her, pushing Phillip out of the way. Shock flashed in his eyes when she cringed away from him. "Chloe?" he asked, his voice baffled rather than hurt.

She hadn't meant to do it, but the last time she'd seen those features, they'd been accompanied by pain.

"Are you guys real?" she asked hoarsely. She badly

wanted to believe they were actually here but couldn't give into another deception.

Mavros landed on the arm of her chair and cawed, watching her with worried eyes. Lykos leaned against her legs, but she couldn't feel it, not with them completely numb.

"Of course we're real," Wesley said, dropping to a knee to start working on her chains.

"Can you prove it?" she asked, even as she felt Mavros pushing relief through their bond.

Phillip laid a hand on her arm. "I'm your brother. We met a couple months ago when Mavros found Lykos hurt behind your house," he told her as she felt the tingle of his magic. It was instantly followed by the pain in her face and stomach easing. She was still weak and dehydrated, but she doubted he could fix that with his magic.

"Who did this to you?" Wesley asked when the first chain released, freeing her legs. "Tell me who it is and I'll tear them apart," he told her, glancing up with yellow eyes. Even his voice sounded more like his bear than him.

She was still too wary to believe it was him and she was too exhausted for true hope. "What's your nickname for me?"

He frowned as he went to work on the chain around her left wrist, while Phillip worked on the right. "Nickname? Which one? I guess honey's more of an endearment than a nickname, but I also call you Boo-boo, usually when you annoy me."

"It is you," she whispered as she looked at all four of them in turn, wanting to cry now with relief. "All of you."

"It's us," Phillip assured her. "And I'm sure you're dying for something to drink, but we didn't think to bring any water. We just wanted to find you," he told her, true regret in his words for that lack.

After her arms were free, Wesley got the chain around her waist released. The moment she was no longer bound to the chair, he stood and swept her out of the chair and against him for a tight hug. Being on her feet caused circulation in her legs to be restored and she was assaulted by the sharp pins and needles sensation once more. It was intense enough to cause her to cry out, and he immediately shifted, sitting her back down. "Tell me a name," he growled. Obviously pissed, his hands were still gentle as he started to massage her legs. It was unpleasant at first, but the painful tingling began to subside.

"It was Erick," she answered as she willed her body to relax. "He kept trying to get me to tell him Dad's name."

"But you don't know it!" Phillip protested.

"I know, but he didn't believe me." She tested her legs, her arms, relieved when it was bearable to use them again. Not pleasant, but she could walk out of here, which was all she cared about.

Wesley drew her out of the chair, less abruptly this time, and cupped her face with one of his big hands. "You're not allowed to do that to me again," he whispered. "I've been going crazy, not knowing where you were for two days."

"Two days?" She was shocked. Erick had said as much, and it had felt like ages, but she'd hoped he had been lying about that.

"Two days," he confirmed. "I can't do that again. I refuse to do that again." Before she could respond, before her brain could even process that, his mouth was on hers. It wasn't a fairytale kiss, not with her lips so dry, her clothes filthy, and the dried blood on her face, but she didn't care. Though she'd forgotten her brother was there, she wouldn't have cared even if she remembered. Erick was gone and she was with four of her favorite individuals.

Phillip cleared his throat after a minute. "We should get her home. She's still dehydrated and weak."

Wesley slowly drew back and nodded. "We should."

But Chloe wasn't quite ready, not physically. Not only

were her limbs still tingling uncomfortably, but her legs were unsteady now thanks to that kiss. She didn't get long to settle or for her legs to stop hurting, not with Wesley wrapping an arm around her waist and starting to guide her out of the room that been her prison for two long days. Mavros joined them, though he didn't settle on her shoulder, too afraid of further injuring her in her condition. Instead, he perched on Wesley's, so he was still close. Lykos wasn't so subdued. He raced ahead of them, darted back to make sure they were following, then repeated the action while Phillip brought up the rear.

The walk was a great deal longer than she would have liked. It took several minutes, and multiple flights of stairs, before she saw daylight. Though it was overcast, she still had to squint as her eyes had adjusted to the dim light of torches.

"Where are we?" she asked, not recognizing the building. It was entirely constructed from stone, and though there was a roof above her and a wall to either side, the far end was open to the elements.

"Apollo's temple," Phillip said, his voice clipped.

She wondered about his tone but found it curious that she'd been kept in a temple. The island had temples for most of the gods, but this was only the second one she'd been in. At least this time the god wasn't there. It hadn't gone so well when she'd visited Zeus's temple, since she'd mouthed off to him.

They walked down the five steps out of the temple and Chloe noticed something odd about the light. It was flickering, sort of like the torches had, but sunlight didn't flicker. Confused, she glanced up and gaped, so shocked that she stopped where she was. The sky above her was full, not of clouds, but of birds. She couldn't even begin to count how many, but assumed it was hundreds, if not thousands of birds. "What the hell?" she breathed, unable to do anything but stare up at them as they circled silently.

Mavros let out a smug caw before he walked down to her shoulder. "Friends. They help."

"Help?"

"After you contacted him, Mavros somehow recruited what I think is every crow within fifty miles to search the island for you. You had the largest murder of crows I've ever heard of hunting for you."

"That's not a murder," she said, shaking her head. "That many crows? It's a freaking massacre."

"A massacre?" Phillip asked, puzzled but smiling.

"Mmhmm. A bunch of murders is a massacre, right? So...massacre of crows." It made sense to her, at least in her still confused state.

"Whatever you say," he told her, still smiling, but shaking his head now.

"Let's get you home," Wesley said, encouraging her to continue walking.

"Home sounds like the best idea you've ever had," she agreed, a little desperate to be back in familiar surroundings.

He smiled faintly, glancing to the bird on her shoulder. "Mavros? You should probably tell your buddies they can go home."

The crow let out an agreeing caw before he leapt from Chloe's shoulder to join the other crows. By the time they reached Phillip's dark gray SUV, the living cloud had begun to disperse.

Wesley opened the back door for her and helped her climb in. She wasn't surprised when he joined her in the back. It was almost more surprising that he didn't just pull her into his lap. Still, she was content to lean against him and just relax for the first time since being taken. For the first time in two days, she felt safe, so it took less than a minute for her to fall asleep, held carefully in Wesley's arms.

Chapter 13

Chloe woke on the couch, a blanket over her and a weight pressed against her belly. She cracked open an eye to see Lykos was curled against her as the little spoon. A quick look around showed her Mavros on the arm of the couch by her feet, Phillip dozing in one chair, while Wesley sat in the other, tapping on his phone and frowning at it.

Her eyes closed again as she took stock of her body. Her face and belly felt okay, but she still felt like crap. She kind of wished they hadn't let her sleep, so she could've taken a shower and had a good meal. One that was accompanied by a gallon or two of water. At least she hadn't had any nightmares, which was common for her after traumatic experiences. And Erick had definitely been a traumatic experience.

"How are you feeling?"

Wesley's voice made her open her eyes once more as she wondered how he'd known she was awake. "Like I need a day at the spa. How long was I out?"

"Not long, just an hour."

It wasn't enough, not even close, but she needed to tell them what she knew. Slowly, she sat up, which disturbed the pup. He yawned and stretched, which made him tumble off the couch. His startled look made her smile before she ran a hand through her hair, grimacing as she felt some dried blood in it, too.

"Need to tell you guys what happened. He needs stopped."

"You do, and he does," he agreed. "I'm not letting you do that until you eat something, though."

"She should hydrate first," Phillip mumbled as he scrubbed a hand over his face.

Wesley rose and went into the kitchen, coming back with a couple bottles of water. He cracked the first one and offered it to her.

She took the bottle and a single, cautious sip. The liquid against her tongue was such an exquisite sensation she almost moaned. The urge passed and she took another drink, fully intending to tip the bottle up and drain it all.

After just a few swallows, Phillip leaned forward and gently pulled it from her mouth. "I'm sorry, I know you're thirsty, but if you drink too quickly, you'll be sick," he told her. "Just sip it for now."

She frowned at him, but knew he was just looking out for her. So she waited a moment then took another swallow, reveling in it. Nothing had ever tasted so good as this simple bottle of water. "I was really gone for two days?"

"You really were," Wesley confirmed.

"I really do need a shower then, but can one of you call Lexi? She was supposed to come over the night Erick took me, so I'm sure she's freaking out."

"That's an understatement," he muttered.

"She's the one who let us know you were gone," Phillip added, but he was smiling with amusement. "But we already told her we found you. She's dealing with a few things but will be over soon. You've got time to shower." He nodded to the water. "You should take that with you."

"Believe me, I will." When she started to stand, they each

took an arm and helped her to her feet. It both amused and annoyed her. Yes, she'd been through two seriously crappy days, but she wasn't made of spun glass. "How long are you two going to be overprotective?"

"At least a few days," her brother said without hesitation.

"A week, minimum," Wesley corrected flatly.

"Great." They did, at least, let her go up to the shower by herself, though Lykos wasn't as cooperative. She tried to keep him out, but he stuck his muzzle between the door and frame, then shoved his way into the bathroom. Giving up, she let him stay. He didn't try to climb in the shower with her, but he also didn't seem inclined to let her out of his sight. Since he was a lot less intrusive than a grouchy grizzly or overly cautious older brother, she allowed it.

It was likely both men were waiting impatiently to find out everything that had happened, but she couldn't resist scrubbing every inch of her twice then savoring the soothing warmth of the water. The drink she'd brought with her was gone long before she was done, but the combination of shower and hydration made her feel better. All she needed now was to stuff her stomach and to sleep. Preferably with Wesley beside her, but at this point, she'd take any restful sleep she could get.

After she'd dried off, dressed, and pulled her hair up, she felt better. Not quite good as new, but this was a definite improvement on how she'd felt just a few hours ago. She went back down to the others, almost tripping on Lykos, and stopped at the bottom of the stairs. Wesley was sitting on one side of the couch, while Phillip had opted for one of the chairs. Mavros was on the arm of the chair, receiving absent pets from her brother. All of that was somewhat normal. What wasn't normal was her coffee table being absolutely covered in food. There were two pizza boxes and a dozen or so to go boxes.

"Are we having a party?"

Phillip looked amused while Wesley twisted to look back at her, a hint of sheepishness on his face. "I wasn't sure what you'd want, and what you'd be able to tolerate," he admitted, "so I got a little of everything."

She grinned and joined him on the couch. "So Yogi can be sweet, hmm?" she asked, kissing his cheek.

"Don't get used to it," he warned, but she saw the corners of his mouth twitch upward.

Peeking in the boxes, she found food from both the diner and Banquet. There were burgers, pizza, soup, pasta, and one thick piece of chocolate cake. Though her taste buds were eager for the cake, she didn't think she'd be able to keep it down, and she wasn't about to waste Francois's delicious creation. Disappointed, she opted for lighter foods and soup, though promised herself she'd eat the cake later.

Chloe expected them to dive right into questioning her about what had happened, but the only words spoken for a while involved food and making her comfortable. Though it felt like she could eat a horse, she found herself actually able to get down very little. It still improved her mood and eased the hunger pangs, but the water she continued to drink helped more.

When she had eaten the last of what she could, she set the bowl of chicken and rice soup on the table and settled back, leaning lightly into Wesley. Lykos curled up on her feet—literally on them—while Mavros abandoned Phillip to rest on her knee.

With Wesley's fingers absently trailing up and down her arm, she finally felt settled. But then he spoiled it. "I know you'd probably rather forget the last few days happened, but we need to know so we can stop Erick."

"And beat the shit out of him," Phillip added dryly, a sentiment Wesley obviously agreed with judging by the sharp nod. "But I'm sure you'd rather only have to go through it once, and there's someone else who should hear it."

She definitely only wanted to tell the story once. "You want to wait for Lexi? Because I'm okay with that," she assured him.

Phillip shook his head. "No, though if you want to wait for her, we can." He drew in a slow breath, released it the same way. "Our father."

It was hard for Chloe to figure out her dominant emotion to the prospect of seeing her father; excitement, apprehension, annoyance, and confusion were all present. "Why now?" Out of all the questions that ran through her mind, that was the one she had to know.

He rose, moved to sit beside her. "The odds of two people wanting to get at you to attack him are slim to the point of being ridiculous. Though Erick hasn't confirmed that you're our father's daughter, it's clear he has a very good idea. Which means there's no point in keeping Dad's identity a secret from you anymore. And keeping you ignorant could put you in more danger, now that we know who's coming after you."

Wesley's arm slid around her shoulders but he said nothing, letting her decide. Given how opinionated he could be, she appreciated his restraint. "I've wanted to know who my dad is my whole life, so I'm not going to tell you to keep it to yourself now. Who is he?"

"I think it's better if he tells you," Phillip said as he rose.

She groaned. "And how long is it going to take him to get here?"

Phillip smiled. "Not long." He closed his eyes for a moment before a flash of light filled the living room. When it died down to normal, a man stood behind the couch. A man she knew very well, as he'd been in her dreams multiple times since she first stepped foot on the island. A tall, handsome blonde man who looked like the stereotypical surfer. A man with eyes the same shade as her own. A man she'd never met in real life, until now.

Her father.

She shot to her feet in shock, gaping at him. His gaze landed on her and his eyes widened before they shot back to Phillip. "What are you doing?" he demanded, sounding mildly panicked.

"She was kidnapped, Dad. I think keeping her in the dark at this point will only put her in more danger," Phillip told him.

Those eyes, so like her own, narrowed before he looked back to Chloe. He studied her as she just stood there, stunned to be in the same room as her dad for the first time in her life. Once he'd found whatever he was looking for, he circled the couch, ignored the confused Wesley, and stopped in front of Chloe. His arms lifted as though he'd embrace her, then stopped and forced them back to his side.

She understood. This was a huge moment for both of them, but also awkward as hell. Anytime she'd imagined meeting her dad, right after being held hostage for two days by a crazy councilor hadn't even made the top hundred scenarios. There was some lingering anger toward him, as well, anger she couldn't quite dispel fully. Knowing he'd stayed away for her safety wasn't enough, not when she'd end up taken anyway. But still, this was her *dad*. The only parent she'd ever get the opportunity to meet, to talk to.

"Chloe," he said in a quiet voice, thick with emotion. Something, some sort of permission, must have shown on her face, because he gathered her up in a hug.

Unable to resist, her arms slid around him and she let out a shaky breath. Feeling tears form, she closed her eyes against them. She knew no one in the room would judge her for crying right now, but she still didn't want to let them fall.

"I'm so sorry," he whispered against her hair. "I stayed away to try to spare you from this. I'm sorry I failed you."

She wasn't sure what to say. Telling him it was all right was out, because it wasn't. Knowing her mind, she would have nightmares for a while. Blaming him didn't feel right, either. Yes, part of her wanted to blame him, so she could blame someone, but a larger part just wanted this. Having a parent hold and comfort her.

He drew back after a minute and smile, his eyes shiny. "I want to spend hours getting to know you, but I can't do that until I know you're safe. Will you tell me what happened?"

"I will. I need to tell all of you. But I'd like you to do something for me, first."

He didn't even hesitate before he nodded. "Anything."

"Tell me who you are." The desperation she felt leaked into the five words. For most people, they weren't defined by who their ancestors were. In Chloe's case, she literally was. To the world, she should be an aether elemental, with a limited set of powers. In the past few months, she'd demonstrated too many abilities she shouldn't have, and she was desperate to know exactly what she was and what she could do. And avoid having more surprise powers pop up. Her dad was obviously powerful, but that didn't tell her who—or what, exactly—he was.

Her dad exchanged a glance with Phillip, then nodded and stepped back. "I suppose it's time for that, too. Though you might want to sit down, first."

"Is it that bad?" she asked, but she did take a seat on the couch. With Wesley beside her, she felt a little steadier. He slid his arm around her and she could breathe a little easier. Mavros settled on her knee once more and let out a caw of greeting for her father, but that wasn't unexpected. Her dad had admitted to sending the crow to her. What did surprise her was when Lykos rose and padded over to her dad, wagging his tail. Her dad smiled and took the last seat before he leaned forward to pet the wolf.

"That depends entirely on your point of view," her dad answered.

"It's not bad," Phillip corrected. "It is shocking, though.

Just don't freak out too much."

"Would you get on with it? Dragging it out isn't going to make it any easier," Wesley growled.

"Brave words from the man who let my daughter get kidnapped," her dad said coolly, glaring at the shifter.

"Are you going to yell at all of us, then?" Chloe countered. "We were all taking precautions."

He cleared his throat and went on. "That's a fair point, as is his." He met Chloe's gaze and smiled, part in apology, part in what could only be parental love. "My name is Apollo."

"Apollo," Chloe repeated dully. "Like the god?"

Amusement shimmered in his eyes. "Not like the god. Or did you not realize that your brother summoned me like any other god?"

Was this a joke? She glanced at her brother who nodded his agreement with their dad's words. "He's telling the truth. He's the god Apollo."

"She's a demigod?" Wesley asked, stunned.

"She is," her dad—Apollo—confirmed.

"I can't think about that right now," she told them, hoping not to overwhelm herself. If she thought of herself as a demigod, she knew she'd spiral. Instead, she blinked and her gaze dropped to the half-grown wolf, happily sitting at her dad's feet. "I named my wolf after my dad," she said flatly.

Phillip grinned. "You really did. It was hard as hell not to laugh when you told me his name."

Apollo's expression was eerily identical to his son's. "You did?"

"Sort of, yeah. It's not Apollo, it's Lykos, but Wesley said that's one of your names."

He still looked extraordinarily pleased. "I'm flattered, even if you weren't aware of what you were doing at the time."

While the men chuckled about the naming of the wolf,

Chloe couldn't help but run it all through her head. If her dad was a god, what did it mean that someone like Erick was coming after her? Did he know he was going after the daughter of a god? Shit. A god. She knew about Apollo. She'd read about him, as he was one of the Olympians. Which meant...

"Holy shit. No, no, no," she said firmly as she shook her head.

The conversation around her stopped and she suddenly had five pairs of eyes directed at her.

"No what?" Wesley asked.

"I cannot be the granddaughter of freaking Zeus!"

"Oh shit," he breathed. "Do you think that's why he forgave you when you got all mouthy to him?"

Apollo chuckled. "It is. He could sense his blood in you. Protecting Pandora's Box might have saved you, but being my daughter made it a certainty."

Chloe groaned and shook her head. "Not thinking about it. We've got more immediate concerns."

All traces of humor fled the room. "We do. Can you tell me what happened?" her dad asked.

Before she could say a word, her front door opened and they all tensed, preparing for a new threat.

Chapter 14

pollo stood and moved to stand between Chloe and the doorway, almost faster than she could track. Even the wolf leapt to his feet and bared his teeth toward the intruder.

"Holy shit. I come in peace," Lexi said as she stood in the doorway, her hands raised in surrender, eyes wide.

Everyone relaxed once the threat was identified and Lykos padding over to her, tail wagging. She bent to pet him before she truly looked at the strange face in the room. Her mouth dropped open and she stared at Apollo in shock and more than a little awe. "Oh my gods, you're Apollo!"

Grumpy, Chloe folded her arms over her chest and asked, "How is it you recognized him when I didn't?" Then again, Wesley hadn't seemed to recognize Apollo either, but then, he'd been a little distracted.

The god in question simply chuckled and stepped back to settle into his chair.

Lexi shut the door behind her as she pointed out, "Well, he's got a statue in his temple, doesn't he?" That surprised Chloe. She hadn't noticed a statue, but she'd also been more focused on getting away than checking the temple out.

After a minute of staring Lexi managed to drag her attention away from the deity in the room to focus on Chloe.

"But I'll figure out why he's here and fangirl over him in a minute. How are you? I need to know how badly I need to beat the shit out of someone," she said, looking Chloe over from head to toe.

The fact that her best friend would ignore a god to check on her lightened some of the despair within Chloe. She may have someone coming after her, but she wasn't doing this alone. "Exhausted, definitely freaking out, but Phillip healed me so I'm not hurting anymore," she admitted.

"Good." She strode briskly across the room and dropped onto the cushion beside Chloe, sandwiching Chloe between her and Wesley. "Don't ever do that shit again," she warned sternly as she grabbed Chloe for a tight hug. "And what's this I hear about it being Erick who took you? Is the role of councilor on this island cursed or something?" she asked when she drew back, looking at the faces of the others, clearly wanting an answer.

"I was wondering that myself," Chloe had to concede. "I mean, Kyra we can't really blame on her. But Daphne? Erick? That's still more than half. I really hope Colin doesn't end up being a psychopathic douche, too."

"At least Diego's only a douche," Lexi said with a heavy sigh as she slumped back. "Now, why is Apollo sitting in your living room?"

Chloe's gaze slid to her father and she arched a brow. She was going to tell Lexi everything, but since he'd been Mr. Secrets since they'd first 'met' in her dream, she was curious if he'd want to keep Lexi in the dark.

He smiled and inclined his head to her encouragingly. "Go ahead. I think the proverbial cat is out of the bag now," he said as he began absently stroking the wolf's head.

His comment only made Lexi look between them, curiosity shining in her eyes, but to her credit, she didn't say a word, just waited.

Taking a deep breath, still not entirely sure this wasn't

some weird dream or one of Erick's illusions, Chloe said, "Apollo is here because…he's my dad."

Lexi's mouth went slack, her eyes widening. Chloe expected a squeal or some rapid speech, but it seemed her best friend had actually been struck speechless. Amused, she watched as Lexi's mouth opened and closed a few times without a sound escaping.

"I think you broke her," Wesley drawled, sounding as entertained as she felt.

"I think I did, too." She reached out, lightly tapped Lexi's forehead. "Do you have a reset button somewhere to fix you?"

"I'm not broken," Lexi snapped. "I'm trying to…Cynthia hooked up with a god and she didn't *tell* me? Oh, and I know Lydia knew, too," she said darkly, eyes narrowing dangerously. "No way was Cynthia having a demigod baby without telling her mom. But this is why she was so secretive about her baby daddy!" She shot an accusing look at Apollo, as though he alone was responsible for them keeping his identity from her.

"They couldn't tell you," he said, continuing to pet the pup. "Even gods have enemies, and the fewer people who knew, the safer Chloe would be."

Lexi seemed to accept that easily enough, for now. "You have powers other than the aether ones, don't you?" she asked Chloe. "I'll bet that's why Lydia bound your powers. It would be one thing if you grew up doing all the things aethers did, but if you busted out with some god of the sun powers, it'd blow the secret."

Chloe blinked at the other woman. "I hadn't thought about that," she admitted. "Emma said Granny wanted me to have a normal life, so I figured that was it. But I only found out my dad's a god a few minutes ago."

"She's right," Apollo confirmed with a nod to Lexi. "Demigod powers are unpredictable, so we couldn't know which ones you'd receive."

"They really are," Phillip agreed. "My mom's a witch, and my powers could all be mistaken for a witch's, though my healing is stronger than most. But I could have had no witch powers at all. Hell, I could have been born with no powers whatsoever."

Lexi shook her head. "I'm going to need some time to adjust to that. I knew Chloe was special, but damn." Another shake of her head. "So, what happened and what are we doing about Erick?"

"We hadn't gotten to what happened yet," Phillip said, leaning back in his chair. "So, why don't we all get settled, give Chloe some space, and let her tell us at her own speed?"

Except that meant everyone was focused on her again. Not only that, but she had to relive those two days with Erick. It needed done, though. She grabbed another bottle of water and sipped. Mavros, feeling her anxiety, settled on her shoulder and rubbed his head against her cheek.

"When I got home, Mavros and Lykos ran around back. Playing, you know. Stretching their legs and wings after being cooped up in the office," she began, looking at the bottle and not at any of the eyes fixed on her. "I went to unlock the door and Erick came up behind me and injected me with something. I don't know what, or why he'd go with drugs, but it felt like a needle was in my neck, then I was just paralyzed." She glanced at Wesley. "Sort of like what Hiro did to me, but whatever he shot me up with also…suppressed my magic, I suppose. I couldn't even feel Mavros."

Wesley's arm tightened around her but no one spoke, so she went on.

"He put me in what I assume was the trunk of a car and gave me a second injection which knocked me out. I woke up in the temple basement, chained. Exactly how you two found me," she said with a glance toward Wesley, then

Phillip.

"Which temple?" Apollo asked.

Grimacing, she met his gaze. "Yours."

His eyes narrowed and she noticed the teal of them going amber. She realized that had to be why her eyes occasionally turned the same color rather than the violet that was the norm for aether elementals. She didn't get a chance to think about it too much as he continued. "He used my temple?" he asked in a low voice, teeth clenched. It was hard to tell whether insult or anger were stronger, but she supposed it didn't matter. Both were understandable.

"Sorry," she told him quietly, knowing it wouldn't help.

He gathered himself and shook his head. "It's not your fault and doesn't matter. Go on."

She arched a brow but didn't call him on the obvious lie. "He started asking me what my dad's name was and didn't believe me when I told him I didn't know. Said he could tell when someone was deceiving him, and I was."

"But you weren't," Phillip said, brow furrowed.

"I kind of was," Chloe admitted. "Said I'd never met my dad, but I sort of had, in the dreams."

"You didn't look like you did because he asked you questions angrily," Wesley interrupted. "What did he do to you?"

This was the part she really wasn't looking forward to. Not just because it would bring it to the forefront of her mind, but because she knew they—Wesley especially—were going to react badly. "Knocked me around a bit. When it still didn't get him the answer he wanted, he left. Then...he came back, looking like you," she said, looking up at the bear who'd become so important to her.

"What do you mean looking like me?" he asked in a light growl.

"He looked like you, sounded like you." She tried to smile, but it came out weak and forced. "I knew it wasn't

131

you, though, even without my magic." When Wesley only growled louder, she hurried through the rest of it. "He pretended to unchain me, like he was going to rescue me, but then started back on the dad thing. When I still wouldn't—couldn't—tell him, he lost it. He used some kind of magic to hurt me. Didn't touch me, just hurt me, even more than Nick did. When he finally stopped, he looked like himself again and I was back in the chair. I'd never left."

Apollo made a small sound, but when she gave him a questioning look, he just shook his head.

"What did he do to you?" Wesley asked again, each word carefully spoken, his voice low.

"Hit me some more. But before I passed out, he…his face changed."

"He hit you while looking like me?"

His voice was dangerous, but despite flinching in the temple, she knew he wouldn't hurt her, so she nodded.

Wesley shoved to his feet and paced quickly, animalistic sounds dripping from his lips, his eyes brilliantly yellow. No, he definitely didn't like the fact that he had been used to hurt her. She said nothing, knowing no words could make him feel better. None of the others did either, giving the bear room and time to rage. Apparently not even a god wanted to face a pissed off grizzly if he didn't have to.

When he moved toward her, Chloe tensed without meaning to, but he just bent down, bracing one hand on the back of the couch, his other hand cupping her cheek gently. Their faces close, he whispered, "I would *never* hurt you," then kissed her. It wasn't a tame kiss, though he was still so careful with her. If it hadn't also been hot enough to fry her circuits, she might have been embarrassed about her family witnessing such a kiss, but she'd forgotten they were there. Love, passion, relief, and anger were shared with her with every movement of his lips, every stroke of his tongue against hers, and she was helpless to do anything but take it and give it all back to him in equal measure. Trembling fingers found his wrist, holding his hand against her cheek as she lost herself in him, took solace and safety from his touch.

A small snicker from Lexi broke through the haze he'd created in her brain, and she dropped her hand on his chest. He drew back, just enough to stare into her eyes. "Tell me you know," he murmured.

"I do," she whispered without hesitation.

"Good." He settled back on the couch, arm around her once more to pull her in close to his side, almost in his lap. Then embarrassment tried to flare, but it simply couldn't get a foothold. It might trickle in later, but right now, she was just pleasantly dazed.

Phillip cleared his throat and asked, "What do you mean his face changed? Another illusion?"

Forcing her mind back to the events of the last few days, Chloe shrugged. "Maybe, or maybe the face we know is the illusion. But he's obviously not just a clairvoyant."

"What did he look like?" Apollo asked, and the set of his shoulders, the tone of his voice, told her it was important.

"Sort of like he normally does, but more like a cousin or brother to his normal face, if that makes sense. His hair was longer and darker. So were his eyes, I think, and his features were just a little off. I think his nose was a little longer, his chin a little shorter. And he had a small scar right here," she said, tapping her left cheek.

"Dolos," Apollo snarled.

"Who?" Chloe asked, mildly relieved she wasn't the only one who looked confused.

"Are you sure?" Phillip asked, his face pale.

"It fits," Apollo answered, though he didn't sound happy about it. "The illusions, the description, and the comment about deception."

"Great, it fits. Now who's Dolos and why in the fuck

would he do this to me?" Chloe interrupted. The name didn't sound at all familiar, and she tended to want to know about people who kidnapped and tormented her.

"He's a god. A minor one, which pisses him off as he's always thought he deserved to be more."

That was not what Chloe wanted to hear, though it made sense. Who but a god would be going after another god? Anything else sounded like a death sentence. "And he's the god of...what? Illusions?"

"Close enough," Phillip answered grimly. "In your mythology books he's listed as the spirit or personification of trickery, but basically, he's the god of lies, illusions...and treachery."

"What the hell does he want with Chloe, then?" Wesley asked, his arm tightening around her.

Apollo shook his head. "He doesn't, at least not how you're thinking. He wants to hurt me. And before you ask, no, he isn't targeting Phillip or any of my other children. Or at least he hasn't to this point."

"Other children," Chloe repeated slowly. She did remember reading about Asclepius—and wasn't it wild that he was her brother, too—but other children made it sound like more than just him and Phillip. "Exactly how many siblings do I have?" She was remembering more about what she read about her father, even if she hadn't had time to go into any depth about any of the gods she'd read about. Other than Zeus, because it had seemed wise to know all she could after their first meeting.

Her father managed to look both sheepish and amused. "A few."

"How many is a few?" she pressed.

"A dozen...or two."

That was something she'd have to think about later. It wouldn't matter how many brothers and sisters she had if this god got his hands on her again. "So why is he coming after me and not any of them?"

"I can't tell you why he fixated on you and not any of the others, but a long time ago he had a daughter who died, Cressida. He believed I should have been able to save her, but I couldn't. Not wouldn't, but couldn't. Even I have my limits." He sighed. "My best guess? He's wanting to take from me what he feels I took from him. Why he's chosen you and not one of my other daughters?" He shrugged. "It could be as simple as you're the youngest, which means you've haven't had the time to develop your powers like they have.

"But according to you, he's been coming after me since I was born!" And it was just starting to hit her that she had a *god* gunning for her. She could feel panic trying to build. She'd barely gotten a handle on her elemental abilities, and didn't even understand the others, but she couldn't see how healing or glowing like a lantern could stop a god.

Apollo rose and crouched in front of her, resting a hand on her knee. "Because losing a child is the hardest thing a parent can go through. But you're not an infant now. Your powers have been growing, and you're not alone. You won't be alone until he's stopped. You've got your sheriff, who is a formidable bear. Your brother, who can do a great deal more than treat animals. Your cousin, who is the guardian of Pandora's Box for a reason." He smiled, but his eyes still shone with remorse for her situation. "And you have me," he went on quietly, touching her cheek with the gentlest of touches. "I know most people tend to focus on the healing and sun parts of my powers, but that's not all I am. I assure you, I'm not going to let that bastard hurt you again."

"I don't want to have to fight a god," she admitted, voice barely a whisper.

"I know, baby," Apollo murmured. "Like I said, you won't be left alone, not until this is done."

"We shouldn't stay here, then," Wesley said, rubbing his

135

hand over her arm. "This house is too small to comfortably fit everyone who's going to want to stay by your side. Mine is bigger."

That felt like retreating. She knew retreating wasn't always a sign of cowardice, but this house was also familiar. To leave all her things—Granny's things—felt like running. But she did have only one bedroom set up, and the couch wasn't a pull-out, so could only accommodate one person, and not exactly comfortably. Though the idea of seeing the god Apollo sleeping on a couch did lighten her mood for an instant.

"It's a good idea," Phillip agreed after a long moment. "Keep everyone in the same place."

"I agree. And I'll be staying as much as I can until this is done," her dad said, giving her knee a gentle squeeze.

"I'm not going to win this fight, am I?" Chloe asked bitterly, half-wishing she could go back to a time when she had more control over her life. But since that life hadn't included the people who had become so important to her, it was a useless wish.

"No," Wesley answered flatly.

She sighed. "Fine."

"I'm going, too," Lexi said stubbornly. "Don't forget, I've got something none of you have."

"What's that?" Phillip asked curiously.

Her lips curved into a smug smile. "Ghosts. I really am a medium like the rest of Salus thinks, it's just not *all* I am."

"Ghosts could certainly be useful," Apollo said thoughtfully. "As far as I'm aware, Dolos has never shown any affinity for the dead. They would make excellent unseen guards, if nothing else."

"Yep," Lexi agreed with a sharp nod. "Besides, you think I'm just going to stand back and hope everything works out?"

Chloe was glad they all wanted to keep her safe, she really

was, but she also doubted she'd get any privacy until Dolos was stopped. "Your house is going to be bursting," she warned Wesley.

He shrugged carelessly. "So?"

No one else seemed to care either, so Chloe sighed and pushed herself to her feet. "So, I suppose I better go pack, because I need some sleep sooner rather than later." The energy the food had given her was depleting rapidly. She was honestly surprised she was still as alert as she was after only an hour's sleep.

"I'll help," Lexi said as she rose. "And Zane said if you need anything, to let him know."

Guilt flooded her as she walked up the stairs. She hadn't thought about notifying any of her other friends. Yes, it probably was due to her mental state, but what kind of friend didn't let people know she'd been rescued from a kidnapper? "How many people know I was kidnapped?"

"Most of the island," Lexi admitted, rubbing Chloe's back comfortingly. "Wesley and Phillip were going nuts. I think they were about ready to start searching every house on the island. And I don't think anyone could miss the crows flying around. I've never seen a murder that big."

"Massacre," Chloe muttered as she grabbed a suitcase. She wasn't sure where her messenger bag was—it hadn't been in the temple with her—which meant she'd need to replace her pistol. Her IDs, too, but with a crazy god looking for her, she cared more about her gun. She should have been wearing it at the time, but when she'd gone off-duty, she'd put it in her bag. That way it would've been close, but she wouldn't have been wearing it for girl's night.

"What's that?" Lexi asked as she went into the bathroom to grab toiletries.

"It's a massacre, not a murder, not when it has that many crows in it," Chloe explained.

"I like it," Lexi said with a laugh. "You should make sure

to take Lydia's grimoire with you," she added as she came out and dumped an armful of stuff on the bed next to the suitcase. "Who knows, she might have had something in there that could help locate Erick or Dolos or whatever we're calling him now."

Since it was a good idea, Chloe retrieved the book from its hiding place and set it on the bed. She grabbed clothes— not really caring what she took so long as it was warm—and dropped them on the bed so she could fold them and set them in the suitcase. Then, seeing the necklace she'd tossed on the nightstand and forgotten about, dropped it on the bed, too. She'd have to remember to ask her dad about it. Maybe he'd given it to Granny? Or at least might know something about it.

Tired or not, her mind didn't want to shut up, but it wasn't all bad. Yes, she had complained about moving to Wesley's house and staying with so many people, but part of her was thrilled. She had gone from having a single family member, to no family, to several family members. And she was going to be staying with them. There might even be a chance for her to actually get to know her dad. And there was no way she wasn't going to be sleeping in Wesley's bed, which was another definite plus. It might be a little awkward with both her brother and dad there, but they'd make it work.

Maybe there a soundproofing spell in Granny's grimoire?

Lexi insisted on carrying the suitcase downstairs, and Chloe was too tired to argue.

"I let the council know about Erick's true identity," Wesley told her when she stopped behind the couch.

"How'd they take that?"

"Not well, but they're going to keep an eye out for him and notify the town to do the same. If anyone sees him, they're to report it to me immediately." He went into the kitchen, returning with her bag. "And we found this outside the other day. I figured you'd probably want it," he told her as he offered it to her.

She grabbed it and looked inside, infinitely relieved to see her gun was still inside. "Yes, thank you."

"Let's get you to Wesley's," Phillip said, watching her face closely.

They went out to the vehicles. Lexi took Lykos and Chloe's suitcase, because Phillip's SUV was full, with three full grown men, a crow, and herself.

As Phillip pulled away from her house, she stared at it, wondering how long it would be before she saw it again.

Chapter 15

After parking in front of the cabin and climbing out of the vehicles, Lexi passed Chloe's suitcase to Wesley. "I'm going to put some wards up around the house, just to be safe."

"I'll help you," Phillip offered. "The stronger the wards, the better."

"Agreed." Smiling at Chloe, she added, "When you're feeling better, you should put an aether ward up, too."

Phillip blinked at Chloe. "You can do aether wards?"

"Don't look so surprised," Chloe said dryly. "Demigod, remember?"

He grinned, half-amused, half-apologetic, and only shrugged.

"I'm not surprised," Apollo said, his posture as proud as his voice. "I knew you would be strong. Your mother was the strongest aether I've ever met. Even stronger than Lydia."

"Fine, you're proud, you're surprised, and you two are going to ward the place up. Do whatever you want, but I'm getting Chloe to bed. She's had one good hour of sleep in two days," Wesley grumbled, grabbing her hand with his free one and half-dragging her inside.

Apollo and the animals followed them in. "Make yourself

at home," Wesley told him absently. "I'll be back in a few."

"I'll be counting," Apollo said, sounding like he was joking.

"I guess meeting the parents is twice as tricky when the parent's a god, huh?" Chloe half-whispered, more than a little entertained by the attention Wesley got from her dad. She had a feeling most of Apollo's comments were said just to rile the bear, since he had expressed approval of the sheriff weeks ago. Then again, she didn't really know him that well, so she could be completely off.

"You're a constant pain in the ass," Wesley replied before he stopped in front of his door.

"Yeah, but you love me," she teased.

His expression was serious when he looked down at her. "Yes, I do," he told her quietly, no traces of humor on his face or in his voice.

That was not at all what she was expecting, and it took her a few seconds to realize exactly what he'd said. Something in her chest flipped and she found herself holding her breath for a moment. "You do?"

He gave her a slow, hot smile that shot through her blood faster than whiskey and was far more potent. "You think I put up with this much crap from just anyone?" He turned to face her fully, brushing his thumb over the back of her hand. "Yes, Chloe. I love you."

It was almost worth the last few days to hear that, and know he meant it, but she couldn't simply tell him she loved him, too. She couldn't even pull a Han Solo, though it was tempting. "You picked a hell of a time to tell me," she replied instead, ignoring how her voice sounded a little choked up.

"I was going to wait until things were quiet, but with you around, things are never quiet, so I had to take what I could get."

She laughed softly and slid her arm around him, leaning against his side. "Fair point. And as it so happens, I love you, too."

His bear flashed in his eyes. "Then I won't ask whether you want a guest room," he said, pulling her through the doorway and into his bedroom.

"Good, because I didn't want to sleep alone." Especially not with the nightmares she expected to follow her into sleep.

He set her suitcase down next to the dresser and lifted her bag off her shoulder, setting it on the nightstand. With neither of them encumbered, he pulled her into him and kissed her. Despite their confessions to each other, it wasn't a hard kiss, not with him so concerned about her well-being after the kidnapping. Nor was it angry, like the kiss after she'd told them what had happened in the temple, but it was certainly thorough, intense, and hot. It left her breathless and clinging to him, forgetting all about her newly found demigod status and the angry god gunning for her. There was only him, the feel of his body, so hard and warm against hers, the taste of him, invading her senses.

"You need to sleep," he whispered against her lips, ending the kiss far too soon for her liking. He wasn't wrong, though. She was on the verge of collapsing. But that didn't mean she had to like it.

"Join me later?" she asked as she forced her fingers to relax and release him.

Grinning, he eased her over to the bed and drew the covers back. "Even your dad couldn't keep me away," he assured her.

She kicked her shoes off and slid into bed, too tired to bother undressing. "Glad to hear he doesn't intimidate you."

"Oh, he intimidates me plenty, since he could crush me like a bug, but that doesn't mean I'm going to stay away," he told her, drawing the covers up. "Now sleep."

He gave her one last kiss, this one light and sweet, then left the room. She saw the door start to close, but he held it open for a moment longer, just enough to let Mavros and Lykos inside.

She smiled as the wolf curled up at her feet and Mavros took a spot on the headboard. Everyone settled, she let exhaustion claim her. She stirred only briefly sometime later, when she felt Wesley crawl into bed with her. But even his presence could only hold the nightmares at bay for so long.

Chloe dragged herself out of the nightmare, partially sitting up in bed as her mind abruptly shifted from the basement of Apollo's temple to Wesley's cabin. Though her breathing was quickened, the nightmare hadn't been as bad as she'd expected. Could sleeping beside Wesley really have helped?

She lowered herself back to the bed and glanced to the side, only to realize she was alone. Except, this time she didn't feel the overwhelming sense of loneliness she'd felt all too often in the past months. Her lips curved as she realized that, when she left the bedroom, she'd find her dad, brother, cousin, and the man she loved. It was a good feeling. A great one.

Rising in the predawn light, she changed into clean clothes and went to find them. Phillip, Wesley, and Lexi were in the kitchen, with the men working on making breakfast. It was curious that they were all up before the sun but was too happy to see them to wonder too much about it.

Instantly, Chloe could feel the tension in the room, though she wasn't sure about the cause. Lexi looked amused, but Wesley and her brother were all but snarling at each other.

"What's going on?" Chloe whispered to Lexi.

The brunette jumped, not having realized Chloe was

there until she spoke. Immediately after, she grinned and answered in a low voice. "Seems your brother doesn't like the fact that you spent the night in Wesley's room. It looks to me like you're getting all the overprotective big brother action in a few days, that most people normally get over several years." And she was clearly loving watching the drama.

Chloe rolled her eyes and raised her voice. "What's for breakfast?" It was kind of amusing, but her stomach was reminding her she'd only eaten a small meal the day before, and nothing for two days before that.

Both men turned to face her, and she saw the annoyance on Phillip's face, the mildly amused resignation on Wesley's. "Bacon, eggs, and waffles," the latter answered. "Coffee's already made," he said, inclining his head to the coffee pot.

"Did you make it?"

He growled softly at her and made her smile.

"No, I made it," Lexi answered. "Even I've heard how bad his coffee was."

"It's not that bad," he protested.

"It really is," Chloe assured him as she walked over and kissed his cheek. She fixed a cup of coffee, surprised and delighted to find he'd gotten caramel so she could have it just how she liked it. "Where's..." It didn't feel right to call Apollo Dad, not yet, but neither was it right to call him by his name.

Phillip seemed to understand anyway and nodded toward the back door. "Outside. I think your wolf and crow are with him."

"Thanks." She sipped her coffee, deemed it perfect, and started for the door. "Try to play nice while I'm gone? I love you both, but I'm not going to deal with any masculine drama," she warned them before she stepped outside.

Apollo sat in the grass cross-legged, unbothered by the early morning chill. The pup was lying beside him, head resting on one of the god's knees, while Mavros was perched on the other.

Though there wasn't snow on the ground, Chloe wasn't going to be able to stay out here long, but she couldn't pass up this opportunity to talk to her father alone. She crossed the yard and sank down onto the grass beside him. Mavros let out a soft caw and stepped from Apollo's knee to hers. As for the wolf, he gave a single thump of his tail, but was too lazy to move otherwise.

"How are you feeling?" her dad asked, absently stroking a hand down the pup's back as he stared out at something.

"Better," she admitted, following his gaze. All she could see was the sun beginning to crest the trees in the distance. But then, as the god of the sun, it made sense that he'd want to watch the sunrise.

They sat in silence for several minutes, just watching the ball of light creep higher. When it had fully cleared the trees, he spoke again. "I know there are a lot of stories out there about gods meddling with mortal women, but I thought you might like to know it wasn't like that with me and your mother." He looked at her, smiling sadly. "I loved her, and I was delighted when she discovered she was pregnant."

Chloe met his gaze and nodded slowly. "I do want to know that. It helps." She smiled, just the barest curve of her lips. "I've spent my life wondering who you were, wondering why Granny refused to ever speak of my dad. Knowing you're a god?" She shook her head and looked back to the small lake. "It kind of hurts my brain."

His smile now was one of understanding and amusement. "I'm sure it does, but I really hope you won't think of me as a god. I can't help being a god any more than you can help having aether powers or teal eyes. It's just who I am."

"But it changes who I am," she said quietly.

"No, baby, it doesn't," he murmured, pushing a stray curl back from her face. "It gives you powers you wouldn't have if you were only an aether, but it doesn't change who you are."

"Are you saying that powers can't change who a person is?"

He sighed and dropped his hand, looking back to the sun. "Powers can change a person, yes, but it doesn't always define a person. Look at your cousin. She can see ghosts, and it's made her more empathic toward others, but there are numerous other mediums who harden themselves, or use the suffering of those ghosts to their advantage. It's the same power, but they choose how it defines them, rather than letting it do the defining."

"Okay, that makes sense." She sighed and trailed a finger down Mavros's back. "I just wish I'd grown up knowing you. Or Mom."

"I know, and I'm sorry you couldn't. I'm even more sorry that you can't meet her."

"Will you tell me what happened? I know...very little, actually. I was told I was born here, but I thought I was born in Boston until a few months ago."

He grimaced but nodded. "Cynthia and Lydia were living here when I met her. Shortly after she learned she was pregnant, I got wind that someone knew I had a daughter on the way and wanted to get their hands on you."

"How could they know, especially that early in the pregnancy?"

"I'm not sure. They could have consulted an oracle. Generally, oracles are mine, but nothing is absolute. Then there are those who see the future. They also tend to be mine, but again, not all of them. However they learned about you, your mother decided to stay on Salus, hoping that acting like nothing was wrong would throw the one searching for you off. But we knew I would have to be careful. Being seen with her could have put her—and you—in danger. So I stayed away. Until Lydia got word to me that your mother was in labor. I couldn't stay away for that. So, you were born in the house your grandmother left you. Since we couldn't let anyone know you were my daughter, it was just the three of us." His lips curved, eyes going bright with pleasant remembrance, with unadulterated joy. "I held you even before your mother, and you were so beautiful. I like to think you recognized me, too. You didn't cry, just stared up at me. It was like you were trying to figure everything out. Figure me out."

She may not have cried at birth, but she did now, tears sliding silently down her cheeks. For so long she had wondered if her father hadn't wanted her, if he'd abandoned her, but now he was sitting beside her, assuring her that she was very much wanted.

Chloe didn't bother to wipe the moisture from her skin, knowing these weren't going to be the last tears she shed this morning. And she still had more she needed to know. "Why did they leave? If they thought it was safe enough to stay here until I was born, why leave?"

"Because the one looking for you somehow found out you were on Salus. Then, one day, your mother was coming back from meeting me, well away from her house, when she was killed."

"Did you know? That it wasn't just a car accident?"

He nodded, and she saw that his cheeks were wet as well. "I did. So did your grandmother. It's why we bound your powers. We didn't want anything, even a tiny hint, leading anyone to you. But your grandmother had gone a step further. I didn't know about it, not until after Cynthia died, but it likely saved your life."

She frowned. "What do you mean? What'd she do?"

"Put one of the most complicated wards I've ever seen on you. It hid you, but she knew it wouldn't be foolproof."

"Is that ward still on me?"

"It is, though it's almost gone. I'm a little surprised it

lasted this long. The last few years she kept having to reapply it to you every so often, because, even bound, you were essentially sucking the magic out of it."

"But I didn't…I couldn't *do* anything, not until I got to Salus! Even then it was just feeling things until that asshole Diego broke the block."

"That isn't quite true," he admitted. "Since you didn't know you had powers you couldn't exactly try to use them, but you've always been able to absorb magic. It's an innate part of you."

"I didn't think I wanted it," she admitted, looking down at Mavros and stroking the back of her finger along the feathers at his chest. "Being an aether and everything that came with it."

"I understand," he told her, his expression, his tone, showing her he likely did. "It's a lot. I think anyone would want things to go back to normal, if all they'd known was a life without the insanity that comes with magic."

"That's the thing, though. My normal kind of sucked. Granny was gone, and I had next to no social life. I had my work and nothing else. And when I was in the basement of that temple, my powers gone?" She smiled wryly. "I realized I wanted them back."

"That's also understandable. They've become part of you," he told her.

Silence stretched between them again until the one question Chloe *needed* to ask refused to let her stay quiet any longer. "When this is over, when Dolos is taken care of, are you going to disappear again?"

"Oh, baby. No," he assured her without a moment's hesitation. "I didn't want to disappear the first time. I even checked in on you as often as I could without putting you at risk. When your powers were freed, I was able to visit you in your dreams, but I couldn't meet you in person without leading Dolos right to you. But now that it's all out in the open?" He shook his head. "I'm not going anywhere. I'm your father, and I want the chance to actually be your father."

She looked up at him, afraid to hope, but unable to allow herself to do anything else. "Do you honestly mean that? I know gods are different from the rest of us…"

He rested his hand lightly on her cheek before she could glance away. "A god is just part of what I am. I'm also a dad who really wants to get to know his daughter."

"But I'm not your only daughter."

"No, you're not," he agreed easily. "And each one of my children is special to me, regardless of whether they're gods or essentially human. I know you might not feel the same way about me, but I do love you, Chloe."

The word she'd been holding back slipped from her lips. "Dad," she whispered, as she leaned into him and wrapped her arms around him. He held her back tightly, cheek resting against her hair, as she wept out her emotions on his shoulder. Her feelings of abandonment, relief, confusion, and joy all coalesced into a chaotic mass that eased with each tear, each pass of his hand over her back.

A soft whine came right before Lykos wiggled between them and licked her face, then Apollo's.

It broke the air of melancholy around them. They separated, Chloe letting out a little laugh. "Yes, yes. We see you," she assured the pup, ruffling the fur on his face.

The door behind them opened and she twisted to see Phillip come outside and cross the yard to join them. "Everything okay?" he asked, gaze fixing on Chloe's face.

She was sure her eyes were red, and she knew her cheeks were damp, so it wasn't hard to figure out why he was asking. "Yeah, it's okay. Just…"

"Clearing the air," Apollo finished for her after she trailed off, unsure of how to answer.

Phillip slowly nodded and looked between them. "And it's all good, now?"

"I think so. Just needed some time to just…talk, you know?" Chloe answered.

"Yeah, I know. And I'm sorry to interrupt, but breakfast is ready, and I know everyone's wondering how we're going to handle Dolos."

"I am hungry." One meal—and a small one at that—was not enough for three days. Mavros said, "Eat," before he nipped at her finger then flew into the trees. She was surprised he was hunting for his own food, since he normally opted to eat with her.

Phillip helped her to her feet, she grabbed her forgotten coffee, and they went inside. Hopefully, they'd be able to figure out a plan that allowed her to keep her father and brother in her life.

Chapter 16

Despite Phillip's words, they hadn't just finished cooking breakfast, but had chosen to keep it warm in the oven until Chloe and Apollo came in. Chloe wasn't sure how long it had been there, but the tension in the kitchen was much lower than when she'd left. Likely because Wesley and her brother had put some distance between them.

You had to love alpha males.

As soon as they got inside, Phillip grabbed plates and set them on the table. He also grabbed the forgotten coffee, dumped it, and refilled it with fresh. He even added caramel, which earned him a smile.

Though Phillip gave him a dirty look, Wesley took a seat to her left, but no one protested when Apollo took the one to her right. Lexi sat across from her and shot her a wink. Lykos curled up at her feet but watched her with hopeful eyes.

After everyone had gotten settled, and before she'd even taken a single bite, Chloe asked, "So…exactly what powers does Dolos have? Seems like something we need to know if we're going to find a way to stop him from coming after me."

"Not just his powers, either," Lexi chimed in. "The more we know about him in general, the better we can understand him, which means we have a better chance of stopping him."

Apollo nodded. "Very true. Unfortunately, I can't say he and I were ever the best of friends, even before his daughter died. As you've already noticed, his primary power seems to be illusions," he told Chloe. "They're also the strongest illusions anyone I know has ever come across. But don't think it means he can only disguise things or make you see something differently like he did with his appearance. I've known other illusionists who could make things seem to disappear or could make you think something existed that didn't. Some can affect just sight, but some can trick all five senses."

"I'm going to verify that last point," Chloe said dryly as she slipped a piece of bacon to the wolf. "That time when he pretended..." She trailed off and gave Wesley a sidelong glance, noting that he bared his teeth at the reminder. "He definitely affected sight, touch, sound, and smell. I can happily say I didn't get to see if he affected taste, too, because no. Just no."

"What about his friends, his family?" Wesley asked, clearly eager to get away from the topic of Dolos's illusions.

"That's where it gets a little tricky," Apollo said with a sigh. "The family tree of gods can get a little...long and convoluted. And after so long, sometimes even we have a hard time differentiating between reality and mythology, unless it directly concerns us. So, while I can tell you who my parents are, my children, all that, I can't promise I'm telling you truthfully when it comes to someone I didn't interact with as much like Dolos."

"Something's better than nothing," Lexi pointed out.

"True. I know he had a daughter named Cressida. She's the one who died and began his hatred of me. That's fact. And I believe that his parents were Nyx and Erebus."

"Are you shitting me?" Wesley demanded.

Apollo shook his head. "I wish I were, believe me."

The vehemence of Wesley's reaction confused Chloe. "Okay, those are two names I don't know. They sound familiar, but they're not any of the ones I've actually studied."

"Neither of them are gods you want to piss off," Lexi told her, brow furrowed in concern. "They're both basically deities of darkness."

"Darkness doesn't sound too scary. Besides, doesn't light dispel darkness? And we've got the god of the sun sitting right here," Chloe said, jerking her thumb to indicate her father.

Wesley shook his head. "Honey, from what I've heard, even *Zeus* doesn't fuck with Nyx."

That took her aback. "Seriously?" How could darkness be so scary that even the all-powerful king of the gods would leave her be?

It was Apollo who nodded. "Seriously," he confirmed. "I think she's the only person my father is truly scared of, though I doubt he'd actually admit it."

"Okay, so hopefully we can keep Mom out of the picture," Chloe muttered. "He have any friends or siblings that could cause a problem?"

"I'm not sure who he's friends with, but if Nyx is his mother, then he has quite a few...formidable...siblings. The Oneiroi, Thanatos, and the Fates are at the top of the list."

Chloe felt sick. "That's great. Dream gods, the god of death, and the freaking Fates? What are the odds they'll help him?"

"In the case of the Fates, very slim," Phillip told her. "They're pretty much neutral. It's hard to do their job if they're playing favorites. About the only person they'll break that neutrality for is Zeus, and even then it's not a sure thing."

"Thanatos is the same, though if he and Dolos are close he might break that neutrality," Apollo continued. "The

Oneiroi could go either way. Some might agree with him, others might decide to stay out of it."

"Anyone else?" Chloe asked, afraid of the answer.

Apollo considered for a minute. "Moros, the god of doom, and Hypnos—"

She cut him off and used her fork to point at him. "Okay, that dude had better not come after me."

"Why not?" Phillip asked curiously.

A slow smile spread over Apollo's face. "Because you returned his Horn to him after those witches stole it."

Chloe pointed at her dad and nodded. "That. And he said he owed me a favor. Can we call that in for this?"

He thought about it for only a moment before he shook his head. "Not likely. If it were anyone but Hypnos's brother, maybe, but I can't see him getting involved on your behalf against his own blood."

Wesley tapped a finger on the table, his eyes narrowed and holding a yellow tinge. "I think Dolos has been causing trouble before he ever kidnapped Chloe."

"We already knew he likely caused Cynthia and Lydia's deaths," Lexi said.

"Beyond that. I mean here on Salus." He turned slightly to face Chloe. "Emma was your grandmother's best friend. If anyone was likely to know Lydia's secrets, it would have been her. Jeremy's cause of death was hidden by an illusion that only you had the power to break. Dolos is Hypnos's brother, which means he could have gotten close enough to steal the Horn and used illusions to hide the fact. And just before Christmas, the amnesia cases? Every single victim ended up having a connection to you, your mother, or your grandmother. And again, something from the Underworld was used. I don't think Dolos would have had a problem getting water from the Lethe."

Every single person at the table went silent as they pondered the feasibility of Wesley's suggestion. It made a frightening amount of sense. And in a strange way, was a bit of a relief. If Dolos was behind it all, then it was really one person causing all the trouble. True, it meant he had allies— or maybe they were minions?—but it would all come down to just him. But could it really be that simple?

"I'll give you Emma, especially since Kyra killed her and mentioned Granny and my mom being murdered, but what purpose would any of the rest serve?" Chloe asked finally, not wanting to believe that so much trouble, so much torment, had been because of her. It might not have been her fault, but she was still the cause.

"I honestly have no idea why he'd help anyone open Pandora's Box, but the amnesia cases..." He shrugged and glanced to Lexi. "You never remembered anything?"

"I wish I did," Lexi said miserably. "I lost a couple days before you guys found me in the cabin, so I have no idea what Daphne was doing."

"And why would Daphne work with him anyway?" Chloe wanted to know.

Wesley shrugged and shook his head. "I don't know. I may be completely off base here, but Salus really was mostly quiet until you got here. It's not your fault, but if Dolos was sure you were Apollo's daughter when you arrived on the island, it could all be connected."

"I knew him interrogating me about my dead grandmother on our date was creepy," she muttered.

Apollo almost choked on the coffee he'd just sipped. "You went on a date with him?" he asked incredulously.

She gave him a narrowed-eyed stare. "Seriously? That's what you're fixating on?"

"I just can't...I..." He took a deep breath, shook his head. "You're right. Not important. Though I'm happy your taste in men has greatly improved."

"I'm going to remember you said that," Wesley said, his eyes fading back to their normal gray.

"Back to what Dolos may or may not have been responsible for..." Chloe said, eager to get the conversation away from her love life. "You said dream gods. Do they just like, monitor dreams, or can they give a certain dream to a person? Specifically, can they give nightmares to someone?"

"That's essentially all they do. They monitor and cause dreams in people," Apollo confirmed. "Why?"

"Because I've had a couple of doozies. Specifically, the two nights before he took me. Just wondering if he might have been responsible."

His brow furrowed but he nodded. "It's entirely possible, though I hope they were normal nightmares, as we don't want them to be siding with him."

Phillip cleared his throat. "If we're talking about family helping, do you think Zeus would intervene?"

"I seriously doubt it, but you know your grandfather has his moods. If I catch him in the right one, he just might. I'll talk to him later."

Wesley looked uncomfortable but determined as he glanced at Apollo. "I know this is probably something you don't really like getting around, but in the event that your father won't intervene and we can't get Dolos off Chloe's back any other way...we might have to consider killing him, and I know it isn't easy to kill a god."

Her dad looked mildly ill. "No, we don't tend to advertise the few ways of killing us. Beyond that, they're not exactly easy to manage. Almost impossible these days. We can't get any hind blood, which would be the easiest way. Nor do we have access to adamantine or Medusa's head." He looked at Chloe, blew out a breath, and ran his hand through his hair. "Sometimes dismembering a god thoroughly enough can do the job, but it would be difficult to manage. If we had a way to get him into Tartarus, it wouldn't kill him, but it could get him out of the picture. Unfortunately, few gods have that ability."

Zeus had that ability, Chloe knew. She'd personally seen him zap a couple of men to Tartarus, after all. Even if Zeus didn't want to really get involved, maybe he could be persuaded to send Dolos there if they managed to subdue him? That wasn't really getting involved, right?

After a minute she noticed her dad staring at her thoughtfully, but when he caught her looking, he smiled. "We'll figure something out. You should finish eating, though. You need to get your strength back."

"I will." And she took a bite of waffle to prove it. "I've just got one more concern."

"Just one more?" Phillip asked.

"For the moment," she retorted. "If he can look like anyone, how the hell will we know if we're talking to who we think we are?"

Apollo nodded. "It's a good concern. For you it should be relatively easy as long as your powers aren't blocked. He won't feel like other supernaturals, and you should be able to feel the illusion if you're paying attention."

"Oh, believe me, I'm definitely going to stay on alert, there." Though she was kicking herself for not noticing something was off about him before. Sure, she'd known he was creepy, but hadn't seen him as anything but a weird psychic.

"For the others…I'm not sure. If he can affect scent, then Wesley's bear won't be useful. His aura may or may not show the magic. I'm leaning toward not, though. He's been on the island for years in this Erick guise, right? Someone had to have checked his aura in that time."

"We could go old school. Have a code word when we see each other. Something to verify that it's really us," Wesley suggested. "He can fake our appearances, our voices, but it doesn't sound like he can get into our heads."

"He can't, or he wouldn't have looked so confused when I called 'Wesley' Yogi," Chloe said with a shake of her head.

"She's right," Apollo confirmed after a moment. "And that's a good idea. It may not be foolproof, but it can't hurt."

"I vote we use hottie," Lexi suggested with a bright smile.

"Anyone who knows you would guess that for a codeword," Chloe countered.

"True," Lexi conceded grudgingly. "Kaleidoscope? That's not a word you hear everyday, even from one of us."

"Works for me," Wesley said.

Phillip nodded. "Me, too."

"Kaleidoscope it is," Apollo said with a faint smile. "Now, you really should finish eating. I'm curious to see you put up an aether ward."

"Same. I've never actually seen one constructed." And Phillip sounded excited about the prospect.

"Don't get too worked up. It'll only be the fifth one I've ever done," Chloe warned, but she finished eating. Part of her tried to be nervous about having them watch her put the ward up, but in the grand scheme, it didn't matter. It needed to go up and she was the only one who could do it, so she'd do it.

A few minutes later, Chloe went outside, followed by a grizzly, a witch, a demigod, a god, and a wolf. She felt like some supernatural pied piper. She also felt extremely nervous. The process for creating an aether ward was surprisingly simple—all she had to do was visualize the ward, fill it with her magic, and focus on it protecting something. But with so many eyes on her, she was worried she'd screw up the visualization or something. She didn't think she could blow anything up, but she had destroyed most of a tree when the block on her powers had been removed, so she couldn't rule anything out.

And Wesley would be pissed if she blew up his cabin.

At least they didn't crowd her, but stayed on the porch. Apollo even made sure Lykos didn't run after her, which she appreciated.

"You should be able to feel our wards," Lexi called. "If you can, lay yours right on top of ours. Layering them like that should make them stronger. Think of it like how a braided rope is stronger than any of the strands by themselves."

"Great," Chloe muttered to herself. Not only did she have to make a ward, she had to put it right on top of theirs? No, she could do this. Aether wards were easy, and she was familiar enough with witch wards. She'd taken down several, after all. How hard could it really be? Maybe if she envisioned it like pouring paint over something rather than trying to press a sheet over it?

She closed her eyes and reached out, relieved that her powers felt like they were almost back to normal after whatever Dolos had given her. Having been to Wesley's house plenty of times, and being familiar with both Lexi's and Phillip's magic, it was easy to spot the new wards. She took a minute to study them, to feel the magic that had gone into them. Once she had the feel of where they were, she took several deep breaths then visualized her own ward settling just outside the one Lexi and Phillip had set, as close to it as she could manage.

She took her time, making sure she covered every inch, and then begin to fill it with power, all the while focusing on how she wanted to protect everyone within from harm of any sort. It wasn't a quick process. Likely she could have just pumped power into it quickly, but she would have risked burning herself out. With a god gunning for her, she couldn't afford to do that.

Even going slowly, she felt her power quickly begin to wane. Her legs grew unsteady as the lack of power began to translate to a lack of physical energy. Except she wasn't done. The aether ward was thinner than tissue paper and would be easily broken through if she stopped now.

A hand rested over hers and she tensed, but then her

father whispered to her. "Don't stop. Draw energy from me to place into the ward."

Absorbing magic from another person was second nature to her now, but she was a little apprehensive about taking it from a god. But since she wasn't done filling the ward, she didn't have another choice. It took a moment for her to split her focus, to both draw power and expel it. When she did, she gasped.

Chloe had taken magic from witches, elementals, and shifters, some of them pretty powerful. She'd even absorbed a spell created by a god. None of them had felt anything like Apollo's magic. Given what he was god of, it shouldn't have surprised her that his magic felt like liquid sunlight; warm, golden, and unbelievably strong. It called to her own power, which wanted more of it, but she forced herself to transfer it through her and to the ward.

It took a great deal less time to finish the ward after that. It was also difficult for her to stop draining Apollo's magic, but she managed after only a brief internal struggle.

When it was done, she nearly fell to her knees, but Apollo caught her, supported her until she regained her balance. "That was very well done, Chloe."

"I didn't have enough power," she argued, aware that her voice was weaker than it had been.

"It takes time, and you're still new to using your abilities. It was also a rather large ward you just put up." He smiled at her. "Your mother couldn't have done better."

"Thanks." She glanced toward the porch, saw the others still stood there. Lexi was smiling smugly, Phillip proudly, while Wesley? He looked like he wanted to throw her over his shoulder and carry her off to bed. The only question was whether it would be for sleep or recreational activities. Her vote would be both, but she doubted she would get either right now.

Still unsteady, Apollo helped her return to the porch.

"You should rest for a little while. I'm going to go talk to my father and see if I can convince him to help us."

"Good luck, because I'm sure you're going to need it," she told him, impulsively giving him a hug. The gesture was repaid by the delighted smile on his face when she pulled back.

"I really will," he agreed, kissing her forehead. "Stay safe until I get back."

He stepped off the porch before he disappeared, once again with a flash of light bright enough to sting her eyes.

Lexi hooked her arm through Chloe's. "And you're going to listen to his advice. You and I are going to sit and talk, while the guys patrol or scout or whatever it is they do," she said in a tone that suggested Chloe not argue, pulling her inside.

Knowing how stubborn Lexi could be, Chloe just went inside, relieved to be doing something as normal as chatting with her best friend.

Chapter 17

To Chloe's surprise, Phillip and Wesley made themselves scarce while Chloe and Lexi settled on the couch. She'd expected them both to hover protectively and was happy they were giving her some space. But Wesley didn't come back inside, which made her worry. Everyone was concerned about her being alone, but what about them? If Dolos couldn't get to her, would he go after them to lure her to him? He was a god, after all, so did he even think twice about killing? Especially killing mortals?

Probably not.

Lexi flicked the tip of her nose, hard enough to sting.

"Hey! What was that for?" Chloe asked, rubbing her nose with one finger and glaring at the other woman.

"Just bringing you back to the here and now. Not sure where you were, but it wasn't here. I was starting to feel unloved."

"Sorry. Was just worrying. Don't want you guys getting grabbed in my place."

"Nope," Lexi began, shaking her head and waving her hands in a 'no, stop' motion. "We're not going there. We're going to sit here and have girl talk for a little bit."

"But—"

"No buts," Lexi said firmly, her eyes hard. "Yes, finding

Dolos is important. Stopping him even more important, but so is keeping your brain from breaking. Not to mention you're still recovering from being beaten and starved for two days. So you're going to sit here, talk about guys or clothes or whatever the fuck keeps your mind occupied for a little bit. And drink and eat until you're full. When your dad gets back, then you can go back to thinking serious thoughts, but right now? You're going to unwind."

Chloe had never heard Lexi's voice that stern or seen her face that severe. She'd seen Lexi scared and hurt, but rarely serious. Then her wolf added his weight, resting his head on her leg, looking up at her and whining softly.

She caved and stroked Lykos's head. "Okay, fine. You two win. So what non-serious topic do you want to talk about?" she asked, forcing her body to relax back into the cushions.

Lexi smiled brilliantly. "I knew you'd see reason. First, you should know that your matchmaking attempts are paying off."

"I don't know what you're talking about," Chloe said, an innocent look on her face. Then just a beat later, "So, things are going well with you and Garrett?"

"How could they not? I mean, sure, the reason I originally went out with him is because he's seriously hot, but he's also really sweet, Chloe. I know shifters—especially wolves—have a rep for being hotheads who react first and think second, but he's not like that."

"I thought that rep was only in books," Chloe said with some surprise. "Though, there was that guy at On the Rocks, but I figured that was just because he was absolutely wasted. I mean, none of the other shifters I've met have really seemed to only act on instinct rather than brains."

Amusement shone in Lexi's eyes. "You think Wesley doesn't have his animalistic moments?"

"That's not the same," Chloe protested, but she knew

that was because most of his animalistic moments resulted in her being kissed brainless. Not something she was going to complain about. "He does plenty of thinking before acting."

Lexi smirked knowingly. "Mmhmm. I think it is the same, you just don't mind it when his wild side comes out."

Giving in, Chloe asked, "If you had six foot four inches of muscular bear sometimes literally sweeping you off your feet and kissing you until you forgot your own damn name, would you mind?"

"Not a bit!" Her smile turned sly, tinged with pure feminine pleasure. "Of course, it's not so bad when it's six foot of muscular wolf, either."

"What happened to him being a sweetheart?" Chloe asked on a laugh.

"Hey, giving me the best kiss I've had in a decade is damn sweet in my book."

"Just the best kiss?"

"Actually, yeah," Lexi admitted, sounding surprised. "I like sex as much as the next woman, but I'm not in a race for the finish line with him. I actually enjoy just talking to him. It's different, but in a good way."

That made Chloe smile. She had hoped Lexi would find someone she didn't want to just use as a friend with benefits. Lexi deserved a man who would be a true friend and partner. Garrett had seemed perfect. He was attractive enough to appeal to Lexi's baser side, but he'd never come across as shallow, egotistical, or dumb. And Chloe had gotten firsthand experience at how smart and insightful he really was. "I'm glad. But he'd better be good to you, or I'm going to figure out how to channel my inner pissed off demigod. There's gotta be something impressive in there."

"Man, that's a kick in the ass," Lexi admitted with a shake of her head. "I knew you were powerful, but figured it was just a good aether bloodline. Lydia and Cynthia were crazy powerful, too. But to be a demigod? That's wild."

"Tell me about it. I'm waiting for it to actually sink in, because it still doesn't really feel...real. I mean a year ago I thought I was one hundred percent human, and now I'm not just an aether, I'm an aether with divine blood?" She sighed and slumped on the couch. "It's insane and feels like it should be a dream or a movie. Or hell, happening to someone else. But most of the last few months has felt like it should be happening to someone who isn't me."

Lexi patted her hand then squeezed it gently. "I'd actually be worried if you just accepted everything right off the bat. I think that would probably mean you were suppressing something or not actually believing it was real or something like that. Something you'd need a therapist for, you know?"

Chloe nodded. "Yeah, I know. "

"And don't think you're completely off the hook for not telling me you had a brother, by the way."

"A brother?" Chloe scoffed. "Don't forget that he said I had a couple *dozen* siblings," she reminded in a flat voice.

"Shit. I had forgotten. Man, that must make Christmas morning insane. Not to mention keeping up with birthdays."

"Yeah, well, Dad seems to know a lot more than he should, so I don't think remembering a few birthdays is a problem."

"What do you mean?"

"The dreams he pops in on. They've been going on since I was a murder suspect a few months ago," she began, brow furrowing as she thought back to some of them. How had he gotten so well-informed? She'd have to ask him later but brought herself back to the present for now. "When he would talk to me in them, he'd know things. Like he knew when I was chasing after Pandora's Box to stop Nick and Hiro from getting to it. He knew Hypnos's Horn had been stolen." She looked down at Lykos, thought of his feathered friend. "He even sent Mavros to me. Though how he knew

Mavros would become my familiar is the really baffling part."

Her brow furrowed for a second before Lexi smiled. "He is the god of prophecies. I'll bet he used that."

Having a plausible reason relaxed something inside Chloe she hadn't known was tense. "That actually explains how he knew everything he did. I think. I'm not really sure how prophecies work." She frowned. "Aren't they supposed to be all cryptic and in bad rhymes?"

Lexi laughed. "You really have read way too many stories. Don't get me wrong, I'm sure some prophets only get the cryptic bad rhymes, but from what I can tell, the weaker the prophet, the more confusing their prophecies get. Someone like your dad? He's like the ultimate prophet. He probably just sees it all as it happens, like a movie or something."

"I don't know if I would want to see the future," Chloe admitted.

Smiling sadly, Lexi said, "I think it's too late for that. Didn't you say you dreamed of the sleep spell before it happened?"

"Oh." She'd briefly forgotten about that, but with everything else going on, who could blame her? One hell of a bad dream didn't compare to having a god wanting to kill you. Or worse. "Yeah, I did. But I didn't really like it, much, remember? It was a nightmare. I woke up screaming. Not to mention it *was* kind of cryptic."

"The future isn't always kind," Lexi murmured. "But you're a cop, now. Couldn't prophecies be useful there? You might be able to figure out who committed crimes no one else can figure out, or even stop them before they happen."

Chloe wrinkled her nose. "That sounds like cheating. And wasn't there a whole movie about that? People getting arrested for crimes they were going to commit? Things didn't work out so well for them."

"Well, yeah, but you don't have to *arrest* people before

they commit crimes."

"Maybe not, but there's also the fact that I can't control the dreams. And it's not like I knew it was a prophecy until I was living it."

Lexi threw up her hands in defeat. "Okay, so it's not super helpful for cop stuff, but it can still be a head's up."

"I'd be happier not to have prophecies." Something occurred to her and she brightened. "I wonder if my dad can take them away. I mean, god of prophecies should be able to do that, right?"

Except Lexi didn't look so certain. "I don't know about that...Have you read the story of Cassandra?"

Chloe had read so many myths it was sometimes hard to keep track. Thinking for a moment, she drew something to the front of her mind. "She also had prophecies, right? But no one believed her?"

"Yeah, but that's not the whole story. If the myth is right, then she wasn't born having prophecies, but was granted them by Apollo. After she pissed your dad off—I don't remember how—he wanted to take the power away but couldn't. Best he could do was make it so no one would believe her, basically making her prophecies useless."

That was unsettling on a couple of levels. "So I will always be receptive to prophecies. Great," she said sarcastically. "And not only that, but my dad apparently cursed someone just because he was pissed off? Not a terrific sign of things to come."

Lexi shrugged. "I don't know the whole story. Maybe she deserved it. It could have been a just punishment for whatever she did."

"Maybe." But she wasn't so sure. She didn't really know her dad. Sure, he'd been helpful and supportive to her, but that could be a fluke, or he could have changed in the last few decades or something. Or maybe he was one of those people who was perfect to their kids but a monster to everyone else.

Or maybe he was as bad as Dolos and just pretending.

Sensing her distress, Lexi smiled and rubbed Chloe's arm. "Just don't judge the guy until you know all the facts, okay? I've never heard of Apollo being one of the dick gods. Has he opened a divine-sized can of whoop ass on occasion? Sure, but sometimes you have to. It's not necessarily any different from Zeus sending Elias and Hiro to Tartarus a few months ago. And Phillip seems like a good judge of character, and he clearly likes your dad."

Once again, the cheerful, often shallow-appearing Lexi had a very good point. One of these days she would stop doubting her best friend. "You're right. I'll talk to him before I do any judging," she promised.

"That's all I ask," Lexi told her. "Now, tell me. How are things between you and everyone's favorite sheriff?"

Lexi couldn't have chosen a better topic to get Chloe's mind off more depressing subjects. She knew her smile was a sappy one but couldn't keep it off her lips. "He loves me."

There was no reaction at first, then Lexi arched a brow, the corners of her mouth tipped up slightly, and she said, "Yes? Is that all? Because I think everyone knew that."

"I didn't know that," Chloe muttered defensively.

"They say the ones involved are always the last to know. But trust me, anyone who has seen the two of you together knew exactly how you felt about each other."

"He only told me yesterday, just before I went to sleep."

"Maybe he was waiting until he thought you were ready, because trust me, that man has been in love with you for a while." She grinned. "Might even have been love at first sight."

"Doubtful. First sight was him checking out a crazy lady whose car was blocking access to the ferry." There was some lust at first sight, though, at least on her end. She'd be shocked if it was mutual, since she probably had seemed like an insane tourist. That day hadn't been a great one for her.

"Maybe he's into that. Some guys love the crazy. And let's face it, things are never calm around you."

"Again, not my fault. Besides, you were involved in two of those cases," Chloe said, emphasizing her point by poking a finger in Lexi's side.

"Not my fault either," Lexi protested. "Let's go back to blaming Dolos. And by the way, I'm sorry for not believing you when you told me he gave you creepy vibes."

"I thought we were avoiding talking about him," Chloe asked.

"Good point. But you're still going to rest. How about a movie?"

"I could really go for a movie," she admitted. Hopefully one she could get lost in and, for a little while, forget about the mess she was in.

Chapter 18

Though Phillip and Wesley largely left them alone, Phillip did bring in some sandwiches, chips, water, and Cokes, telling Lexi to make sure Chloe ate at least one sandwich and finished a full bottle of water. It didn't take much prompting for Chloe to take that advice.

She didn't see Wesley ever come back inside, but Phillip just said he was checking on some things and told her not to worry. Easier said than done, but she tried.

They'd just started on the second movie when Apollo returned, appearing in the living room and startling the two women.

"I apologize for scaring you," he told them and took a seat in one of the chairs, accepting Lykos's greeting with affectionate pats. "At least I don't appear with that loud crack of thunder my dad prefers, though."

"True. And I'll get used to it, eventually," Chloe told him, hoping she was right.

He smiled. "How are you feeling? Recovering sufficiently?"

"Considering they've been stuffing my face with food and wouldn't let me do anything but sit here? Yeah, I have," she answered, flashing Lexi a smile. She didn't mind. A little pampering after a traumatizing experience was never a bad thing. Pampering by her favorite people? Even better.

"As well they should," he said, giving Lexi an affectionate look as well. "I should also tell you that I'm pleased she was able to find family during a time when neither I nor her brother were able to be here. I'm more pleased that it was family who was also a friend."

Lexi flushed under the praise from the god. "It's not like it was difficult to become her friend or anything."

"Still, it made me feel better that she had you." The front door opened and Wesley stepped in. "I suppose I feel okay that she had you, as well."

"Good?" Wesley said, clearly not having caught the first part of the conversation.

Chloe laughed. "I think my dad just gave his blessing to you dating me," she told him. Though Apollo was a new part of her life, it still thrilled her that her dad liked her boyfriend. It thrilled her more when Wesley ignored any intimidation he may have felt from having a girlfriend with a deity for a dad and bent down to kiss her. It was a light kiss, but it meant a great deal to her.

He straightened and looked at Apollo. "I'm hoping that means you're not going to toss me into the sun for doing that, then?"

"Not today," Apollo said dryly. "Tomorrow might be a different story. Just don't get too handsy. At least not in front of me."

"Fair enough."

"Where have you been?" Chloe asked Wesley.

"Talking to some people. The council, for one. I think I told you they're pissed another one of them has turned out to be dirty. That hasn't gotten any better. But I didn't tell them that it might have been Erick manipulating people the whole time. Don't have any hard proof, and it wouldn't have made a difference right now. Zane said to tell you to let him know if you needed anything. He wanted to come see you but thought too many people crowding around you right now might be too much."

She smiled. Zane was more likely to understand books than people, but she truly adored the lanky bookworm. And he was certainly dependable as hell. "I'll text him later. That was sweet. But you said the council was just one group you talked to. Who else?"

Wesley ran a hand over his short hair. "Anyone I could find who was friendly with Erick. The number was shockingly low. He made a good show of networking and making friends, but it seems to have just been on the surface. It seems he spent the most time with other councilors…" He hesitated, glanced to Lexi, Apollo, then back to Chloe. "And it sounds like he and Peyton have been close in the past. As in a few people thought they were in a relationship for a while."

"Are you fucking kidding me? I swear, the next time I see that woman, I'm going to break her pretty little nose," Chloe snarled. "She tries to get me locked up as a murderer, makes me the other woman, *and* she's been playing nice with a god in disguise who wants to do see me tortured or killed?"

"I'll hold your coat while you beat the bitch," Lexi offered immediately, sounding almost as pissed off as Chloe felt.

Wesley smiled faintly. "As much as I'd love to let you do that—and honestly I'd pay to see it—I'd just have to arrest you for battery."

"I'd just let her get the first swing in so it was self-defense," Chloe shot back.

"Is this Peyton someone we should be worried about?" Apollo asked, frowning.

"You mean there's actually someone on the island you don't know?" she asked, needling him as much as she was genuinely curious. At this point, she truly believed he was aware of everyone who lived on Salus. He'd come across as close to omniscient, after all.

Slowly, he nodded. "I didn't think there was, but yes," he answered, sounding disturbed. "Somehow she slipped past me, and given how closely I've been keeping an eye on the island whenever I could, that shouldn't be possible."

"Do we think she could have been working with Erick? Could she know he's really Dolos?" Lexi asked, anger fading to concern.

"At this point, I think anything is possible," Apollo admitted quietly. "It would explain how I couldn't see her."

"You said you were going to talk to Zeus, right?" Wesley asked.

"I did. My father is a busy man, but I'm a persistent one."

"What'd he say? Will he help us?"

Chloe knew by her dad's face that Zeus hadn't hopped on board the Get Dolos train, even before he said a word. "Not as much as we would like, but that isn't unexpected. He's never been fond of Dolos, since he's caused a lot of trouble with his illusions in the past. He's also well aware of what he owes you," he said, looking directly at Chloe, "for preventing Pandora's Box from being opened again." He sighed. "But he considers this largely a mortal matter, and Dolos being Nyx's son makes things trickier. However," he said, when her face fell, "he has promised that if we're able to subdue Dolos, that he will imprison him in Tartarus."

Though Chloe had hoped he'd agree to just that, her voice was still bitter. "That's something, I guess. Seems like he doesn't care much about his grandkids, huh?"

Apollo chuckled, and she heard a second laugh before she saw Phillip enter the room. "Do you know how many grandkids he has? Hell, do you know how many kids he has? Dear old granddad seems to feel like he needed to populate the Earth all on his own."

"I know you were…taken aback when you learned how many siblings you have," Apollo continued, "but I honestly couldn't tell you how many brothers and sisters I have. It's

173

probably well over a hundred. I wouldn't be surprised if it's hundreds, plural. And grandkids? Has to be in the thousands. That's not even touching on the great-grandkids. But I would recommend not bringing that up if you ever talk to him again."

"Oh. Yeah, I guess with that many grandchildren, one isn't much in the grand scheme," Chloe said, slumping back.

"For him, it may not be. But as I told you this morning, each of my children—and grandchildren—is special to me. You do matter, and I do care."

"I know," she told him, surprised when the smile came easily to her lips. She might doubt a lot of things in her new life, but she didn't doubt that every person in this room cared a great deal for her. "But how are we going to find Dolos? And once we do, how do we stop him?"

"We keep alert, especially anyone around you," Wesley began. "I'm checking places where he's been known to hang out, but I doubt he'll go anywhere we might expect him to be. I wouldn't be surprised if he staked out this place though, once he realizes you're not going back to your house."

"Will the wards really keep him out? I mean, if he's a god…"

"Indefinitely?" Lexi shook her head. "Probably not. But he won't be able to just stroll in like he belonged here."

"Okay, so we need to find him before he can break through, then." Though this was home turf, familiar, she didn't want to risk Wesley's house getting destroyed.

"Until we come up with a more feasible plan for finding him, we should definitely keep an eye on anything unusual around the perimeter of the wards. And don't just be looking for people, either," Phillip said. "If his illusions are as good as we think they are, then he might be able to disguise himself as an animal or someone we might expect to come visit. Like Zane."

"We should make sure our friends know not to come by

the house," Chloe said, suddenly anxious for people who might drop by innocently, only to be confronted by an angry bear or god.

"I'll take care of that," Lexi promised. "Zane, Cole, Reece...everyone. You don't have to worry, they'll get the head's up. And I have ghosts keeping an eye out around here, so we're covered."

Chloe rubbed her hands over her face and groaned. "I'm going to be a pariah in town again."

"Hey, stop that shit," Wesley snapped. "You were only a pariah when you were new and they thought you were a killer. No one's going to blame you for having a crazy councilor—or god—after you."

"You have such a sweet, gentle way about you," she said blandly, though he did have a knack of snapping her out of her funks.

He shrugged, completely unapologetic. "You don't need sweet and gentle, and that's not why you love me, in any case. I'll be sweet when you need it, and have, but what you needed right now was someone to give you a little kick in the ass."

"I'm liking you more and more," Apollo said thoughtfully as he studied Wesley.

"Good, because I'm not going anywhere."

The rest of the day was spent tossing around theories and plans, though none seemed truly feasible. They could try to set a trap, lure Dolos in, but as the god of deception, he'd probably be able to see through it. Nor could Chloe just go wandering around town, with backup following closely or not. If it even got Dolos's attention, there was no guarantee he'd try to kidnap her again. This time, he might just go for the kill shot.

Phillip and Lexi made dinner, but the conversation continued through to the end of the meal. Mavros made an appearance, grabbing some food as well, but he was insistent he stay outside and keep watch. It was sweet, how protective the crow was.

Afterward, they took a little bit to relax, watching a movie, and Chloe ended up watching her dad more than the movie, but it was just as enjoyable. Despite being a god, he didn't hold back in his reactions. He laughed, his face tensed with concern or anticipation, and she even saw him jump once, which was entertaining as hell.

It also made him seem more human. More like someone she could truly call Dad.

Despite the rest and food, Chloe didn't protest when Wesley pulled her to her feet for bed. In the room they shared for the moment, he touched her tenderly as he pulled off her clothes then laid her on the bed. She found a new burst of energy when he shed his own clothes and joined her. He stretched out beside her, clearly intending to simply hold her and sleep, despite the hard flesh she felt pressed against her hip.

She grinned into the dark. Her sheriff was a shocking contradiction sometimes. Gruff bear one moment, gentle lover the next. Fortunately, she loved both equally.

Turning toward him, she pushed at his shoulder until he rolled onto his back, his expression curious in the dim light from the moon outside. She slid a leg over him and straddled his hips, her breath catching as that hard ridge pressed between her legs. For a moment she wished there was more light so she could really see him, but there was also something so intimate about being like this with him in the dark. Like they were the only two people in this world or any other.

Her hands slid over his chest, feeling the light dusting of

coarse hair over his pecs. Leaning down, she pressed her mouth to his, kissing him lazily, reveling in the feel of him beneath her fingers, the taste of him against her lips. His hands found her hips and clenched against her flesh, proving that he wasn't as relaxed as his kiss might indicate.

There had been emotion when they'd come together before, but this was just a little different. As cheesy as it might sound, even in her head, this was what making love felt like, and their bodies weren't even joined yet.

Lips curved before she deepened the kiss, sinking into it, into him. Her hips lifted, then lowered again, taking him into her, body and soul. Their groans melded as she slid slowly onto him until he was as deep inside her as possible.

One of his hands left her hip, tangling in her hair as he took control of the kiss, though he let her set the pace as she rocked against him. Her breath caught and she trembled as he ravaged her system. And still she moved over him, unable to resist the tidal wave of sensation rushing toward her. There was nothing like this in the world, no magic that could replicate the way he made her feel.

When he bucked his hips, the building pressure within her broke. He swallowed her cry as her body fractured into a million shards, each piece consumed by pleasure.

The climax was still battering her senses when he wrapped his arms around her back and abruptly reversed their positions without allowing their bodies to separate. "Again, Chloe," he growled against her lips as he partially withdrew, then drove into her.

"With me," she panted when she could catch her breath enough to get the two syllables out.

"Always," he promised before his mouth crushed against hers once more.

Their sweat-damp bodies moved together and Chloe thought she was a fool for not having realized he loved her sooner. Or that she loved him. There wasn't any other way such a physical thing could affect her on such an emotional level or feel so huge, so important. Nothing else felt that way, not her magic, not her lineage, not even Dolos. Everything was insignificant next to the power of this simple act.

His fingers stroked over her cheek as his movements lost their finesse. She turned her face toward the touch and arched her hips to meet his. "With me," she said again before she gave in to her body's demands. Groaning, he buried himself in her and his forehead fell against hers as he emptied himself into her.

Before the rest of the energy could drain from his body, he slid off her, resting on his side beside her and drawing her close. He gave a kiss to her shoulder before sighing contently.

She could feel his heart, still racing, against her back, and she smiled, even as her eyes began to droop. But she needed to tell him something, first. It may not be the first time she'd said it, but she needed to let him know she meant it. That this mattered to her.

"I love you, Yogi," she murmured, aware tiredness caused her voice to slur slightly.

Lips curving against her bare shoulder, he replied in an equally sleepy voice, "Love you, too, Boo-Boo."

Chapter 19

It came as no surprise to Chloe when she had another nightmare. She'd been constantly stressed for the last few days, after all. This one was odd, though. Not quite as vivid as some of them, though it still played on her fears, but it didn't feel like the ones they suspected had come from the Oneiroi. It wasn't sharp, but more like she was viewing it all through a gauzy veil. Even when it ended with Dolos in his Erick guise telling her to come to the Oak or he'd go after her loved ones, it felt vague, thin.

Because of that, she didn't wake up screaming or tense, but more confused. The bewilderment grew when she realized she hadn't woken on her own, but because there was a lot of noise coming from outside. It took her a minute to realize it was voices.

Yawning, she found some clothes, pulled them on, and left the bedroom as she dragged her hands through her tangled hair. She found everyone in the living room—animals included—with the exception of Wesley. "What's going on?" she asked brain still fuzzy from sleep, but she was struggling to fully wake.

Five faces turned toward her, and all of them were concerned. "Ah...you sure you want to know before coffee?" Lexi asked uncertainly.

Chloe's eyes narrowed. She was still half-asleep, yes, but not so out of it she couldn't tell something weird was going on. "What's going on?" she repeated, voice firmer than before.

"Do you remember how you were worried about being a pariah again and Wesley told you it wasn't going to happen?"

Oh, she didn't like where this was going. "Yes…"

Lexi's shoulders slumped. "He may have spoken a little soon."

Chloe's eyes closed and she rubbed her hands over her face. "What, are they all jumping on the Chloe is a troublemaker bandwagon? Someone out there calling for my arrest again?"

"Not exactly…"

"It seems everyone on the island—with the exception of myself—all shared similar nightmares. They lived out their worst fears and were told to take you to the Oak or those fears would come true," Apollo told her, sounding as worried as the rest.

A chill spread through her. "Shit. I had one, too. I mean, I got told to go to the Oak or he'd go after you guys, but it was weird," Chloe admitted.

"Weird how?" Phillip asked.

"Usually, my dreams are really clear. It's just like real life, if you ignore the stuff that is too weird for real life. But this time it was kind of blurry." She started to ask what nightmares had to do with the din outside, but then it clicked. "The people outside are wanting to take me to the Oak, aren't they?"

"Some are," he admitted.

"How many are out there?" she asked, starting for the window.

"A few," Lexi hedged.

Twitching the curtain back just enough to look out, Chloe's eyes widened and her jaw went slack. "You consider that a few?" she asked incredulously as she stared out at the dozens of people crowded into Wesley's front yard. There had to be thirty, minimum, and that was just the ones she could see through the gap in the curtain.

"A few dozen?" Lexi corrected. "But from what I heard, most aren't actually wanting to take you to the Oak. They're just wanting to know what's going on. Why they're all having the same dream, why you need to be taken to the Oak."

"But a few of them do want to just give me to Dolos, giftwrapped, perhaps? Maybe with a bow?" Chloe asked sourly.

"They're just scared," Apollo said as he rose and joined her at the window, laying a hand on her shoulder. "That's why Wesley's out there, calming them down. They just want answers. They don't want to see their worst fears brought to life any more than we do."

She tensed. "Shit, Wesley's out there by himself?"

Before she could dart toward the door, her dad grabbed her arms in a firm hold. "Wesley is more than capable of handling them. And if they get out of control, he not only has his grizzly, he also has us."

"Maybe I should go out there…"

"I'm not sure that's a good idea," Lexi said, shaking her head. "The ones who are calming down might get worked back up. You going out there could cause them to turn into a mob," she explained, apology laced through her words, but her voice was firm.

"If you're that concerned, I'll go out there," Apollo offered. "Not only can I teleport, but being a god does afford me some respect. If they know you're my daughter, I have no doubt that a good number of them would back off."

Chloe wasn't sure she was ready for people to know she had a god for a father. It wasn't that she was ashamed of Apollo, because she wasn't, but she knew people would look at her differently. And how could they not? The people on the island knew the Greek gods were real. They had spoken to them, interacted with them. They revered them, even if they didn't worship them. Those who had seen Zeus had certainly afforded him a great deal of respect. Even Hiro and Elias had been affected by his presence. True, it was more fear than respect, but the effect had been similar.

"I'm not sure that's a good idea. Wouldn't that be putting them between one god and another?"

"I assure you, it will be fine. And they would much rather anger Dolos than me." It was said without a hint of pride. He was simply stating a fact from his point of view. Probably a fact all around, actually. Dolos was a more obscure god, where most people had heard of Apollo. Hell, if she remembered right, he the only Greek god who hadn't gotten a new name when the Romans adopted the gods as their own. Even Zeus had gotten a makeover as Jupiter.

"I can also protect your sheriff if need be," he promised her, kissing her forehead before he walked to the door.

Before he could close it fully behind him, she caught it, leaving it open just a crack. It was enough to allow her to hear the voices outside, though part of her wished she couldn't. Some of the gathered people definitely wanted to just sacrifice her to Dolos to save themselves. They were adamant about it. But those voices died down when Apollo strode out to stand beside Wesley. The fact that he didn't push in front of the sheriff made her feel even better about him. For a god, her dad really did seem to be mostly a normal guy. That only made the whole situation weirder.

Chloe heard her dad's name whispered through the crowd as the last of the yelling subsided. When it had gone silent, Apollo spoke.

"I know you are scared, that you all had a nightmare containing your greatest fears. A nightmare that ended by telling you to bring Chloe to Zeus's Oak." He paused for a moment and Chloe saw several heads nodding in agreement.

"This will not happen," he told them, voice firm, his gaze sliding over the crowd. "Chloe Chadwick is my daughter, and as such, is under my protection."

That started them going again, but it was more shock than fear this time. Apollo gave them a few moments to digest that news before he went on. "This is nothing more than the actions of a bully, one who is hoping you'll do his dirty work for him. Giving into threats, into bullying, never actually solves anything. If someone learns that you can be intimidated into doing something once, they'll assume they can continue to coerce you."

"I was told that if I didn't take her to the Oak, that I'd be going *against* the will of the gods. Why would I be told that if you're protecting her?" a man called out, but Chloe couldn't see who it was.

"There are many gods," Apollo answered evenly. "As you know, we do not always agree. I'm sure all of you have heard at least one story where we…disagreed. You were, indeed, told to take her to the Oak by another god, but he does not speak for all of us."

"I want to know why your daughter is worth more than mine!" a woman cried out. Chloe's heart clenched as she realized the woman had a point. One life wasn't inherently worth more—or less—than another. She wasn't worth more than anyone else on this island.

"Because she is…to me. I never said she was worth more than yours. But again, if you give in once, it's so much harder to hold out the next time. This time he's asking for my daughter. What is to stop him from asking your daughter next? Or yours? Or yours?" he asked, looking from one person to another, pausing to meet each person's gaze.

"We know you don't want whatever you dreamed about to happen for real," Wesley interjected. "We also know you don't want to get between two gods, but think about something. Gods are powerful, but only within their skill set.

Apollo is a healer, but he can't cause tidal waves or make crops grow. The god who did this sent you a dream, so what does that tell you about his skill set?"

That, more than anything else that had been said, seemed to sink in. It took a few more minutes, some more convincing, but people started to leave, one by one, until only two figures stood in the yard. Fortunately, these two figures she not only knew, but was fond of. Zane and Reece, a fox shifter she'd literally rescued off the side of the road after Daphne had taken his memories.

"Is she okay?" Zane asked, his brow knit with worry. His eyes kept flicking to Apollo, though he was obviously addressing Wesley. That made Chloe smile.

"I know Lexi said to stay away, but when I found out so many people were coming to hassle her, I needed to come," Reece added as they stepped toward the porch. "I wanted to make sure at least a few people in the mob were on her side."

Chloe started to open the door, but her brother put a hand on the knob before she could. "Make sure it's them before you go out there," he suggested quietly.

Though she started to protest, it only took a moment to realize he had a point. What better way for Dolos to get to her than by mimicking her two best friends who weren't currently in the house. She leaned toward the crack in the door and called, "Where and how did I meet you both?"

Apollo and Wesley glanced back toward her, the latter looking mildly irritated, but he nodded to the men in the yard. "If you can answer her question, you can see her."

Zane looked startled but answered quickly, raising his voice to carry inside the cabin. "You called me because Lexi suggested I could teach you to use your powers. I invited you to the bookstore. We made plans to meet up in Olympus Park for your first practice session because I didn't want the store getting wrecked."

Phillip looked to her and she nodded, confirming the

accuracy of Zane's answer.

"And you?" Wesley asked Reece.

"She literally picked me up on the side of the road. I couldn't remember a damn thing and was wandering around the woods. She took me to the hospital and came back the next day to bring me clothes and my e-reader. She also made me shift into my fox."

"Let them in," Chloe said with a smile, relieved it was really them.

Wesley motioned for them to go inside and Phillip opened the door. To Chloe's shock, Zane actually initiated a hug. It was a little awkward, sure, but the entire time she'd known him, he'd never hugged anyone first, only returned them. That, more than anything else, told her just how worried he was about her. "I'm okay," she assured him.

He stepped back and pushed his glass up with a finger. "Are you sure? I heard how long he had you. What he did to you."

"I'm sure. Phillip healed me, and they've been stuffing me with food."

"Don't think you're getting away without giving me a hug, too," Reece said as he walked up to her and wrapped his arms around her. "And don't think I've forgotten how you helped me when I needed it. It's my turn to help you," he murmured.

Chloe felt her eyes burn but refused to let any tears fall. She had people who were firmly on her side, and it felt wonderful. "Thank you," she told him in a choked voice as she stepped back.

"I just have one question, if I may," Zane said, glancing to Apollo as he joined them inside, along with Wesley.

"What's that?"

"Um...how long have you known Apollo was your father?"

She couldn't help but grin. Of course he was going for

information. "Since a few hours after they rescued me," she admitted. "But tell me, how are things out there, really? I don't mean the mob, I heard enough there, but people in general?"

Zane and Reece exchanged looks, neither looking particularly comfortable. To her surprise, Zane answered, his voice flat and factual, more like a professor giving a lecture than a friend giving news. "It's not good. There are more scared people than what you saw a little bit ago. The council has had a number of calls. Dozens, really. Some people are simply frightened and seeking information to comfort themselves. A few are demanding the council vote and take you to the Oak ourselves."

Chloe could feel the blood draining from her face. "And what does the rest of the council think of that?"

"Colin flat out refused. He said he wasn't going to be doing anyone's dirty work, and especially not for a criminal who betrays the council he sits on."

"I did always like that guy," Wesley muttered, sliding an arm around Chloe's waist and pulling her down onto the couch.

"Me, too," Reece agreed, perching on the arm of Lexi's chair.

"Natalia wasn't quite as…well, growly, but her thoughts ran along the same lines," Zane continued.

"And Diego? I bet that bastard was all too happy to hand me over," Chloe grumbled, folding her arms over her chest.

Zane's cheeks went lightly pink and he scratched his jaw lightly. "I wouldn't say he went that far, though he did insinuate that one person was better than the whole island."

"That fucking prick," Wesley snarled. "I'm going to rip him apart the next time I see him."

"Not if I get to him first," Apollo said coldly, his eyes and skin glowing faintly.

"You boys can take turns tearing him apart. Later," Lexi

said, shaking her head. "Right now, we still need to figure out what we're going to do. It's one thing to just deal with Dolos. It's another thing to be fighting the whole island."

"What do you know so far?" Zane asked, not batting an eye at the name of another god. Either Lexi had told him, or the dreams everyone else had gotten had included their source.

"Not much," Phillip admitted, looking just as angry as Wesley and her dad. "We know why he wants her, but that doesn't help us find him, much less take him out of the equation."

"I meant it, Chloe, when I said it was my turn to help you," Reece said. "I'd be more than happy to go searching for him in fox form. Most people don't pay much attention to animals they expect to see in the area, and I can get into places you guys can't. You're just too big."

Instead of taking him up on the offer, Chloe shook her head. "Maybe I should just leave the island. If I'm not here, maybe he'll leave Salus alone."

Every single person—and crow—in the room immediately shot that down.

"We know he's on Salus, right now," Wesley said. "If you leave, we lose even that bit of information. Not to mention you'd be exposed and wouldn't have the number of friends surrounding you that you do now" He shook his head firmly. "No, you're staying here."

"Then I'm definitely going to go hunt for him. I'm not much in a fight between gods, but I can absolutely do this," Reece decided with a sharp nod. "I'll let you know as soon as I find anything," he told them as he stood and left the cabin.

"Good deeds really do get rewarded," Chloe murmured to herself.

"I'm going to do some research, see if I can come up with anything that might help you," Zane said. "But let me know if there's anything specific I can look into." He patted Chloe's shoulder lightly, smiled stiffly, then followed Reece out.

"I'm going to head out, too," Lexi said as she rose.

"You are? Why?" Chloe asked, suddenly worried that each of her friends who left would end up enjoying Dolos's 'hospitality'.

"First, I'm going to see Garrett. He knows a lot of people on the island, and you said you met Erick at his gym, so he might have some insight. Second, I'm going to gather some supplies, including my grimoire. I'm not sure how well tracking spells would work on the god of deception, but you can damn sure bet I'm going to try." Lexi grinned. "Besides, I can take care of myself. No one wants to mess with an army of ghosts," she added with a wink.

"If you get kidnapped, I'm going to shove my foot up your ass," Chloe warned.

"Duly noted," Lexi said, blowing a kiss to Chloe before she, too, left. Which meant Chloe was alone with nothing but men. All men she adored, but also all men who were just itching for a fight.

"I feel useless," Chloe complained, letting her head drop to Wesley's shoulder. "I get why I'm stuck in the house, but it feels like I'm causing problems rather than fixing them."

"Do I need to call you on your bullshit again?" Wesley drawled.

"No, you need to give me something to *do*," she replied.

"Want to go out back and spar?"

She was about to take him up on that when Apollo smiled. "Actually, I think I might have a better idea. Chloe, how would you like to work on the powers you have that you didn't get from your mother?"

As tempting as it was to spar with Wesley, knowing how to use the rest of her powers could not only be useful, it could also potentially be the difference between life and death.

"As fun as it would be to let you work your frustrations out trying to hit me, that is a better idea," Wesley admitted. He didn't manage to hide all his disappointment, but she got it. Sparring was, for them, a little like foreplay. No different from their bickering, really. It got them hot and bothered. She wondered what it said about them, but decided she didn't care. It worked.

She kissed his cheek. "It is, but I'll spar with you soon," she promised.

Apollo beamed, and for him it wasn't a figurative thing. His skin brightened again, though this time it wasn't with anger. "Wonderful! It would still be a good idea to go out back, though. But not until you put on a coat."

How he had settled so quickly into the role of her father was beyond her, but as she rose to get her coat, she found herself saying, "Yes, Dad."

Chapter 20

Chloe was glad she'd added a hat and gloves by the time she got out back, because it was *cold*. And since she wasn't going to be moving around like she did when sparring with Wesley, she was going to feel every degree.

Apollo, of course, was just dressed in his jeans and a long-sleeved tee, but didn't seem bothered. Something to do with his sun powers, she assumed, though she wondered why couldn't she have gotten that handy talent from him. Or had she and just didn't know how to use it?

He made Lykos stay inside, but Mavros was perched on his shoulder when she joined them in the middle of the yard. Chloe wasn't sure whether to be amused or annoyed by the defection, but finally settled on amused. She didn't need any more annoyance in her life right now. Besides, it could only help her if all the males in her life could get along.

"Are you ready?" Apollo asked once she was in the middle of the yard with him.

"As I'll ever be, since I don't exactly know how this is going to work. I'm guessing it won't be exactly like when I learned to use my elemental powers?"

"It actually might not be so different," he assured her with a smile. "Have you displayed any powers that you know aren't from your mother?"

"Yeah, two of them," she admitted with a nod. "I'm pretty sure I accidentally healed Lexi after Nick and the others hurt her, and did it again when I, ah, accidentally broke Wesley's finger while we were training."

He chuckled. "You're not supposed to actually injure your boss and sparring partner, you know. Especially when he's also your boyfriend."

"I said it was an accident!" she told him indignantly. She still felt a little bad about it and that put her on the defensive.

"I know, and you did heal him, so that helps. We can work on healing on purpose later. What else?"

She hesitated, still a little scared by the other thing that had happened, though she was pretty sure she understood it now that she knew who and what her father was.

"A couple of times, I've glowed. No," she corrected almost immediately, "not just glowed. I freaking turned into a sunlamp. Sort of like how you did a little bit ago."

He cocked his head, intrigued. "Tell me," he encouraged.

"The first time was when Kyra was attacking me. She'd bitten the hell out of my neck and Mavros attacked her, but she swatted him away and hurt him. I couldn't find my gun and couldn't do much more than just sort of…lay there and bleed. I got pissed off that she'd hurt what I thought was just a helpful crow and started…glowing. It hurt her, enough that she passed out. I'm guessing it hurt her because it was actually sunlight, given that you're the god of the sun and all."

He nodded, his eyes luminous now. "Fascinating. Yes, that does make sense, though I can't think of any of my other children who can do that as a defense mechanism. You said that was just the first time, though?"

"Mmhmm. When I walked in on my ex banging another woman, I got pissed off and noticed that my skin was starting to glow then, too. Except it was different that time."

"Different how?"

She hesitated as she tried to think of how exactly to explain it. "When my powers were unblocked, they exploded out of me. Literally. I'd been leaning against a tree and it was pretty much destroyed. Knocked Zane and Diego out for a minute, too. Then, a day or two before I walked in on Diego and Peyton fu...having sex, Wesley and I had found one of Daphne's amnesia victims in the woods. An elemental. She was so scared that she lost control of her powers and was knocking trees down left and right. Big ones, too. I had to absorb her magic so we could be sure no one was going to get flattened. I must have taken too much, because I really think I might have exploded if I hadn't siphoned some of it into Zane and Diego."

She smiled tightly. "So, when I walked in on Diego banging that bitch, it felt a little like when Kyra was attacking me, and a little like when I absorbed the elemental's magic. Glowing but like that was a precursor to exploding. And, you know, I definitely didn't want to explode, and I sure as hell didn't want either Diego or Peyton to see me glowing."

Curiosity shifted to concern and he rested a hand on her shoulder. "What happened? It sounds like you managed to avoid...exploding."

Smiling faintly, she shrugged. "I went to the Oak, stopped fighting the glow, and poured all the power into the tree. I figured it couldn't hurt the Oak, and it might help strengthen the wards."

"Probably the smartest thing you could have done," he agreed, giving her shoulder a comforting squeeze. "How did you feel afterward?"

"Drained," she admitted. "The power didn't just flow out of me, it felt like it was being pulled out, ripped even. But drained was better than exploding."

"Indeed. And we can absolutely work on controlling the sunlight. It's like any other power. You'll need practice and time, but it *is* in your control."

"I know, it just wasn't something I could practice before. I didn't know what exactly it was, and I was trying not to let anyone else know I was more than an aether. Especially since I'd already been told that hybrids didn't exist."

He grinned. "They don't, but when god DNA mixes with supernatural DNA, the results can be...unpredictable, though the child is a demigod, regardless of their powers. Like Phillip said, his powers are entirely those of a witch, he just got a boost in certain areas. Some demigods only display powers from their divine parent. Even demigods whose parents were human are a surprise. Some just live longer, some take on divine powers. And not always those from their parent. Or not obviously so."

"Like what?"

He shrugged. "I could have a child who could control fire, which isn't something I could do, but since I am connected to the sun, it isn't really all that different, either."

"Oh. Yeah, that makes sense."

"Was there anything else that's happened that you couldn't explain?"

Chloe considered for a moment, sifting through all the weird stuff that had happened since that day in the lawyer's office. "Did you sent me those dreams? The ones about the island dying?"

"When Pandora's Box was in danger?" When she nodded, he shook his head. "No, I would never intentionally frighten you like that. I would have sent something different, more informative and less...traumatizing. Which means it's likely you inherited some of my prophecy powers, too."

Her nose wrinkled. "Is there any way I can turn that off?" she asked hopefully.

"Unfortunately, no," he admitted. "But if that is the only prophetic dream you've had, then it's not likely that you'll be dealing with them on a frequent basis. Not enough to truly call you a prophet. There are some who have dreams every night, or even multiple times a night. Some have visions even when they're awake."

"I'm definitely glad that's not me, then." She hesitated, then asked, "How likely is it that I'll have other things pop up? Or is there any way of knowing what other powers I have?"

"The right person can tell what powers a person has, but I would say that's probably all of it. Most demigods only have a couple of powers, though there are exceptions, of course." Then it was his turn to hesitate. "You should know there's also a roughly fifty-fifty chance that you're immortal, as well."

She groaned and rubbed her gloved hands over her face. "I was just getting used to living longer than a human."

He chuckled and tugged her hat down over her ear. "You'll adjust to it. And you might not be immortal. It isn't something you'll have to deal with for quite a while either way. And no way of knowing for a while either."

"Great," she muttered. "Okay, can we just work on the sunlight thing? I do want to learn how to heal, but without someone who's hurt, I don't see how we can work on that."

"I could help with that."

Chloe looked over to see Wesley leaning against the doorframe, arms folded over his chest. "No," she said firmly. "I'm not going to hurt you just so I can practice healing. Besides, one of us gets hurt often enough that I'll have the opportunity before too much longer."

"True," he agreed with a grin. "I'll leave you to play with sunlight then," he drawled before going back inside.

Apollo stared at the closed door for a moment. "I know I keep giving him a hard time for being in a relationship with you, but he really does seem to be a good man, and good for you."

"He really is," she murmured, unable to keep the smile off her lips.

Even Mavros bobbed his head, still on Apollo's shoulder, and said in his croaking voice, "Good, yes."

She grinned. "It's a consensus, then. But right now...how do I control the sun?" She wasn't quite to the point where talking about her love life with her dad was comfortable.

Apollo laughed. "It's not the entire sun," he corrected, "it's unlikely you have the same control over it I do, but yes, let's work on that."

Chloe shook her arms around and stood in a loose, relaxed pose. Mostly relaxed, in any case. This was essentially a new magic, so there were some nerves, but she thought she'd be okay. She hadn't blown anything up with it, which was a good start. And since it was sunlight she was dealing with, she was sure Apollo could prevent her from doing anything catastrophic. "Okay, so what do I do?"

Humor brightened his eyes. "You're not about to fight anything, so first you take a breath."

Even though she understood he was teasing her, she took him literally, inhaling slowly, exhaling the same way. It helped relax her further. "Fair enough. But what's step two?"

He ran a hand over her arm and stepped back. "It's just like your aether abilities. It's already a part of you. As you've seen, it's just beneath the surface, quite literally, waiting to be used. All you really need to do is learn to bring it to the surface. So let's start with you telling me how you use your elemental powers."

"Depends on which part of the power. When I'm sensing magic, I don't really have to do anything, I just feel it. Different magics feel different on my skin. But if I need to sort of search out magic, or separate one from another, I generally close my eyes so I can focus and...it's going to sound weird."

He smiled and shook his head. "I doubt very much that it's weird."

She shrugged. "If I close my eyes, I can see magic. It's like

195

lights, bubbles of light specifically. More powerful magic is brighter in my mind. If it's connected to a person, I can see a sort of tether between them and their magic, unless it's surrounding them. When I'm trying to search for magic, or narrow my focus to a specific one, it's like I turn out the lights without breaking them."

"Interesting, but not weird. And when you absorb or dispel magic?"

"Dispelling I just pop the bubbles. The stronger the magic, the harder I have to jab it, but I just reach out and…" She held up a hand, finger extended, and poked the air in front of her. "Most of the time, anyway. When everyone was asleep, I had to sever the tether to a person to wake them up, block the flow of magic to them. Then I absorbed it, which I…" She didn't bother protesting, just blew out a breath. "I pull it into me, like I'm a black hole of magic or something. Which probably isn't at all accurate, but the visual helps me."

He grinned. "I don't know that it's inaccurate. Like I said, even with your powers blocked you were still absorbing magic. But I'd say you should treat the sunlight as you do absorbing magic, just in reverse."

"How do you mean?"

"Instead of drawing magic into you, gently push it out of you, via your skin."

Considering that, she nodded slowly. "So kind of like when I gave power to the Oak?"

"Exactly, but instead of trying to get rid of the power—or give it someone or something else—just think about wanting to change that power to light."

"It's worth a try. Tell me if it works?"

"I will."

She closed her eyes and checked magic in the area out of habit. It was no shock when Apollo lit up like, well, a sun. It was distracting and amazing, but not a surprise.

Forcing that to the back of her mind, she found the power within her and began to gently coax it to the surface. She didn't try to expel it in a rush through her hands like she did when transferring power to another, but prodded it to the edge of her body. It wasn't easy. This felt like trying to shape dry sand. She'd get it in place, but when she grabbed another handful, the first would slide away.

Trying a different method, she gathered her power and just pushed outward. She didn't push hard, just steadily, until her skin felt swollen with it. Biting back a gasp of triumph to have gotten that far, she pushed a little harder, trying to remember to visualize the light.

"That's it. You're doing it."

Her father's voice sounded far away, but it was clear enough. Bolstered by her progress so far, she dug down and pushed a little harder.

"Wonderful. Simply wonderful," her dad said, his voice full of pride. "Open your eyes. Don't stop, but open your eyes."

Almost afraid to listen, worried it would fracture her concentration, she cracked an eye open. Though it was already daylight outside, the yard now looked as though it had a dozen floodlights fixed on it. Opening her other eye, she glanced down at her skin, saw it was, in fact, radiating that light.

Grinning with success, she looked up at her dad. "I did it! On purpose!"

"Yes, you did," he told her, grabbing her in a tight hug. Mavros squawked and flapped his wings to relocate to a nearby branch.

The combination had the light dimming, then disappearing, She didn't care, though. She'd done it once, she could do it again.

Apollo released her and smiled down at her. "It will get easier with practice, especially now that you've figured out how it works for you. I would even imagine that, with enough practice, you could use it as a weapon."

"Like what I did with Kyra? Against vampires?"

"Yes, but not only against vampires. You might be able to channel it, focus it through, say, your hands. It doesn't have the heat of regular sunlight, but it could certainly blind someone, even if only for a moment."

She shrugged. "Sometimes you only need a moment."

"Exactly."

"I'm not sure I'm ready to try that yet, but I would like to try summoning the light again."

He smiled and nodded, taking another step back. "As often as you need to."

Chloe learned that he meant it. For a couple hours she practiced summoning and extinguishing the light, illuminating the yard to varying degrees. When she began to tire she expected him to call it quits, but he just offered her more power. Since she wanted to master every power she could before Dolos cooked up his next plan, she accepted.

It wasn't until Lexi returned to the cabin that they finally called it quits. By that point, the sun had begun to set and, when they went inside again, they found that Wesley had made dinner.

An unspoken agreement had them shying away from the topic of Dolos, since no one seemed to have anything new. Instead, they just shared a nice dinner. It was a novel experience for Chloe, but one she thoroughly enjoyed.

When Lexi stole a buttered roll off Apollo's plate, and Wesley flashed her a grin, she thought she'd fight a dozen gods if it meant she got to keep nights like this one.

Nights where she was surrounded by the ones she loved.

Chapter 21

It didn't surprise Chloe when she had another nightmare. It was less blurry around the edges but otherwise it was very similar to the dream from the night before. This time, Dolos promised that if she didn't come to him, didn't give herself up, that he would systematically kill all her friends, her family, but only after making sure they were fully aware that she could have prevented it. If that didn't convince her, he'd kill everyone on the island.

When she woke it was still dark. There wasn't even a hint of daylight breaking through the night. Solid warmth beside her told her that Wesley was actually still in bed, and the even sound of his breathing made it clear he was asleep.

She didn't move, enjoying the feel of his body against hers as she stared up at the ceiling. There was no doubt everyone in the house would tell her she was dumb to even consider giving in to Dolos's demands, but at the same time, he'd given her some powerful visuals. Images of how he would kill Lexi, Phillip, Zane…everyone she'd gotten close to.

For a psychopathic god, he certainly was creative, but that wasn't a plus in her book. But that wasn't what her mind kept dwelling on.

How could she save herself if it meant her friends, her *family*, had to suffer in her place? No, she couldn't let that happen. She wouldn't be that selfish. As much as she didn't want to be anywhere close to Dolos, definitely didn't want to be tortured, she'd rather him hurt her than hurt the others.

Carefully slipping out of bed, she dressed in the dark, being as quiet as she could. Though Wesley normally mentioned his sense of smell, she was pretty sure all of his senses were well-honed and sharper than a human's. This morning, she managed not to wake him, even when she left the bedroom, closing the door silently behind her. Even more impressively, neither Lykos nor Mavros noticed her leaving, either.

Apollo, she knew, had taken the room right across from Wesley's, and Phillip had graciously given the other guest room to Lexi—such a gentleman—which meant after she managed to sneak down this hallway, she only had to worry about her brother on the couch. In order to avoid waking him, she opted to slip through the kitchen and out the back door.

A few of the boards in the hallway creaked when stepped on. Not loudly, but in this house that could be enough to get her caught. Creeping along the wall prevented that until she put her weight on a board near the end. She froze, her nerves making the soft sound into an explosion. Listening intently, she didn't hear anyone get up, but still waited for a full minute before continuing.

Once in the kitchen, she peeked into the living room, relieved to see Phillip on the couch, completely out. Steeling herself, she went to the back door, pausing with her hand on the knob.

They really wouldn't agree with her decision. She knew that. Hell, she wasn't entirely sure she agreed with it. It wasn't likely that Dolos could do anything to her father, and she knew the rest of them were more experienced than she was—with their powers as well as in general—so it might be harder for them to be abducted, but could she take the chance? Wouldn't it be more selfish of her to stay here, safe, while putting them at risk?

But they would be so pissed off at her. She knew they loved her, each and every one of them, and had no doubt they'd step in front of an angry god for her, but didn't it all come down to simple math? One person getting hurt was infinitely better than three—or more.

With her mind made up—again—she turned the knob and eased the door open before she stepped out. That was as far as she got before a hand wrapped around her upper arm, tight as a vise.

"Tell me you're not thinking of going to Dolos," a voice hissed quietly behind her.

Phillip hadn't been as out as she had thought.

Body still, she turned her head to look at him. "I'm not going to let him hurt you. Not you or Wesley or Lexi, not anyone," she whispered.

He made a sound that would've been more at home coming from Wesley's throat, and pushed her out the door, following her and closing it behind them. Even with the barrier between them and the rest of the sleeping household, he kept his voice down, but it didn't disguise the fury in it. "Do you really think that little of us? That we can't take care of ourselves? Or worse, that we aren't willing to take the risk for you?"

"That's just it, you shouldn't have to! He doesn't want any of you, he just wants me. If he gets me, you'll be safe."

He shook his head. "I had the nightmare, too, I know what he said, but you're wrong. We won't be safe because he wants to cause Dad pain. He thinks taking you and doing…whatever the hell he has in mind will hurt Dad and make him feel better. It won't. So when he's done with you, what do you think he'll do next? Retire to Florida?"

She hadn't thought of what would come after. The here and now had scared her too much for that. "What good would it do for him to hurt any of you?"

"Well, for starters, I am also Apollo's kid. Wesley and the others?" He shrugged. "They might be left alone, or he might go on a rampage, hurting anyone he thinks would upset Dad. Which could be anyone on this island, any of our brothers and sisters, or freaking sunbathers, doctors, and archers, for all I know."

"But I can't just sit here and do nothing!" she protested, though the resolve that had compelled her to give herself up was weakening. She wasn't stupid and he had good, logical points.

"You're not doing nothing. Didn't you spend hours today learning how to use a new power?"

"I doubt glowing is going to stop Dolos."

Another shrug. "Maybe it won't, but Dad told me you could easily blind someone with it. Could be that blinding him at the right time could be just the edge we need. Or maybe the grimoire you and Lexi have mentioned has something in it. From the sounds of it, your grandmother was a pretty fucking powerful and smart lady. Or maybe," he went on, voice fierce, "you need to realize you're not alone anymore and learn to work as a team." She started to protest, but he spoke over her. "Each of us has our strengths, Chloe. No one, not even the gods, can do everything. When we find where he is, then we can make a plan to deal with him. Since he is a god, it won't be easy, and we'll need all of us—and I do mean all—to handle him. My magic, Dad's sunlight, Lex's ghosts, your magical absorption, and Wesley's bear. And how could we use all of our powers if you're not here?" he asked, the last three words spoken between gritted teeth.

Though her intention had been noble, selfless, his words shamed her. Especially the ones about her trying to act like it was still just her. Except, had it really been selfless? She'd been wanting to spare them pain, yes, but also to spare herself the guilt she'd feel if they had gotten hurt. And she hadn't thought it through, not like he had. "I'm sorry," she breathed, the two words almost disappearing in the darkness.

His expression softened, as did his hold on her arm. "Just promise me, Chloe, that you won't play the martyr. It's not what any of us want. And if you don't promise, then I'm going to tell the others what you tried to do," he warned.

And they would be royally pissed. Shoulders slumping, she nodded. "I promise."

"Good. Then why don't you go back inside and try to get some sleep?"

"I don't think I could," she admitted. "I'm too awake, now."

Accepting that easily, he nodded. "Then how about I make us some hot chocolate and we just talk? Either way, can we get inside? My feet are ice."

Glancing down, she saw he hadn't bothered to put shoes on before coming after her, and socks didn't do much against the January chill. "That sounds good."

They went back inside and he left the lights off—aside from the small one over the stove—as he rummaged around in Wesley's cabinets. When he found the box of instant cocoa mix he looked mildly disgusted. "Sorry, going to have to use the cheap stuff," he told her as he started heating milk.

"When exactly did you get on Salus? Were you here when I got here?" she asked as she hopped up on an empty section of counter, so they could talk without waking the rest of the house.

He shook his head. "No, I arrived right after Dad told you he was sending you a present. Which is still a really weird way to say it since I'm your brother."

Despite herself, she felt her lips curving. "True. Where do you live, then?"

He smiled. "Here. When he told me about you, about the problems you'd been having, I moved here. The stuff in my house is really my stuff. I do have some in a storage unit in

Washington, but I live on Salus." He glanced over to her. "Wanted to be close to my baby sister so I could get to know her."

Since that gave her a warm feeling in her chest, she returned the smile. "Have you met any of our other brothers or sisters?"

"A couple," he confirmed. "I can't say I'm all that close to any of them, though."

"Why not? Do they all suck?"

"Well, a few do. But mostly we just don't have a lot in common. Most of them are really old."

Cocking her head, she asked, "How old?"

"I'm more than three hundred years old and some of them are ancient compared to me."

She blinked. "Sometimes I feel like I'm still a baby and not a grown woman."

He made a soft, noncommittal sound. "Compared to some of us, you are, but think of it this way. Some people get better with age, getting wiser, more powerful, whatever. Some people just get older. That doesn't change just because you extend the lifespan to centuries or more."

Considering Dolos had to be close to the age of her father, she couldn't argue that.

"Did you leave anyone behind in Washington?"

He chuckled and shook his head. "I know what you're thinking, and no, moving here to keep you safe did not separate me from the love of my life or anything like that," he promised.

Since that had been exactly what she was fearing, she let it go. "Were you a vet in Washington, too?"

He laughed softly. "No, I wasn't. Dad knew you were going to find Lykos, so we figured the vet thing would be the easiest and most natural way for you and I to meet. In Washington I was treating people in a hospital."

"That seems like a weird shift. I mean, I know healing is

healing, but wasn't it bizarre going from dealing with people to animals?"

Grinning, he shook his head. "Not really. Since I heal with magic, it doesn't matter if my patients can tell me what hurts or not. And as a vet, most of my patients now are a hell of a lot cuter. A lot of times they're more cooperative, too. They definitely can't lie to me, and I don't have to try to hide what I'm doing, covering magic with medicine. Besides, I've always had an affinity for animals. Canines especially, but that sort of makes sense, given wolves are one of Dad's animals."

When the milk was hot, he dumped packets of the cocoa mix into two mugs, filled them with the milk, stirred, then offered one to her. She took it, sipped, then grinned. "I don't know why you were looking like someone who lost their toy. This tastes like cocoa to me."

"That's because you've apparently never had *real* hot chocolate before," he muttered. "I am going to have to teach you so many things."

"And you, apparently, are a food snob," she told him, realizing her mood was vastly improved from where it had been when she'd first left Wesley's bedroom.

"I'm not a snob," he protested. "I just like things to taste good, and how they're supposed to taste!"

"I don't know. I think I'm going to stick with food snob until I see evidence to the contrary," she mused, feigning a serious expression. She couldn't keep all the humor out of her voice, though.

To her shock, he plucked one of the tiny marshmallows out of his cocoa and tossed it at her. His aim was good, because it hit her right between the eyes before bouncing onto her knee. It was so out of character for him that she gaped for a long moment rather than wiping the chocolate-flavored residue from her skin. Only when it began to drip down the bridge of her nose did she rub the heel of her hand over it.

"I can't believe you did that," she said incredulously.

He grinned smugly. "That'll teach you to think you know everything about me. But you'll learn. One marshmallow at a time, if need be."

"Oh yeah? Well, I'm telling Dad." It surprised her, how good those words felt, even if they were said in jest.

Phillip only laughed. "You should. He'd get a good chuckle out of it."

"Just don't tell Wesley. He'd never let me hear the end of it."

"Way to make it less tempting."

Though she groaned, she was enjoying the byplay. This was the first time he'd truly felt like her brother, and she liked it.

Chapter 22

Chloe and Phillip kept talking until the sun began to rise and the others woke. They talked about everything and nothing, without any awkward silences. It was…nice. Really nice.

To no one's surprise, Apollo was the first one awake. She had a feeling he always rose with the sun. Or maybe the sun rose with him? She wasn't entirely sure exactly how all that worked and wasn't sure she wanted to. At some point there was going to be so much information that her brain broke. Easing into it might help, or that was her hope.

She offered to make breakfast, but Phillip—in true food snob fashion—refused, saying he wanted to be able to eat it. He also did tell Apollo about the marshmallow incident as he made sausage, biscuits, and eggs. Unfortunately, he told their dad just as Wesley was joining them in the kitchen, so he heard every word. That led to playful ribbing all throughout breakfast. Even Lexi and Mavros joined in. Lykos? He just waited patiently until he was fed bits from people's plates. They were well on their way to spoiling him rotten.

They were just finishing breakfast when Wesley's phone rang. He rose and stepped into the living room. Conversation continued around Chloe while she watched the displeasure grow on his face. "I've gotta go," he told them when he hung up and walked back to the table.

"What's wrong?" Chloe asked.

He smiled faintly. "I'm still sheriff, honey, and Jack can only take the night shift, which means I'm on duty." He kissed her lightly. "It might take a bit. People are pissy about the recurring nightmares, and it's caused some tempers to get heated."

"I should go with you."

Though everyone still at the table said or indicated a disagreement with that statement, Wesley's voice cut through them all. "No, you shouldn't. It could be another diversion, like the fire at the Oak. Consider yourself on leave until we get Dolos out of the picture."

He gave her another kiss, though she glared at his retreating back as he went to handle things. "I hate it when he's right." And hated it more when he was going out there by himself. Yet she knew if she suggested one of them go with him, that would get shot down, too. Stubborn jerks, all of them, but she loved them all.

"It's not so bad. There's still plenty to do here," Lexi offered.

Chloe blew out a breath. "Yeah, I know."

"You wanted to spar yesterday with Wesley before Dad offered to teach you to use your demigod powers. So how about you and I spar?" Phillip suggested. "Burn off some energy, get some more practice."

She considered him for a moment. He wasn't as bulky as Wesley, but he was far from skinny. He was also three times Wesley's age. That didn't necessarily mean anything, but he'd had three times the amount of time in which he could have been honing his hand to hand training. But either way, it could be a lot of fun, and definitely a good distraction. "Sure. Why not? And I don't even want you to warn me if you're going to royally kick my ass."

He gave her a wide grin. "Of course not. It wouldn't be any fun if you were prepared."

They went to change before meeting in the back yard. To her chagrin, Lexi, Apollo, Lykos, and Mavros all joined them, though they remained on the patio. The animals didn't bother her, as they'd been present before, but Lexi and Apollo? Especially when she didn't know how good Phillip was? This could really get embarrassing, and now there were witnesses.

"What style has Wesley been teaching you?" Phillip asked when they had stepped into the middle of the yard.

"Ah…no real style, I don't think. At least none that he said. And it didn't look like any kind of martial arts or anything. Not that I'm an expert or anything."

"Brawling then," he said with a nod. "I can work with that." The grin returned. "Now's your chance to repay me for the marshmallow," he invited, settling into a defensive stance.

"And if you hurt him, you can always practice your healing," Apollo called out helpfully.

"Thanks, Dad," Phillip replied dryly, even as Chloe grinned. "Whenever you're ready, attack me however you want," he told her.

They started off slow, just as she did with Wesley, though this was as much testing each other's skill as it was warming up. Seeing him, she realized Wesley really had been teaching her to just brawl. Not that it was a bad thing. With the fights she tended to get into, brawling was probably her best bet. It was hard to use finesse when you were bleeding from a ragged bite to the throat or trying to tackle a crazy witch. Though she wouldn't argue if someone wanted to teach her how to get out of holds, since both vampire and witch had managed to latch onto her too well for her to escape. But she'd wanted fast and had doubts she could learn any kind of martial arts in just a few months.

Their pace quickened as muscles warmed and he adjusted to her skill level. It was still slower than a real fight would be, but she didn't complain. It was good, fighting someone new. If the only person she ever fought with was Wesley, she'd get used to his style, his preferred moves, and she needed to be able to defend herself against anyone who came at her.

Chloe threw a fist toward his face, fully expecting him to block it, but just before it connected, his eyes went unfocused and he stilled. She tried to pull it but didn't have enough notice and her knuckles rapped against his jawbone. Her first instinct was to pause, to apologize, but he didn't seem to notice he'd been struck.

"Phillip?" she asked, worry replacing the thrill she'd felt during their fight.

"Someone's testing the wards." His eyes cleared and settled on hers, then shot over to Lexi.

"I feel it, too," the brunette said, scrambling to her feet.

"Where?" Chloe asked, scanning the edges of the yard. She hadn't felt anything but didn't know if aether wards gave a warning like witch wards apparently did. Or maybe whatever was being done was focused on their wards and hadn't yet gotten to hers. She'd tried to put hers outside theirs but could have made a mistake.

Neither gave her a verbal answer but started running toward the left side of the house and the trees beyond. Both she and Apollo followed, and she had just enough time to order Lykos and Mavros to hang back. The crow didn't like it, but listened, and Lykos stayed with his friend.

Phillip and Lexi stopped ten feet from the woods. Chloe didn't see anyone—or anything—in the trees, but knew that didn't mean anything. A man who could look like anyone could probably make himself look like nothing. That thought terrified her, because how did she fight an invisible enemy?

They lifted their hands, almost in tandem, palms out and nearly identical looks of concentration appearing on their faces. Shoring up the wards, she assumed, but she didn't want to ask and risk distracting them.

Apollo must have thought the same, because when he spoke to her, he kept his voice quiet. "Gently give them some power, if you can. If this is Dolos—and I suspect it is—keeping him out will require quite a bit. If you need more, let me know, and you can channel it through me. Just make sure you keep it gentle so it doesn't break their focus."

Chloe nodded and stepped behind them, resting a hand on the back of their necks, as it was the only skin she could easily reach. Both were so tense they felt like stone, and she could feel that sweat had already sprang to their skin, proving just how hard this was on them. Being careful, so she didn't overwhelm or distract them, she began pushing power into them.

A quick check told her it wasn't going to be enough. They were already weakening. She gradually increased the flow, giving them more and more of her magic. At this rate, she was going to be tapped out in another minute, ninety seconds at most, and glanced at her dad. Understanding, he rested his hand against her cheek. It took precious seconds for her to shift, to pull from him and send it directly into Phillip and Lexi, but she did it, able to feed them the more potent magic from a much deeper well.

It wasn't going to be that easy, though. Only a few seconds after she became a conduit, she felt a jolt. Not physical, not even directed toward her, but an echo of what Lexi and Phillip were feeling. Someone was pounding hard on the wards, much like she had when Hiro had placed a ward around the Oak. She could only hope they weren't as successful as she had been.

After a few seconds, there was another jolt, this one strong enough to cause Lexi's body to jerk, and even Phillip twitched. Before they'd recovered from that, there was another, and Chloe realized each blow against the wards drained a lot of power from the witches.

"Brace yourselves," she whispered, hoping they could hear her. Drawing in a deep breath, she gave her dad an apologetic look. He nodded, obviously understanding what she was intending. Relaxing her hold on the magic, she let it flood into her brother and cousin. Lexi gasped, but she felt them both harden themselves against the assault.

It wasn't easy on Chloe. Though the power was simply passing through her, she had to direct it, and fight against her own power's instinct to cling to it. Her fingers started to tremble, and she pressed her hands more firmly against the witches, trying to pretend like it wasn't happening.

Dolos—or whoever he'd conned into helping him— didn't give up easily. Minute after minute passed, until Chloe wondered if this was going to be a siege. While she suspected Apollo had a great deal of power, she didn't know if it would be enough to outlast an attack like this. Except, could Dolos really outlast an Olympian? That shouldn't be possible, right?

After what had to be half an hour, there was a wordless, furious yell from deep within the woods. It was followed by a single, vicious strike against the wards before the pressure on them eased, then disappeared. As quickly as she could, Chloe cut off the flow of magic, not wanting to overload Phillip or Lexi. Only when she stepped back did she realize she was panting, her limbs shaking lightly. The witches weren't any better, looking as though they'd just climbed a mountain. Only Apollo looked unaffected, but even he had concern on his face.

"He's going to know I'm here now, if he didn't before," the god warned the trio.

"Couldn't be helped," Phillip said, out of breath as he shook his head. "Without your magic, I don't think we would've lasted long enough for him to give up."

"Maybe not," Apollo agreed as he gently herded them back to the deck and the chairs resting there. They all collapsed and, to Chloe's surprise, her dad went inside and returned with three bottles of water, handing one to each of them. It was such a mundane task for a god, but she could only smile and gratefully drink.

"Do we think he's going to try again?" Chloe asked as she rested her head against the back of the chair. Lykos whined softly and nudged her hand, so she stroked the top of his head as they spoke. Mavros wasn't going to be left out. He landed on her knee and gently pecked her other hand until she set the bottle aside and he got the same treatment.

Apollo considered for a moment before he shook his head. "No. He definitely won't try a frontal assault on the wards like that again, and I'm not even sure he'd try a stealth attack either. Crazy and vengeful he might be, but he's not stupid. This didn't work, and probably cost him quite a bit, so he'll try another tactic."

"Lexi, do you know why the ghosts didn't warn you he was coming?" Chloe asked.

Lexi sighed and glanced to a spot in the yard. "They didn't see him, not until after he started attacking the wards," she admitted.

Chloe nodded and considered for a moment. "I'm worried he's going to try to grab one of you when you leave the house," she admitted.

Lexi shook her head. "He might try, but first, we know that's a possibility. Both the grabbing and who the grabber is. Second, none of us are easy prey. And before you start getting a complex," she added, somehow correctly guessing where Chloe's mind went, "you weren't expecting a god to be after you, and you only have a few months of experience being in this world. I'm the youngest here and even I have a lifetime of experience."

"And he's a god," Chloe reminded her.

"But not all gods are created equal," Apollo interjected. "Like I've said, his powers revolve around illusion and

213

deception. I know you're worried about your sheriff, but I don't think Dolos would go after the most physically formidable of your circle." He hesitated, then smiled faintly at Lexi. "I hate to say it, but you're the one he would most likely go after. As you said, you're the youngest and you're female. He doesn't know you're also powerful enough to be the Keeper of Pandora's Box, so I think you would be his top choice."

"You're not leaving here by yourself," Chloe told Lexi firmly. "I don't care if I have to cuff you to my wrist, you're not leaving the wards by yourself."

Lexi sipped on her water as she studied Chloe coolly. "Normally, I'd tell you to fuck off, but under the circumstances?" She shook her head. "I don't want to end up as a bargaining chip for a pissed off and crazy god."

Chloe understood the reaction. It was essentially the same reaction she'd had to being cooped up here. Then again, if it was good enough for her, it was good enough for Lexi, so she smiled faintly. "Good, because I'd feel guilty, then you'd feel guilty for making me feel guilty, and a bad time would be had all around."

Phillip chuckled. "Sometimes I think you two act more like sisters than cousins. It's kind of adorable."

"I'm not sure if I like being thought of as adorable," Chloe told him, eyes narrowed.

"Why not? Adorable's not a bad thing."

"For puppies and babies," she shot back. "When it's women, it tends to mean men think they're harmless."

"Only if they're stupid men," he replied with a grin. "Wise men know that small kittens may be cute but still have claws."

"Suck up," Lexi said under her breath.

"I think all three of you act like siblings," Apollo said, a warm, almost proud smile on his lips. Sure, he had dozens of children, but maybe he didn't mind having an extra, honorary daughter to go with the biological ones? She kind of liked that thought. A lot. "How are you all feeling?"

Chloe did a quick check and realized the distraction and rest had helped. She felt like she was a quart shy of full, but it was bearable. "A little tired, definitely a little drained, but I'm okay."

"Same," Lexi echoed.

"Nothing that a few hours and a good meal won't fix," Phillip answered.

Apollo nodded then turned to Chloe. "Do you want to rest some more, or get in some more practice?"

She considered. "I don't think I'm up for more sparring, but if you wanted to spare a little more power, I'd probably be okay for practicing some more of the demigod juju."

He smiled. "I can do that, though I'd like to check something before I do."

Curious, she cocked her head. "What's that?"

He crooked a finger, and she was intrigued enough to follow him into the middle of the yard, until they were both bathed in warm sunlight. "Since you can radiate sunlight, you might be able to also take power from it," he explained. "You might also find that you're stronger when the sun is up, and weaker in the middle of the night, especially during a new moon, when it's darkest."

"Really?" She closed her eyes and tipped her face up to the sun. As her skin warmed, she focused on her aether senses, the well of magic inside her. It delighted her when she realized that she was, in fact, getting power from the sun. Not much, but enough to notice. A laugh burst out of her. "I'm a damn plant now," she said when she opened her eyes, fixed them on her father's.

"Really? A photosynthesis joke?" Phillip called, but he sounded just as amused as she did.

The fact that he got her joke earned him a bright grin. "Can you think of a better one? I'm getting energy from the sun!"

Even Apollo chuckled. "Prettiest flower I've seen."

"Wait, that means I can call you Buttercup and it actually make sense?" Lexi asked gleefully.

"Only if you want me to steal every single left shoe in your closet," Chloe warned.

A horrified look passed over Lexi's face. "Right. No Buttercup. Promise," she said, drawing an X over her chest with her index finger.

"Are you ready to get some more practicing in, now that the Buttercup matter is settled?" Apollo asked, still entertained rather than impatient.

Chloe nodded. "Absolutely." The mood was lighter now than it had been, and she'd like to keep it that way. And keep her mind off Wesley until he was home safe.

Chapter 23

Apollo was serious about her practice and had her work at it for several hours. Not just radiating it from her skin like she'd done before, but he also wanted her to try emitting it from her hands and turning it on and off quickly. She agreed, but also tried to shoot beams of it from her eyes. Not that she managed that particular feat, no matter how hard she tried. It was probably something best left for the movies, anyway. But by the end of the session, she was actually pretty good at calling and dismissing the light at will. She'd even managed, several times, to concentrate it in her palms, though that took more focus and was surprisingly hard to aim.

Once she had the sunlight down, at least well enough to be able to work with it sufficiently solo, he switched to healing. Despite her loud and determined protests, he insisted. Both Phillip and Lexi volunteered to be practice dummies, but Chloe couldn't watch as they took turns injuring themselves.

Fortunately, before anyone took a blade to their own skin, all of them explained about healing. How it felt, how they did it, how to search for wounds or illness. She was mildly surprised when it sounded like they all healed in essentially the same way. Apollo's ability seemed to be a little more innate, but the how was the same.

Most surprising was how similar it was to her aether abilities. Searching for wounds or diseases was a variation of searching for specific magical signatures. Healing was simply sending her magic to the injured area and directing it to heal.

Only after she'd wrapped her mind around that did she give in on anyone cutting themselves, but she'd put her foot down and forbidden anything major. Despite that, knives and blood were still involved. It turned out to be shockingly good incentive for her to learn quickly, though. The faster she caught on, the fewer times they'd need to hurt themselves.

The first few cuts were a little nerve-wracking, though the wounds were small and shallow. Apollo promised he was ensuring they didn't feel pain, which helped. Healing a few of those cuts helped, too, but she still forced them to call it quits after healing three cuts each. Painless or not, she simply couldn't stand to see her brother or cousin injured again for her. Besides, she had picked up on it rather quickly. The similarity to her aether powers made the learning curve better for her.

They didn't go inside until the sun started to set. Wesley had checked in a few times, which Chloe appreciated, though she continued to worry. It affected her appetite, but she didn't turn down Lexi's offer to order pizzas. Not only was pizza the perfect food, but it meant no one had to cook or leave the cabin.

The pizza arrived at the same time Wesley did. He carried the boxes into the house but stopped when Apollo shot him a hard look.

"Forgetting something?" the god asked, arms folded over his chest.

Wesley frowned in confusion. "What?"

Her dad's meaning clicked for Chloe the moment Wesley spoke. Living like this wasn't exactly the norm for any of them, so she could forgive Wesley for forgetting. "Code word," she explained as she watched his face.

His expression cleared. "Oh, right. Sorry. Kaleidoscope."

Apollo's face relaxed and he smiled, arms dropping. "Had to be sure."

"No, you're good," Wesley assured them as he set the boxes on the table. Now familiar with the kitchen, Phillip grabbed some plates and napkins while the sheriff went right to Chloe's side. "I'd rather you be safe," he murmured before giving her a light kiss. "How'd today go?"

She exchanged a look with her dad. "Someone tried to get in the wards earlier," she told him. Beating around the bush would just drag it out, and it was going to be bad enough already.

In a blink, Wesley's eyes went full bear. "Why didn't you call me?" he asked, yanking her to him and into his arms.

It felt like he was trying to wrap himself protectively around her. While she appreciated the sentiment, it was also a little suffocating. Literally. She shifted until she was able to breathe and wound her arms around him. "Because we dealt with it. Lexi and Phillip shored the wards up, I pumped power into them, and my dad gave me more to give to them. It was enough that Dolos gave up."

"And we checked the wards," Phillip added. "They're intact. Probably stronger now, since Dad's power was added to the mix."

"And even if he'd gotten through the wards, I wouldn't have allowed him to lay one finger on my children," Apollo said, voice mild, though his eyes were faintly glowing.

"I still wish you'd have let me know," Wesley growled softly.

"It was done by the time I could have called you, and I didn't want to distract you while you were outside of the wards," Chloe admitted, stroking a hand over his back, trying to soothe him.

"I need more deputies," he muttered.

"Temporarily, maybe, but I'm hoping not for good. I don't want to be cooped up inside these wards for long."

He said nothing, just continued to hold her while the others grabbed slices of pizza or transferred salad to their plates. Eventually his bear receded and he was able to release her. "Next time, let me know?" he asked softly, looking into her eyes as his faded back to gray.

"If I can," she promised. And she meant it, but to her mind, if telling him would put him in danger, there was no way she'd be able to tell him. Part of her felt guilty for the omission, but she wouldn't lose him. She was sick of losing people.

Except he seemed to realize she was holding back, the understanding on his face made that clear, but only nodded and kissed her again. "You should eat something," he said, pulling a chair out for her.

She sank into it and snagged a couple slices of pizza, as much to appease him as to appease her stomach. "You should, too," she told him as she nudged a chair out with her foot.

He followed her lead and took a bite before he focused on Phillip. "How close was it?"

Her brother glanced at Lexi, who only shrugged and continued chewing. "Not as close as you're afraid it was, but closer than I would have liked," he admitted. "Without the extra power, I think he would have broken through."

Wesley cursed softly. "We have got to find where he's holed up and do something to stop him."

"Believe me, we know," Lexi said blandly. "It's kind of hard to find a god, though, especially when it's a god whose primary powers are all about hiding. We'd almost have better luck finding a specific grain of sand on a beach."

"I'm going to look in Granny's grimoire," Chloe said as she got up to grab a Coke from the fridge. "I know she created a bunch of spells already, but since she knew my dad was a god, it's entirely possible she looked into making spells that involved the gods." She dropped back into her chair and took a drink. "No idea how successful they would be, though." She lifted a brow, focused her gaze on Apollo. "Unless she used you as a guinea pig?"

Like the others, he was busy chowing down on the pizza, and it relaxed something inside her. Meeting gods for a couple minutes at a time didn't really give her any indication as to how different they were from supernaturals, but this did. Seeing him doing something as blessedly normal as enjoying the world's greatest food was refreshing. He may be an immortal with divine power, but he wasn't completely alien.

Though now she had to wonder about Francois. How did a man whose primary diet was blood cook such fantastic meals? Could vampires actually eat real food, despite all the myths? She'd have to remember to ask later.

Apollo chuckled, his expression mildly pained. "I can thankfully say that no, I wasn't a guinea pig. Though I would have offered if I'd have known we'd be in this particular situation."

"Does that mean you'd be willing to be guinea pig for us now?" Lexi asked curiously.

The god cocked his head, his gaze intent on the witch. "That all depends."

Amusing Chloe, Lexi squirmed in her seat and lowered her pizza to her plate. "On what?"

"On what exactly you're wanting to test on me."

"Oh! No, nothing bad," Lexi told him quickly, her voice mildly panicked until a grin curved his lips. She blew a raspberry at him. "Tracking spells and stuff. Things that could help us find Dolos, or protect against him."

He nodded. "If it's something that can keep Chloe—and all of you—safe, then yes, I'll agree to being your guinea pig."

Lexi smiled and started to speak, but he lifted a hand. "But," he continued, "you have to give your oath that whatever spells you come up with, whatever information you may learn about gods, will not go any further than the people at this table."

"Of course," she agreed without hesitation. "The way I see it, you're family. Okay, so it's a distant connection, but you're the father of my cousin, that's still family. I don't screw over family." She looked to Phillip. "Can you handle the oath?"

"I can," Phillip answered.

"Wait, why do I get the impression you mean more than crossing your heart or a spit shake or something?" Chloe asked curiously.

"Really?" Wesley asked, bumping her knee with his. "You, who have some movie or book equivalent to everything you've learned, don't have anything for magical oaths?" he teased.

Chloe resisted the urge to stick her tongue out at him, but he wasn't exactly wrong. Her brain hadn't gone in that direction immediately this time, but normally it was a way of marrying the familiar with the unfamiliar. No way she was going to admit that to him, though. "Of course I do, but I'd still like to know about these magical oaths. Like, how binding are they, can you break them, and if you can, what are the consequences to breaking them?"

"All good questions," Phillip chimed in. "And the answer to all three questions is…it depends." He smiled at the frustration on her face. "I know, not what you wanted to hear, but there are different levels. But essentially, the more binding they are, the harder they are to break, and the more dire the consequences. It ranges from maybe a mild headache to death. Something like this?" His shoulders lifted, dropped. "Extremely binding, so very hard to break, and yes, if she did break it, it would kill her."

She felt herself go pale. "Kill her?" Shaking her head, she told Lexi, "No. Not happening. I'm not risking you like that. What if you broke it but were forced into it? Or tricked? Dolos looked and sounded exactly like Wesley, remember? I could only tell it wasn't Wes because of the nickname."

"Relax," Apollo told her soothingly, resting a hand on her arm. "It doesn't work like that. In a way, the oath would protect her. It's magic, remember? Yes, Dolos could trick her, but unless he tricked the magic, too, the oath wouldn't allow her to tell him. And if he did manage it, the oath wouldn't come back on her because it wouldn't realize it was broken."

The heartbeat that had quickened began to slow. "You make it sound like it's intelligent, sentient."

"It's not, not how you're thinking. It's more…" He trailed off, considered a moment. "Like a very complex computer program."

That made her feel better. The sleep magic that she'd fought months before had felt sentient and had creeped her out. The magic from the Oak was almost at the same level, though it felt more comforting. But she'd like to keep her contact with magic that felt like it could think to a minimum. "Gotcha." She mulled it over then told Lexi, "Up to you. You know the risks better than I do."

Lexi smiled. "I do, and I think it's worth it. Besides, you should know that neither your brother or dad would intentionally put me in danger." She leaned forward, dropping her voice to a stage whisper. "I think they're afraid of pissing you off."

Chloe laughed, but Phillip nodded while Apollo said, "She's not wrong." That made her pause, and after she'd processed their reactions, it made her smile. She didn't think they were afraid of her, but afraid of going the next twenty-seven years without her again. It was a nice thought. A good thought that cemented the fact that she had family who truly cared about her.

She leaned toward her dad, resting her head on his shoulder. The small act of affection still felt a little weird, so she only left it there for a moment before she straightened. It still clearly affected Apollo, who looked both pleased and touched. Since that was how they had made her feel, she couldn't blame him.

"I'm not going anywhere," she promised, not just to her brother and dad, but everyone at the table.

"You'd better not," Lexi said as she plucked a pepperoni off her pizza and popped it in her mouth. "You think I've got the time to find a new best friend before things get good with Garrett?" She shook her head. "Because I don't, and I'll need a best friend to listen to me ramble and help me pick out the best dress for blowing his mind."

Chloe grinned. "I don't think you need help on that last part, but I promise, not going anywhere," she repeated.

"Very glad to hear it," Wesley whispered in her ear before lightly kissing her cheek. "Now eat. You haven't eaten enough."

She let out a deep sigh. "See how he bosses me around?" she asked as she picked up her slice.

Her family only laughed, just as she had intended.

Chapter 24

Though Chloe slept pressed against Wesley's side, with Lykos against her legs and Mavros on the back of a chair, nightmares still found her. She had hoped that Dolos would have weakened himself with the attack, that she'd get a night of peace, but she wasn't that lucky.

Knowing it was a nightmare didn't make it any better, not when she was trapped in her own body, unable to do more than follow along with the script Dolos or one of his allies had written.

She walked into the diner, found it packed with people. No strangers, no slightly-familiar faces, not this time. No, this time it was full of those she cared for. Wesley sat in a booth with Phillip and her father. Lykos lay on the floor at their feet, while Mavros had perched on Apollo's shoulder. Another booth was occupied by Reece and the others Daphne had abducted. Lexi was behind the counter, setting a couple of plates in front of Zane and Cole. Further down were Deirdre, Colin and Garrett.

Normal noises filled the small restaurant. Conversations, cups being set on counters and tables, silverware against plates. She felt her lips curve into a smile as she took a few steps, but once the first face glanced toward her, recognized her, all those sounds stopped. Every single person turned toward her, some with forks poised at their lips, others with cups halfway to their mouths. And none of them looked happy to see her.

Frozen in place, she tried to figure out what she could have done to anger them, then a soft growl broke the silence. To her shock, Lykos was slowly getting to his feet, teeth bared as he growled in her direction.

"What's going on?" she felt herself ask as the wolf approached, stalking her like she was a wounded rabbit and not the woman who had rescued him, taken him in.

Lykos didn't stop, and no one answered. Instead, they all got to their feet as well, equally aggressive expressions on their faces. Their paths led them into a close group which reminded her too much of a mob. Worse, she noticed all the predatory shifters had claws tipping their fingers and their eyes had gone the color of their animals. She had no doubt that if she could see their teeth, she'd see fangs.

She didn't realize she was backing away until she was pressed against the glass door. Though it was supposed to open out, it didn't move, even with her weight against it. Unwilling to look away from the people and animals approaching her, she fumbled for the lock, wondering if one of the witches has turned it, but wasn't able to find it through touch alone.

Her heartbeat quickened as they drew closer, and her eyes darted from one face to another, seeing hatred in each one. Even her father's face. Even Wesley's.

"No," she whispered, shaking her head. "Don't do this. Please, don't do this." She hadn't thought the nightmares could get worse than when she was all alone or everyone was dead, but this broke her heart.

"Dad...Dad, what's going on? Why are you acting like this?" He didn't register that he even heard her, so she looked to Lexi. "Come on, talk to me," she begged. Nothing. "Wesley?" Tears pricked at her eyes at the animosity she saw on his face. Not him. Please, not him. Families fought and argued, but Wesley? It was too much. Then, when he bared his teeth and she saw they had lengthened, she felt her heart stutter.

Phillip lifted his hand, palm up, and magic began to coalesce into a ball. Zane's eyes turned white as all the forks and knives in the diner were lifted by his wind, the points aimed toward her. A glow began to emanate from her father, just before Wesley lunged toward her.

Unwilling to defend herself against these people, unable to hurt them to save herself, she closed her eyes, letting the tears fall as she waited for their attacks to connect. She felt a rush of wind, braced to feel the utensils stab into her body, but it never came. Nor did Wesley's claws or Phillip's magic.

After a minute passed with no pain, no sound, she opened her eyes and saw only darkness. Perfect darkness, without even a pinprick of light to mar it. It was like she was blind, but after a moment she realized she couldn't feel anything either. A line formed between her brows as she shifted her feet, but she couldn't even feel the ground beneath them. No, there wasn't ground beneath them, as there was no resistance, but she didn't feel as though she were falling, either. She swept her arms out in front of her, to either side, but they didn't connect with anything.

Fear began to build, and she tried to shove it down. She didn't feel threatened, not like she had in the diner, but the utter lack of sensation was beyond disconcerting.

"Hello?"

Her mouth moved, her throat vibrated, but no sound left her lips, which only added to the fear. Despite not being able to see anything, she closed her eyes. It helped, took something away from the absence of anything *to* see, and let her concentrate on slowing her breathing, allowing her heart rate to start to return to something resembling normal.

What could she do, when there was nothing to interact

with? No one to interact with?

Her eyes popped open as she realized she didn't need a light. She *was* a light. Hadn't she spent hours working with her dad on controlling that particular power? She called on that practice now, but it felt like it took three times as long for her to even manage a faint glow. But it did work, eventually, every inch of exposed skin shining against the darkness. Except nothing was revealed. Refusing to allow herself to stop now and give up, she pushed more power into her skin, until she shone so brightly she could see nothing *but* light.

There was a slight jolt, which she realized were her feet hitting something hard. It startled her so she quickly shut off her glow, only to be shocked to find she was actually someplace real. Though it was night, the moon offered enough light to see she was at the Oak.

And she wasn't alone.

Dolos stood in front of the tree, his expression smug, arms folded over his chest, looking as though he'd already won. There was a shadow beside him, but not his shadow. This one—no, there were two dark smudges—stood nearly as tall as Dolos and moved independent of his actions.

Her legs began to move, to carry her toward the god of deception. His lips moved, but she couldn't hear a word. No, she still couldn't hear anything, but was relieved at the return of her other senses. Anything was better than the void she had experienced.

Chloe's arm raised, and she found her pistol in it, but before she could fire it, the most intense pain she'd ever felt crawled across every inch of her body. Screaming without sound, her hand spasmed on the gun, jerking the trigger, but the bullet hit one of the thick branches of the tree.

Her legs buckled and her body fell toward the frozen earth. Before her knees could connect, the tree, the god, and the pain were all replaced. She was back in the basement of her father's temple, chained to a chair and staring at the face of the man she loved. A face she knew was false. He spoke. She remembered the lies well, and this time she was happy not to be able to hear.

The chains loosened around her legs and 'Wesley' looked up at her, which was when the memory shifted. Though she'd known it wasn't the sheriff at this point, the illusion had been flawless. Now it shimmered, so three faces were all superimposed over one another; Wesley's, Erick's, and Dolos's true visage.

The dream moved her again, to her couch, with a warm fire burning silently in the hearth. Granny's grimoire lay in her lap, a strip of paper resting between two pages to mark it.

Then she was in the back yard of Wesley's house, her skin glowing while her father looked at her with love and pride.

Only seconds later, she sat at Banquet, Erick in the chair across from her, a hint of annoyance in his eyes. As soon as he hid it, she moved again.

Granny's Boston house, having dinner with her grandmother.

The storage room of Granny's Salus home, staring at slip of paper.

In Diego's workshop, watching him prepare a spell.

At the Oak, screaming as she poured power into it.

In Zeus's temple, hurting and looking up at the most powerful of all Greek gods.

Back at the Oak at night, on her hands and knees as she tried to suck in air.

In the woods, trying not to explode after draining a terrified elemental.

As the dream continued to flash quickly from one scene to another, some memories, some unfamiliar, sound began to filter back into her awareness. At first it was just an indistinct murmur, but it gradually grew louder, more coherent. Then she made out her name. It didn't match what she was seeing, and it was hard for her to keep up with all the images bombarding her. As soon as her brain started to process what was in front of her, it changed.

She tried to close her eyes, to block out the sight and focus on the words, but she couldn't. Her body refused to cooperate.

Quickly overwhelmed, she latched onto the sound of her name, using it to anchor her to sanity. It still took precious minutes more before she recognized the voice as Wesley's.

"Chloe. Chloe, wake up, honey! Come on, Chloe. Don't do this to me."

Right, she was dreaming, which meant she could wake up and leave all this behind. But how did she do that? She wanted to, she really did, but she wasn't sure how.

"She won't wake up. Do something!"

Another voice, this one different, but it was little more than a buzzing in her head.

The slideshow lightened, growing brighter and brighter until all she could see was white. She squinted against it, though it didn't actually hurt her eyes. Before she could lift a hand to shield them, something felt like it hooked in the vicinity of her navel and tugged sharply.

She slammed into consciousness, her breath expelled in a sharp gasp as she blinked into the darkened room. Wesley hovered over her, fear and anger for her showing in every line of his face. Behind him, she could see her father, an equally worried look on his face. A soft rustle of feathers had her looking up to see Mavros on the headboard, sending relief into their bond. Knowing Lykos wouldn't have abandoned her either, she glanced down to see him with his head on her knee, whining quietly in concern.

"Chloe," Wesley growled, distracting her from everyone else as he wrapped his arms around her with far more gentleness than a man of his size should be able to manage.

With stiff limbs, she lifted her arms to circle him, frowning in confusion at Apollo. "What was that?" she asked, her voice raspy, which made her wonder if she'd been screaming in her sleep. Again.

"I'm not entirely sure," her father admitted.

"Forget what the fuck it was, is she okay?" Wesley demanded as he leaned back to look at her, searching her face for signs of distress or injury.

Leaning over the bear, Apollo reached out to rest a hand on her cheek. She felt the warmth of his power for a full minute before he straightened. "I don't sense anything lingering. As far as I can tell, you're in perfect health, though you may want to check yourself for magic."

It was a good idea, and one she might have had after the fog of sleep had fully lifted. She closed her eyes and struggled to focus enough to do as he'd suggested, but it took some time to get her mind and powers on the same page. It was then that it clicked. She was in bed, with Wesley, and her father was in the room. A small shift of her hand reminded her that she'd gone to bed in a tee-shirt and shorts, so she was covered. Relieved, she searched for magic on her, and found only the slightest residue, already well on its way to fading completely.

Opening her eyes, she shook her head. "I'm good. But I don't understand what happened."

Apollo ran a hand through his hair, the first time she'd seen him make any sort of nervous gesture. "You were trapped in a dream. I don't know how. Or rather, I don't know who was responsible for trapping you in it."

"Then how am I awake?" she asked as Wesley slid out of bed—fortunately wearing cotton pants—and into the bathroom.

"I was able to enter your dream and force you out. Otherwise, I'm not sure how long you would have stayed there."

Her brow furrowed. "Did you see it? The dream?"

"Bits and pieces, but I was focused on waking you, not the dream," he confessed. "It also looked rather...fragmented."

"It was. At the end. Too many pictures, like someone took a hundred video clips and spliced them together."

Wesley returned, sitting on the bed and offering her a glass of water. She took it with a murmured thanks and carefully took several swallows. The fact that it eased her throat told her she probably had screamed at least once. Likely no more than that, or the bedroom would have a few more people in it.

"You can tell us about it in the morning," Wesley told her, running a hand over her hair.

"But—"

"He's right," Apollo interjected. "You need rest. You're healthy, but I could tell you didn't sleep well. That or the dream drained you. Either way, you need a few more hours sleep."

Since she did feel like she'd been up for a few days, she didn't protest. Taking one more drink, she set the glass on the nightstand and sank back down to the bed. "Okay."

Apollo bent to kiss her forehead and she felt a tingle of magic. She had a feeling it was something to help her sleep, and she was grateful. "Sleep well," he told her before leaving, closing the door quietly behind him.

Wesley pulled her half on top of him, his arms holding her close. "Sleep," he told her, kissing her hair.

Eager to comply, she rested her head on his shoulder, closed her eyes, and plunged back into the dark.

Chapter 25

Because of the scare with the wards and the nightmare that followed, Wesley didn't go into the office the next morning. While Chloe enjoyed having him nearby, she was starting to feel a little smothered. Unless she was in the bathroom, there was always someone within ten feet of her. She couldn't even say one of them was worse than the others, because they were all equally guilty.

Over breakfast, she told them what she could about the dream, but beyond the nightmare portion, it was all jumbled in her head, making it hard for her to relay it with any kind of clarity. Which meant the best anyone could figure is that Dolos or one of his brothers had messed with her, and whatever they had done had morphed into something else. A prophetic dream, maybe, but if that was the case, it was nothing like the last one had been. That one had been more cohesive, even if it had been metaphorical in places rather than literal. Not that it had helped her at all, not until she'd been living it. Still, it was better than snapshots that didn't seem to have anything to do with one another.

As they all went about their different tasks, Chloe couldn't help but try to piece together something useful. Ignoring everything in the beginning, she focused on the last bits. The darkness and all the images that came after. Except her brain just couldn't fit the pieces together in any kind of meaningful fashion.

She decided to clear her mind and hope that not thinking about it actively would help spark something. Which meant going for a run. A difficult task when she was confined to the area within the wards, but not impossible.

When she went into the front yard to stretch, she was followed by her brother and cousin. As she bent forward, fingers and ponytail brushing against the ground, she looked to where they were lounging against the porch railing. "Aren't you guys missing work?"

"Called in," Lexi answered with an unconcerned shrug. "Joel gets it. Besides, he's super happy with you, since you saved me from Daphne."

"Pretty much the same for me, too," Phillip told her.

"Just don't lose your jobs because you're babysitting me," Chloe said as she straightened, though she knew she'd worry about them constantly if they were going to work. Too many chances for Dolos to screw with them. Or worse.

Phillip only smiled. "Technically, I don't need to work. I just enjoy helping people—and animals—and it was an easy way to slip into the community and ensure I met you."

"I'm not worried, either. I mean, yeah, I have to work, but Joel loves me." Lexi grinned impishly. "And I think some of the customers would riot if I got fired."

Chloe laughed, because she had a feeling Lexi was absolutely right about that. "Fair enough. But are you two going to run with me? I'm not actually going anywhere, but I'm too restless to stay still."

"If you're not going anywhere, where are you running to?"

"I'm not. I'm doing laps. Very boring, very short laps around the house."

Lexi wrinkled her nose and sank into the porch swing. "I'll stay here."

"But I thought you told Garrett you loved running," Chloe asked innocently. When Lexi's reaction was to give her the finger, she laughed once more before she started jogging around the house. After a few steps she realized neither wolf nor crow were running with her, which was surprising. Mavros, of course, didn't run, but they'd been accompanying her essentially everywhere.

When she reached the back of the cabin, she saw the reason for their absence.

Mavros was perched on the back of the chair Apollo was sitting in. Both god and bird were avidly watching as a bear and wolf wrestled around on the grass.

Chloe's steps slowed as she stared at the two furred bodies. Wesley was obviously taking it easy on the much smaller wolf, as neither had blood on their pelts. Lykos was thoroughly enjoying himself, pouncing on Wesley and knocking him on his side. When the wolf growled and 'attacked' Wesley's neck, she felt her heart leap, but realized the fur of a grizzly had to be thick, and a play bite was hardly going to break skin. It probably also wasn't the first time Wesley had been bit by the smaller animal.

But it was the first time, as far as she knew, that Lykos had met Wesley's grizzly, and she'd worried—a bit—that the wolf would react poorly. Wouldn't instinct kick in when faced with a predator so much larger and stronger than him? But she knew enough about canine body language to recognize that Lykos was just having fun. Besides, Apollo wasn't likely to sit by while either of them harmed the other. Especially not when they were both so important to her.

Walking over to the deck, she inclined her head toward the wrestling match. "How long has that been going on?" she asked quietly.

Apollo smiled and looked away to meet her gaze. "About five minutes."

"And before this?"

He shook his head. "It's the first time Wesley has shifted for Lykos." The smile turned proud as he looked back to the wolf. "He's a smart one. Realized right away that it was still his friend, so there was no fear or posturing."

"Really?" Ridiculously pleased, she watched them in silence for a moment. "So you really know I was going to find him, huh? Lykos, I mean."

"I did."

"Did you know he'd be hurt?"

His voice betrayed his displeasure when he answered, "I did, but I also couldn't prevent it. I didn't know exactly when it would happen. As soon as I realized it was time, that he was hurt, I sent Mavros to find him."

Her head whipped around, only for her to see the crow with his head ducked, very intent on cleaning his feathers. "What happened to no more secrets?" she muttered darkly. He continued to ignore her, but she felt him push love through their bond. "Being sweet won't get you off the hook," she warned him.

Apollo grinned. "Don't blame him. At the time, he was probably just concerned about the wolf. And after? Well, you did have a great deal on your plate."

She glared at Mavros for a moment longer before returning her attention to her father. "I did. But I wanted to ask, do you know exactly what happened to him? He had two broken legs. They're fine now, obviously, but if it was some sort of trap or whatever, I want to make sure they're cleared out of the woods. He still plays there, and I'm not going to risk him getting hurt again, even if I can heal him now and have a couple other healers on tap."

"I'm sorry, I don't," he told her with a sad smile. "But I can check for traps when I know you're safe."

"I wouldn't argue," she admitted. "When all this is done, I want us all safe for a very, very long time. I think I've had enough excitement for even a supernatural's lifetime."

"I know you have, and I'm sorry for that."

His face was so full of grief and guilt that she walked over to him, bent to wrap her arms around him, and rested her head on his shoulder. "It's not your fault. The only thing you could have done to prevent all this was not have a daughter, and I'm kind of happy being alive."

He let out a soft, surprised laugh and rested his hand on her arm, patting lightly. "That's always a good thing. But I get the feeling those two distracted you from something?"

She straightened and leaned against the railing. "Eh, I can get back to it in a minute. I was just going to do a few laps around the house. Wanted to clear my head, and I've been a little restless, being cooped up like I have been. Running helps with that." She smiled. "Besides, watching those two is even better than a run. It's just so happy and…I don't know. Carefree? Since none of us are actually carefree right now, it's nice to see."

"That it is. Though I think Lykos is getting tired. He's still young."

Chloe watched for a moment and saw Apollo was right. The wolf was lunging more slowly, less often. His growling was less forceful. Wesley noticed as well, because he carefully flopped onto his side, either giving up or playing dead. Lykos must have believed it was the first, because he sprawled across one of Wesley's legs. It was so adorable, she dug her phone out of her pocket and snapped a few pictures.

As she slipped her phone away, she turned her focus away from the cuteness in front of her and to her dad and less pleasant topics. "Any thoughts on finding Dolos?"

Apollo shook his head. "Not yet. Lexi and Phillip have been working on some spells, off and on, but they haven't found anything yet that will even track me."

"Do you think they can?" While she knew about tracking people digitally, and she could follow someone in the city, she knew nothing about tracking a god.

He didn't answer right away, his brow furrowing lightly as he considered. "I'm not sure. They're both very talented witches, and your brother does have a connection to the divine, but tracking any god would be difficult. Not impossible, and I'm sure other people have devised locating spells in the past, but very difficult. Adding in Dolos's powers?" He drew in a deep breathe, released it on a shrug. "I honestly don't know. I hope so. I think they have a good chance of achieving something, but that's the best I can do."

It was honestly no more than she was expecting, but less than she was hoping.

"I'm going to get back to my run."

"Enjoy."

She'd taken no more than a few strides when she heard a yip. Pausing, she glanced behind her to see Lykos scrambling to his feet. Even Wesley rolled onto his. The pup raced toward her, tail wagging happily while Wesley followed at a more sedate pace. Bending, she rubbed at the wolf's fur, until Wesley nudged her back with his forehead. Straightening, she gave him a curious look. He gave her another, slightly harder, nudge. It only took her a moment to realize what he was trying to convey to her and grinned. Scratching between his ears, she said, "Okay, Yogi."

While she would have been content running by herself, doing it with Wesley on one side of her and Lykos on the other was infinitely more fun, especially when Wesley made a game out of it. He started to lightly bump his body into hers, which caused her to bump into Lykos. Catching onto the game after only a few gentle hits, Lykos started running into her, reversing the game. Caught between them, Chloe could only laugh as she was turned into a living pinball. They didn't stop, which only made her laugh harder. Running became impossible, but she couldn't mind. Life had been so stressful since the fire at the Oak, so to have these few precious moments to simply enjoy life was not only fun, it was necessary.

One particularly enthusiastic bump from Lykos had her stumbling, but Wesley was right there, catching her on his back. Chloe didn't even bother to rise, just lay across him, breathless, ribs aching from the laughter. It wasn't until Lykos pressed against her legs and whined in concern that the laughter began to ease. She sank to the ground, grinning when she ended up with a lap full of wolf and a face wet with kisses.

"I'm okay, I'm okay," she assured him, only to giggle when Wesley joined the new game by sniffing at a ticklish spot on her neck. Between the two of them, it was several minutes before she was able to relax and catch her breath. By that point, Wes had laid down and she collapsed against him, Lykos's head in her lap.

She absently pet the wolf's head as she grinned, feeling better than she had in a week. No, she hadn't run far, not even a single full lap around the house, but this had been so much better. She barely felt the cold ground beneath her butt, not with the heat of both bear and wolf, so stayed where she was, relaxing.

A shadow fell over her face and she glanced up to see Lexi smiling down at her. "That doesn't look like running to me," she teased.

"Yeah, well, these two had other ideas. Turned out to be kind of better, though," she admitted, resting her head against Wesley's back for a moment. "What about you? I thought you and Phillip were going to work on a spell?"

"We were. Hit a block. Could use your help. Well, you and your dad, but he's already agreed."

Part of her just wanted to continue to lay here and ignore the world for a minute but knew that wasn't possible. "What kind of help?"

"The kind where you transfer power from your dad to the two of us?"

Chloe sighed but nodded and started to sit up. Wesley helped by heaving himself to his feet, which caused her to gasp in surprise, even as the movement lifted her onto hers. "Let's go," she told Lexi, running her hand across Wesley's broad back before following the other woman inside.

And spent the next several hours recharging both witches as they spent massive amounts of power trying to figure out how to track a god.

Chapter 26

I f Chloe dreamed that night, she didn't remember it, for which she was grateful. Wesley had to leave in the middle of breakfast to deal with a call, which worried her, but she couldn't tell him not to do his job. She did make him promise to be careful, though. If she thought it would work, she'd have insisted he take Lexi or Phillip with him but knew that wouldn't fly.

Since she still hadn't figured out the dream, she spent an hour practicing with her powers, then another hour sparring with her brother, then with Wesley after he returned. It left her tired and sore, but in a good way. Afterwards, Phillip and Lexi decided to work on the tracking spell again, as the previous night's work hadn't yielded any positive results, and she opted to go take a shower.

She didn't know what it was about showers sparking inspiration, but it did the trick. With her mind empty, the hot water surrounding her, she closed her eyes and just relaxed. Unbidden, the dream returned to her mind, flashing to the various images, the short clips. At first, they came as rapidly as they had in the dream, but then they slowed, until she focused on one particular image. That was when she realized what she'd been missing.

Granny's grimoire.

Several of the images she'd seen had contained the grimoire, including one she was sure had been a memory. The only question was, what part of the grimoire had she been reading at the time? Which one was important enough to have a place in a prophetic dream? If it was, in fact, a prophetic dream and not just jumbled memories.

She hurried through the rest of her shower and got dressed, pulling her damp hair up in a ponytail. It would be crazy later, but that wouldn't matter, not if she could figure out the missing piece of the puzzle. If she could figure out how to stop Dolos from coming after her.

Grabbing the grimoire, she made her way to the living room. It wasn't exactly how she'd seen it in her dream, but it was as close as she could get without going home. The dictionaries had, unfortunately, been left at her house, but there was still a large chunk of the grimoire left that she could read. And if she was right, at least one of the images of the grimoire was a memory, which meant she was looking for a page she'd already read. If she was wrong? She had no doubt either her brother or father could help translate.

Lexi, Phillip, and Apollo were in the kitchen, cooking up a new spell. Mavros was sitting on the back of a chair with them, but she caught him looking at her. She smiled to assure him she was okay, then looked for the remaining two members of her family.

Seeing neither Wesley nor Lykos, she checked the thin strand of power that connected to the wolf's collar and told her where he was. Moving to the front window, she smiled as she saw them in the front yard, with Wesley clearly working on training the pup. No, not a pup anymore, she thought. He was close to full-grown now. And it was good that Wes was working with him. At first, she'd been hesitant about having Lykos work with them, but the idea had grown on her. He was a smart wolf who picked up things quickly. And, while she'd prefer to be partnered with Wesley, she could see the wisdom in her being able to track scents when he wasn't around.

And when full grown, Lykos would be a formidable partner as well. While some people might think they could take on an aether elemental easily, they might think twice about taking on an elemental with a wolf.

Satisfied that everyone was home and safe, she curled up on the couch and ran her fingers over the cover of the grimoire. She both loved and hated reading this book. Love because it was a piece of Granny she still had, a piece that showed her a different side of the grandmother who had raised her. Hate because it was a side Granny had deliberately kept hidden from her. She had to wonder if she could have handled everything on Salus better if she'd known how to use her powers when she first stepped onto the island. Even just understanding the supernatural better might have made a difference.

But then, maybe leaving this book, all this information, hidden in a way only an aether elemental—or a god, she supposed—could find, was Granny's way of trying to make it up to her. She could always ask Lexi to find out. Her cousin had spoken to Granny's ghost at least once since she'd died, but even then she'd been secretive, so it might not help. Unless she'd only been secretive because Chloe hadn't yet known the identify of her father.

Chloe shook her head, opened the book, and focused on the writing before her. Though she did want to know more about Granny's life, there would be time for that later. For now, she focused on the spells and explanations of aether abilities. Though she was tempted to skip the smaller spells, she resisted. She did, however, start with the ones she'd marked the last time she'd been through this book. They all looked useful, but she needed to find the one that would be applicable to the fight she knew was coming. Which meant sorting through centuries of spells.

She flipped past all the silly spells, the ones meant for vanity or fun, and focused on the ones she'd noted as interesting. The problem was they were all interesting, they just weren't all equally useful. Being able to speak to Lykos would be good but wouldn't help with Dolos. Making a ward to prevent the use of magic was definitely useful, but without knowing where Dolos would be, it wasn't something she could use now.

She came across one spell that could potentially be helpful. It was intended to hide the presence of magic, even from all but the strongest aether elemental. Likely such a spell had been used when Granny had hidden Pandora's Box beneath Zeus's temple. Chloe didn't see how the powerful wards could have gone unnoticed for so long without such a spell, even with no other aethers on the island. If they worked up a plan to sneak up on Dolos, she would definitely make sure they used it. Except it looked like a long, complicated process, and she couldn't identify a couple of the ingredients. Great. She shook her head and moved on to the next spell.

It wasn't until her fourth marker that she paused, frowning at the handwritten spell title. To Defend Against Divine Magic. She remembered this one. While it had looked important, it hadn't seemed like something she'd need at the time. But now that she knew a god was after her, protecting herself from godly powers was definitely something she could use. If it worked, anyway, and Granny had added a note saying she hadn't been certain it would. Still, Chloe would be willing to give it a try. It couldn't be any worse than dealing with him without any protection, right?

She'd just started to read through what went into a spell like that when her phone dinged to alert her to a new text. A glance at the window told her it was getting dark, and everyone who normally texted her was here. Curious, she set the book in her lap and picked up her phone. Reece. Had he found Dolos? Her pulse quickened and she opened the message. There was only a single image, and it made that rapid pulse falter.

It was a close up of Reece, bound, obviously unconscious and lying on the ground. Bruises darkened his skin and one eye was swollen shut. Several cuts were visible on his face, including a large one across his lower lip that had covered his chin with blood. She searched the picture for some clue, some idea as to where exactly he was, but the picture had been taken in a way that all she could see was Reece, dirt, and dry leaves. It could be almost anywhere on the island.

Before she could call for the others, another text came in.

'Reece': Now maybe you'll meet me at the oak to save your friend. If you don't, he will die, and it will be long and painful. And make sure you come ALONE and within the hour.

Her breath caught and her eyes closed for a minute. Reece had been searching for Dolos because of her. No matter what Phillip had said to her the other morning, she couldn't be selfish. She couldn't just let Reece die, not when there was a chance to save him. But she also knew, without a doubt, that this was absolutely a trap. She'd also promised her brother she wouldn't play the martyr. It didn't leave many options.

Hoping not to draw the attention of the others, she put a slip of paper between pages, quietly closed the grimoire, and set it on the coffee table. She carefully walked back to the bedroom, slipping on her coat and holster. A gun may or may not be any good against a god, but it was the one weapon she was comfortable with.

When she left the bedroom, she heard Wesley's voice in the kitchen. A soft yip told her Lykos was there as well. Checking, she felt Mavros was now somewhere in the woods, hunting, and she was careful not to let him feel what she was about to do. She just had to hope none of them noticed her departure, especially not Wesley or Apollo.

She never thought she'd have to worry about her dad catching her sneaking out.

Chloe made it out the front door undetected, only to realize her car was still parked in front of her house. It was a problem, but not an unsurmountable one. Unfortunately, she'd never learned how to hot-wire a car, but the Oak wasn't really that far from here. It would take a great deal longer to reach it on foot, but she could still make it in an hour.

Determined not to let Reece down, not to let him die because of her, she started walking, being careful of the windows, just in case someone decided to glance outside.

She made it to the tree line and stopped. This was wrong. She wanted to save Reece, but she couldn't do it like this. Reece wouldn't thank her for it, and her brother would never forgive her. So what the hell did she do?

"Should I ask where you're going, or is this where I'm supposed to ground you?"

Chloe froze at the too-mild voice behind her. She wasn't fooled, though. Her dad was pissed. She hunched her shoulders and slowly turned around. "I don't think grounding works when I'm twenty-seven."

He was leaning a shoulder against a tree, his arms folded over his chest, eyes blazing brilliant purple. "Well, I never got the opportunity when you were a kid, so perhaps I should make up for lost time." He pushed away from the tree, started toward her. "But we'll start with option A. Where are you going?" he asked, the four words measured, and without a hint that he would let this slide.

"She studied his face in the fading light then sighed. "I hadn't actually decided to go anywhere. I made a promise," she admitted as she drew her phone out of her pocket. As soon as she unlocked the screen, the text was visible, and she turned it around to show him.

He took the phone and the calm mask fractured. "He has

the fox," he said, voice vibrating with anger.

"He does," she agreed as she took the phone back. "I can't let him die, Dad. I just can't."

"No, you can't. But you can be smart about it. He says you should come alone, which means it's a trap."

"I know it is," she admitted, "but that doesn't mean I can just avoid it."

"No, it means he needs to *think* you're alone."

She wasn't against that idea but had to ask. "How? We've only got an hour for me to get there."

"To begin with, we go back to the house, get everyone together, and the five of us work up a plan."

Since she wasn't keen on dying in Reece's place, she only nodded and walked back to the cabin with him, hoping they could come up with a damn good one.

Chapter 27

When they went back inside, Lexi was standing in the doorway between the kitchen and living room. "Where'd you go?" she asked, frowning.

Chloe's mouth opened to admit what she'd done, but Apollo spoke first.

"We were talking. She's gotten some unpleasant news."

He was covering for her? That felt...good. Really good, actually. Surprising, but she wasn't going to question it. Besides, she had decided not to go alone before she'd been caught, so it wasn't a complete lie.

"What sort of unpleasant news?" Phillip asked as he came out of the kitchen.

Chloe pulled her phone out and walked over to them, showing them the photo. "Dolos has Reece. He sent me a text from Reece's phone, telling me that if I don't meet him at the Oak in one hour, alone, he's going to kill Reece."

Lexi cursed under her breath. Phillip did too—or she assumed it was cursing, but it wasn't in a language she knew, or even recognized. Maybe it was the unfamiliarity, but it sounded even angrier than English cursing.

"You can't go in there," Lexi said flatly. "You do realize it's a trap, right?"

"Yeah, I know," Chloe confirmed with a nod. "But I also

can't just leave Reece to die. He was only hunting for Dolos because of me. I won't let him die because he was doing me a favor."

Phillip's face was grim. "No, you can't," he agreed. "You're not going in there alone, though," he said before he disappeared into the kitchen again.

"No, she isn't," Apollo agreed. "He says alone, but I have no doubt we can find some way to hide and be her backup. One of us can sneak in and get Reece out, which will leave Dolos with no bargaining chip. Once Reece is safe, we can settle this for good."

"The Oak always has at least a few ghosts around it. I'm sure I can convince them to help us," Lexi said, though her brow was furrowed with uncertainty. "But I'm not sure how we're going to fight a guy who can make us think we're seeing stuff that isn't there."

"I wish I could say that I wouldn't be fooled by his illusions, but unfortunately, god powers do sometimes work on other gods," Apollo said.

"Like Hypnos being able to put Zeus to sleep," Chloe murmured as her gaze slid to the grimoire, still resting on the coffee table.

"Exactly," he agreed, nodding. "And as much as I'd love to go in your place, as it would keep you safe, I have a feeling that would result in Dolos killing your friend immediately." There was a strain on his face she wasn't used to seeing, and a grief in his beautiful teal eyes.

"Dad? What is it?" she asked, and saw Lexi step into the kitchen, giving them some privacy.

"I'm just so sorry that all of this is happening because you're my daughter," he murmured. "Not that I would trade being able to know you for anything, but I am sorry I'm the cause of so much trouble for you."

She shook her head and found herself stepping forward to hug him. "It's not your fault. You can't blame yourself for other people's crazy. Besides, the five of us have to be able to beat one crazy god. Especially since your dad said he would lock Dolos up and throw away the key." She leaned back enough to see his face. "And as far as dads go? I think I lucked out okay there. Some dads flat out don't care about their kids. Some are even worse than that. It may have taken twenty-seven years, but I've got a dad who genuinely cares for me and wants what's best for me. If I had a different dad, I might not have that."

Apollo smiled, his eyes now shimmering slightly as he rested his hand on her cheek. "I definitely care. I love you, Chloe. You and your brother, both."

"I know. And we're going to get past Dolos's illusions and..." She trailed off as that tickle returned, stronger this time.

"Chloe?" he asked, when she didn't continue. "What's wrong?"

Slowly, she shook her head. "Nothing. In fact, I think something is very right." Quickly, she rounded the couch and snatched up the grimoire, flipping frantically through the pages to the last one she'd read. "Remember that dream that you guys thought could be prophetic? I have to agree. It had me looking in here earlier, right up until I got Dolos's text. At first, even when we were talking, I thought it was just one spell, but it might be two. So I think Lexi might need to pass a message on to Granny."

"What about Lexi?" the brunette in question asked, poking her head in.

"You might be delivering a message to Lydia, it seems," Apollo answered, head cocked as he watched Chloe.

"Always happy to help, but why?" she asked as Phillip rejoined them.

Chloe's lips curved into a huge grin. "Because she's got two spells in here that might help. One hides magic, which..." She shrugged, wiggled a hand in the air. "May not be as useful, and it looked like it would take a long time to cast. But she's got one to protect against god powers. Like, say, being able to possibly see through illusions."

"Seriously?" Lexi asked, jaw dropping in surprise.

"Seriously," Chloe confirmed.

"Damn, Lydia," Lexi breathed, her lips curving into a smile. "I know you're pissed about her keeping secrets, but she was good."

"She was," Chloe agreed. She held the book out to her dad, tapping her index finger on the page in question. "What do you think? You're most familiar with god powers. Will this work?"

Apollo took the book, read over it, his expression unchanging. His gaze lifted, met Chloe's. "Your grandmother...was brilliant," he said, slowly smiling. "I think it will. But it will take some time to cast, so I'm not sure you can cast it more than once before you need to leave, which means only one person can be protected."

"As much as hate it, I think you should cast it on yourself," Phillip said grimly. "You're the one who's going to be closest to him, and you're also the only one of us who can potentially break those illusions, which would protect the rest of us."

"He's right," Lexi agreed, looking equally unhappy. "But I'll help you cast it."

Her dad handed her back the book and looked to Phillip. "Where is Wesley?"

"He's working off being pissed and making a few phone calls," Phillip answered.

Apollo nodded. "I'm going to go get into touch with my father, but I'll be back before you're ready to go," he promised, before disappearing in his usual brilliant flash.

"What sort of phone calls?" Chloe asked.

Phillip shrugged. "Not sure, but I wasn't about to tell him not to. Back up, maybe? Information?"

Since they were going to be spending some time on the spell, he had time to make those calls. For all she knew, they could be the tipping point between life and death tonight. Anything they could do to stack the deck in their favor, she'd do.

Lexi helped Chloe gather the ingredients needed for the spell. Though a few came from the supplies Lexi had retrieved a couple of days before, Chloe was surprised at how many were relatively common household items that even Wesley had. Only one ingredient gave them pause. They needed something made of citrine and silver, which would rest against the skin.

"What the hell is citrine?" Chloe muttered, unable to remember even hearing the word before.

"Clear yellow stone, sort of like yellow quartz," Lexi answered absently, frowning as she dug through the supplies she'd brought. "I don't think I have any with me. I've got some silver settings, but no citrine."

"I think I might. Be right back." Chloe hurried to Wesley's bedroom and dug through her bag for the necklace she'd tossed in there on a whim. It was well established that she had prophetic abilities, minor ones, from her dad, but had it been possible her grandmother had, too? Or had someone else given it to Granny, knowing Chloe would find it?

Finding the necklace, she lifted it by its chain and studied it. She was no gemstone expert, but that was definitely a clear yellow stone. Hopefully Lexi would be able to identify it.

Her cousin was still hunting, so Chloe let the pendant dangle a few inches in front of Lexi's eyes. "Is this citrine?"

Lexi blinked and leaned her head back so her eyes could focus on the stone. "Yes, it is. Where did that come from?" she asked as she took it.

"I have no idea," Chloe admitted. "Found it in a hidden compartment in one of the trunks at Granny's. Had a note that said it was for protection, but it wasn't signed and I didn't recognize the handwriting. It also doesn't have any magic on it, so I couldn't figure out how it would protect anyone." She paused a beat then added, "It was one of the things I saw in my dream, too."

"Huh. Show me the note later? But for now, this should work." She set it with the other ingredients. "Ready to do your first non-aether magic?"

Chloe had to grin. "Technically, I've already done that. Healing and turning into a nightlight, remember?"

"Smart ass," Lexi deadpanned.

"That I am. And yes, I'm ready."

"Good. Then let's go outside and get comfortable," she said, gathering up the supplies while Chloe grabbed the grimoire.

Pausing at the door, Chloe thought about the chill in the air, especially now that the sun had set. "Why can't we do it in here?"

"A couple of reasons. More room, for one, and there's also less...residue outside, which means less chance of interference," Lexi explained. "People who cast a lot of spells generally designate one room in their house where they ensure it's kept clean of...stray magic and impressions. Things that can potentially alter a spell, just enough to make it dangerous. Think of it like a clean room, except we're not worried about dust or bacteria."

Since that made sense, sort of, Chloe only grimaced and followed Lexi outside. Wesley was still on the phone, though when he saw them he said something into the phone and hung up. "Everything okay?"

Seeing as how his eyes were yellow, she took a moment to go to him, sliding her arms around his waist, her cheek resting against his shoulder. "It's fine. There's a spell in Granny's grimoire that should protect me from the powers of a god. We're casting it before we go."

His arms tightened and he rested his cheek against the top of her head. "Good. I don't like you going in." Before she could argue, he went on. "I know you have to, I do, which is why I'm happy you've found a spell that could protect you."

"Me, too."

His lips settled on hers gently, lingered for a few seconds. "Get your spell cast. I'll find your brother and start planning."

"Okay." She watched him for a moment as he went inside, then walked to where Lexi was already sitting and sank down to the cold grass.

Phillip must have grabbed Lykos, because she didn't see either of them, though Mavros landed on her knee the moment she was sitting on the ground. "Let me guess. Familiars can help with spell casting?" she asked as she tickled the feathers at his neck.

He let out a coarse sound that she'd realized months ago was his version of a laugh.

Lexi grinned. "Some can, but it depends on the familiar and the spell, though all familiars can help keep you focused. But him being here won't hurt anything."

"Okay, good. So…let's see this spell. Is it just like a cooking recipe?"

"Pretty much. Except if you screw up with this, you won't just end up with food that tastes horrible or doesn't come together right."

"What does happen if I screw up?"

She smiled tightly. "It can vary, but the least objectionable thing I've heard of happening? A drain of magic and a hell of a headache."

"And the worst?"

"Let's just not screw it up," Lexi advised, even the strained smile dropping away.

The dire tone had Chloe agreeing. She blew out a breath

and picked up the grimoire, happy Lexi had thought to turn the outside lights on so she could see the words. A sense of deja vu distracted her for a moment, and she realized this had been another image from her dream. Hoping that was a good sign, she skimmed over the spell. It didn't look too complicated. Mix a little of this, drizzle a little of that. Chant some Greek, smear the paste onto the necklace, then push a steady stream of power into the necklace while chanting…indefinitely…until the power 'broke over the jewel like a wave over the beach'. Very poetic, Granny, she thought. Poetic, but not super helpful.

Lexi's warning had her nervous, but she thought about Reece, currently at the mercy of a deranged deity and pushed past the nerves. She could do this. She *had* to do this.

She began mixing the ingredients together, under the watchful eye of Lexi, who offered suggestions here and there. The resulting gunk was an unpleasant shade of yellow-brown and smelled oddly like fish, though nothing fishy had been used. She chanted the lines of Greek, still shocked that she could speak the language. Then came the gross part.

Her nose wrinkled as she dipped a finger into the paste and wiped it carefully over the pendant, ensuring that no bare spots were left. Now came the potentially endless chanting. She hoped her throat would hold out, as would her power.

It was easy at first to direct the power into the crystal, barely more than a trickle, as she started to repeat the chant. After a minute, then five, it felt like she wasn't getting anywhere, so she used a little more power. More minutes passed, but she wasn't sure how many, as they were beginning to blur together. But then she felt something, magic within the pendant starting to build, and rapidly now. It wasn't just her magic being held within the stone, as it had altered, become something else, something more.

Sweat beaded on her forehead as she fought to keep the

flow steady, her words even. The rest of the world faded, until it was only her, the necklace, and that growing power. Then she truly understood Granny's words. The power built, surrounding the pendant, until it felt like it would slip out of her control. Desperate not to let this fail, she clung to it, built upon it, before it finally collapsed inward, filling the small crystal until it felt so full of magic it might burst.

The instant after the magic ended, she slumped forward, her hands on the cold ground to keep her face from smacking into it. She heard a low hum of sound, and after a moment, she realized someone was talking to her.

Warm hands cupped her cheeks, tipped her face upward, and she looked into eyes identical to her own. His mouth was moving, but she could only blink at him. Apollo paused, smiled, and it felt as though sunlight was washing over her, warm and soothing. The sounds around her sharpened, until she could make out Lexi's voice, as well as Wesley's. Sensation came back to her, and she could feel Mavros pressed against her leg.

"Is that better?" her dad asked.

"Yeah, much better." Slowly, she straightened, surprised none of her muscles were stiff, but then, her dad had healed her. "Is it always like that, casting a spell?"

"Not usually," he admitted, shaking his head. "That wasn't a small spell, though. It's meant to block the power of gods. If you didn't feel like you'd just run a marathon, I would have thought you'd done something wrong." A proud smile curved his lips. "But I felt the power you raised. You definitely didn't do anything wrong."

"But did it work?" she insisted, hoping they had that, at least, to defend against Dolos.

"We can certainly find out." He glanced to the necklace, which had fallen to the ground when she fell forward. To her surprise, none of the gunk remained. It looked as pristine as if it had just been polished. "Put the necklace on, and we'll see if I can affect you."

With fingers that were like ice, she slipped the chain over her neck and settled the chilled metal against her skin. With it in place, she looked up at him and nodded. She wasn't sure what he was going to do, so was surprised when he began to glow. It wasn't like when she did it, a gentle yet noticeable illumination. He was the god of the sun and became a small freaking star himself, lighting up the back yard. But she could see him, at the center of it.

A few seconds later the glow dimmed and he cocked a brow. "What did you see?"

"Light, with you at the center."

Apollo looked pleased, but Phillip spoke up, from where he was standing with Lexi and Wesley. "She has some of your sun powers, though. Are you sure that's not the reason she could see you?"

"No," Apollo admitted, "I'm not. But I am hopeful." He offered his hands to her, and when she took them, he pulled her to her feet.

"What if we tested it on me or Wesley?" Lexi suggested. "Neither of us have any kind of sun powers."

"Me," Wesley insisted. "As a shapeshifter, I don't have any defenses against magic, so it would be the most accurate test."

Apollo nodded and glanced to Chloe. She slipped the necklace off and handed it to Wesley, his fingers brushing hers. He held it clasped in his hand and kept his gaze on hers for a moment before he said, "I'm ready."

Once again, Apollo glowed. Even before Wesley spoke, Chloe knew the spell had worked. Yes, she still saw her father at the center of the light, but she had to squint, and even then he wasn't as clear as he had been with the pendant against her skin.

"It works," Wesley confirmed as he handed the necklace back. "The first time, I couldn't see you. I did this time."

MEG M. ROBINSON

"Good." Apollo waited until the necklace was back around her neck before asking, "Are you ready to go rescue your friend?"

She looked to the other three, their serious faces, the worry on them, and nodded. "I am." She didn't see the wolf, asked, "Where's Lykos?"

"Inside," Wesley answered.

"Good. He should stay here. I don't want him hurt." She wanted to ask if Wesley would keep him, take care of him, if something happened to her, but thought it would be tempting fate to even voice a concern like that. It would also piss the bear off, making it sound like she was expecting defeat.

Mavros leapt from the ground, flapped his wings, and settled on her shoulder. "I go," he told her firmly, before giving her ear a small bite for emphasis.

"I had a feeling," she told him dryly, but she smiled. He was as loyal and protective of her as she was of him, and she hoped he understood how much she appreciated it.

When the thought was followed by the crow pressing his head against her cheek, she knew he'd felt the emotion and agreed.

"While you were...busy...we fine-tuned the plan a little. No big changes, just clarifications," Wesley told her as he strode toward her and Apollo.

"Hey, I'm all for fine-tuning. It's not like I'm exactly experienced with going up against a god," Chloe pointed out.

"If he is responsible for the big messes since November, you kind of are," Lexi pointed out.

Chloe couldn't argue, so just asked, "What's the plan?"

"You'll take Lexi's car. I think it's plausible that you might have borrowed it and snuck off. The rest of us are going in Phillip's SUV, though we'll ditch it well away from the Oak and go on foot. You'll approach the way most people do, from that little parking area. We'll spread out but stay back as far as possible while still being able to see and hear you. Lexi's going to send her ghosts in, to watch and to interfere if there's a good opportunity for that. You? Distract Dolos. Get his attention away from Reece and whichever of us is closest will get him out as soon as we can. Once he's out of the area, the rest of us will move in." He held up his cuffs. "Everyone, with the exception of your dad, will have a pair of these. They may not work as effectively on him as they do on us, but they should help dampen his powers. If we can get them on him, we will. If we can knock his ass out, even better."

"Once he's subdued, I'll call my father to imprison him," Apollo continued.

"And how do we get him in the cuffs?" Chloe asked, doubting it would be as simple as beating the crap out of the guy until they could get the bracelets on his wrists. For all she knew, mortals couldn't hurt gods that way, not without help or special weapons.

For some reason, everyone looked at her dad, but he was quiet for a full minute, studying her face. "I never spent much time around Dolos, but even if he's a fantastic fighter, his greatest talent is most likely going to be in his illusions. Avoiding the fight, the attacks. We—I'm hoping that you can potentially counter his illusions, since your powers aren't blocked like they were in...like they were before."

Chloe was sure she paled, but it made sense. It was probably the best shot they had at ending this tonight. Closing her eyes, she took several deep breaths before she nodded. "I'll do my best."

"That's all anyone can ask," he said, giving her arm a gentle squeeze.

Wesley carefully pulled her away from her dad and wrapped her in a tight hug. "Just be careful, because if you get yourself killed, I'm going to be pissed," he whispered against her temple.

For some reason, that eased a little of her panic. "I'll do my best."

The presence of her father and brother didn't stop him from kissing her breathless, and she got it. Despite their preparations, it was entirely possible this might end badly. If it did, she wanted that last kiss, too. When he finally drew back, he rested his brow against hers. "Then let's go save Reece and finish this."

Chapter 28

A familiar feeling of loneliness slid over Chloe when Phillip's SUV pulled over to the side of the road and its lights went out. It was temporary, she knew that. They weren't going to abandon her to her fate, to Dolos's wrath. But it was hard, going to face off against a god with only a crow and a nine millimeter at her side, even if both had saved her life before.

It didn't help that the sky was cloudy, often blocking what little light the moon might have otherwise provided. Normally she wasn't jumpy, didn't mind the darkness, but tonight she *knew* bad things were going to happen, and some of them were likely going to happen to her.

Mavros had sensed her unease and spent the entire drive pressed against her belly, making the soft sounds she knew were meant to be soothing. Oddly enough, over the months they'd been together, the awkward noises had actually began to comfort her.

Her life had certainly changed since coming to Salus.

She pulled into the parking area near the Oak, unsure what it meant when her headlights didn't land on anything but trees. "Okay, Mavros. Time to face a crazy god with a grudge against my dad," she muttered, turning the car off. He let out a soft caw and walked up to her shoulder, determined to stick close. She appreciated it, even though she was also worried he'd get hurt. Birds, even crows, were so much more fragile than people, and he'd already been injured protecting her once.

Her right hand dropped to the butt of her pistol, though she had a feeling it wasn't going to win tonight's fight for her. She wasn't even sure it was going to leave the holster. Her left hand lightly touched the necklace hidden by her shirt and coat, ensuring it was still touching her skin. Hopefully Granny's spell worked as intended. She did wish they'd been able to test it more thoroughly, but had to trust in Granny's ability and the fact that it had protected Wesley from Apollo.

Slowly, she walked toward the Oak, keeping alert, not just with her eyes and ears, but her powers. If someone so much as thought about using magic, she'd notice. Except, when she started paying attention, she realized someone already was. Great. On the plus side, maybe she'd figure out immediately how well the necklace worked.

It wasn't until she reached the actual clearing, with nothing between her and the Oak but darkness, that she saw the figures. An image from the dream flashed in her mind even as a chill spread across her skin, one that had nothing to do with the winter air.

Dolos was there, of course, wearing his Erick disguise, and she saw Reece on the ground nearby, still bound, gagged, and unconscious, but they weren't the ones that made her stop and frown.

Diego and Peyton were standing beside Dolos, and neither looked like they were under any kind of duress. Actually, when the clouds parted for a moment, Chloe could see the smug look on Peyton's face. Worse than that was the smirk on Diego's lips.

Her skin began to glow faintly as her emotions sharpened, as anger toward her ex and fear for Reece built.

"I was starting to think you weren't coming," Dolos

drawled, folding his arms over his chest.

"You know I couldn't let you kill Reece, not when you don't give a damn about him," she retorted.

"True," he agreed easily. "But if you cooperate, I'll take you to him, and you can be the hero. Again."

Take her to Reece? It wasn't dark enough to hide his still form, and he wasn't far enough from the trio for Dolos to think Chloe hadn't seen the fox.

Was the spell on the necklace working? Was the magic she felt an illusion cloaking Reece from view?

She suppressed a thrill at that realization and fought the urge to shift her gaze to her friend. Tipping her hand too soon could cause Dolos to flat out kill Reece. But just because she could see through the illusion didn't mean the others could. And she wasn't sure how to signal them to let them know where he was.

"And how do I know he's even alive?" she asked, trying to stall him while she figured out a plan.

Dolos shrugged carelessly. "You don't. But do you really have a choice? If he is alive, and you refuse to cooperate because you didn't get what you wanted, he'll still die, except he'll know you *chose* not to save him."

Her fingers flexed, brushed against her pistol. "And what exactly is it you want me to do?"

Thinking he'd already won, his lips curved into a smirk. "Nothing too strenuous. All you have to do is surrender yourself to me."

Chloe arched a brow. "And if I go with you, how exactly can I get Reece home?"

He lifted a hand, wiggled a finger at her. "Now, now, I never said you could take him home. I said I'd take you to him. You can release him from his bonds and he can find his own way home."

Debating what to do, she studied him and the pair that flanked him, silently gloating. She needed to stall, to give the others time to get into place. Except they hadn't counted on Dolos having backup, which, in hindsight was stupid. Crazy attracted crazy and while she hadn't noticed that trait in Diego, she wasn't surprised Peyton was on board with the insanity. No, Chloe had to stall. They'd come up with something, one way or the other.

"Before I agree to go with you, I just want to know something first." Didn't villains always monologue? Maybe he would be the reason that stereotype existed.

"And what's that?" he asked, sounding bored.

"Are you responsible for all the crap that's happened on Salus? The deaths, the sleep spell, the amnesia?"

Diego finally reacted, clapping in a way she could only describe as sarcastic. "Took you long enough."

"She's guessing," Peyton argued, shaking her head.

Dolos looked rather proud of himself. "Of course I am. But I suppose you want details?"

Chloe shrugged and nodded. "Would be nice. I'd also like to know what those two are doing here. Did you not think you could handle me on your own?"

He didn't take the bait as she'd hoped. "You were right, my dear," he told Peyton without taking his gaze from Chloe, "it doesn't seem like she's figured it out."

"So why don't you educate me?" Chloe goaded.

Peyton started to speak, but Dolos shot her a look before he smiled at Chloe, but the expression chilled her more than the winter air. "To begin with, Peyton is my daughter. Where else would she be but at her father's side?"

That explained Peyton's bitchy attitude. It was written in her DNA. "And Diego? Please tell me he's not your son. That would be more than a little gross."

Diego laughed and shook his head, but didn't speak until Dolos inclined his head. "Not his son," he confirmed, "but soon to be his son-in-law."

"And a god," Peyton said grandly, draping herself over

Diego's side. Though they were both clothed, and she didn't obviously grope him, she still somehow made the pose look lewd.

Well, that explained exactly how Diego had turned out to be such a complete dick. He was hooked up with the princess of all dicks. She didn't get the god comment but wasn't going to admit her ignorance. "So...you were okay with your future son-in-law cheating on your daughter?"

"I might have been a little upset...if he had actually been cheating," Dolos answered with a shrug.

"It was distasteful, certainly, but not cheating," Diego confirmed with a nod, his hand sliding down Peyton's back, no doubt grabbing her ass judging by the position it landed in. "It was just all part of the plan. It let me watch you, closely, and get inside your head."

"You see, I love my dad. I would have helped him regardless, but how could anyone turn down a chance for ambrosia?" There was a pause, then Peyton laughed. "I'll bet you don't have the slightest clue what ambrosia is, do you?"

"It's the food of the gods."

"And the food that *creates* gods."

Incredulous, Chloe looked at Dolos. That was such a bad idea. She was of the school of thought that power only heightened whatever was already inside a person, good or bad. She'd hate to see Peyton's vindictiveness and Diego's deviousness increased. They'd be insane dictators with divine power. Not a pleasant thought. Which meant they definitely had to stop Dolos, here and now, before those two could grow more powerful.

Reaching out with her powers, she felt for magic, beyond Dolos's illusions, beyond Peyton and Diego's latent magic. When she felt four nearby signatures—including one that felt like fur—she was relieved. It also meant it was time to end this. Now.

"You're seriously going to make this bitch and complete

asshole gods? And you think Zeus and the others are just going to be okay with it?" She snorted and pushed as much disbelief as she could into her next words. "There's no way anyone would be okay with those two fuckwads becoming gods. Hell, from what I hear, the other gods aren't exactly thrilled that you're a god."

His eyes narrowed and she began to act, mentally grabbing at the magic hiding Reece from view. When this all blew up, the others would need to be able to see the fox.

Dolos's voice was low and tense with an anger that was building toward rage. "What the hell do you know about the gods? Until a few months ago, you didn't even know they existed. According to Diego, you still don't know much of anything."

"She's shockingly ignorant," her ex confirmed. "I honestly don't know how she managed to stop Hiro from getting the Box."

"Oh yeah, so ignorant that I figured out your daddy-in-law was behind four deaths, the plot to get the Box, and the amnesia cases," Chloe sneered, fighting to break through the illusion as quick as she could. She was almost there. If she could just keep them talking for another minute, she'd have it. "Though I can't imagine what good you thought depriving the world of hope would do."

"Why should Apollo have hope when I don't? I lost it all when my daughter died!" Dolos roared before he flung a hand at her. She braced, but nothing happened. Almost laughing with relief, she realized she was protected from his illusory pain as well as the false images. Except her lack of screaming infuriated him more. "I want her dead!" he snapped.

Just as the illusion hiding Reece shattered, Peyton stretched her hand out and vines shot out of the earth, winding their way up and around Chloe's legs. They were half as thick as her forearm and threw her off-balance enough to pitch her forward. Her hands barely managed to shoot out in time to catch herself before she ate dirt, rocks scraping deeply across her palms. It was enough to dislodge Mavros, who let out a shriek of rage and flew toward the witch, talons extended. Chloe didn't even have time to worry that he'd be hurt like he had with Kyra.

As quickly as she could, she shoved herself up and started sucking up Peyton's magic, but only had a second to work before Diego attacked. He didn't go for magic, not when he knew how good she was at absorbing it, but instead crossed the distance between them in the blink of an eye. She didn't see the knife until it was inches from her. Though she hadn't trained with weapons when practicing with Wesley, her arm swept out to knock the blade away from her. It still slid across her side, though that was better than letting it sink into her belly like her ex had intended. Even knowing he was a bastard didn't stop the shock of betrayal she felt. Cheating on her was a far cry from having him try to kill her.

How had she missed so much about Diego? This was a man she'd allowed into her bed, into her life, and she hadn't seen any of this.

The moment she registered the sharp sting of metal against flesh she also heard an enraged roar. It should have been terrifying, but instead was the sweetest sound she'd ever heard.

Wesley, in his grizzly form, charged into the clearing, running faster than she'd realized a bear could move. His target wasn't Dolos, who was arguably the more dangerous target, but Diego.

Nor was he alone. Mavros was diving at Peyton, over and over, and the redhead bore several deep gashes that proved the crow had connected more than once. A glow came out of the darkness, preceding her father, who grew brighter as his eyes fixed on Dolos.

She saw Phillip darting out of the trees, not moving quite

as fast as Wesley, but he'd spotted Reece and was going for the unconscious fox.

Chloe didn't see Lexi, but felt the eerie brush of magic over the back of her neck, telling her that her cousin was likely summoning every ghost she could reach.

Dolos was pure fury as his plan began to unravel, and he let out a scream of both anguish and rage. It sounded even less human than Wesley's roar had. Before she could do anything, he lifted his arms above his head, swept them downward. She saw a dozen ephemeral copies of himself appear. More illusions, and to her they seemed like faint ghosts, but she knew that the others wouldn't be able to tell which was real and which was false.

Ignoring the vines still holding her in place, she drew her pistol and fired at the god. She only got one shot off before Mavros and Peyton stumbled into her line of fire, but she was almost positive that bullet had connected. Whether or not it would slow down a god was the bigger question.

After that, it was sheer chaos. Wesley was attacking Diego viciously, but though Diego was several times smaller than the sheriff, he was a very talented witch and lasted longer than most would when faced with a pissed off bear. Peyton was contending with Mavros and what must be Lexi's ghosts. Phillip was nowhere to be seen, probably still getting Reece out of the line of fire. Apollo, however, had manifested a bow from somewhere. It seemed as though he wasn't able to distinguish one copy of Dolos from the other, but was firing arrows rapidly into them, hitting each one dead in the chest. While it would have been nice if the arrows caused the illusory men to dissipate, they remained, unharmed by the golden arrows.

Chloe couldn't say they were winning, but neither were they losing. She also knew she'd be more effective if she could move and, on a burst of anger, shredded Peyton's spell. As the vines disintegrated, she darted forward, heading for the real Dolos. Before she could reach him, he let out a yell then disappeared. She skidded to a stop and turned in a circle, wondering if this was another trick or if he had run away.

Somehow, she doubted he'd retreated. Not with his goal so close. Then she felt a sensation that made her blood run cold.

Several gods had just teleported in, and she doubted they were on her side.

There was Dolos, standing a good twenty feet away from both her and her father, and flanking him were three other men. She didn't recognize them, but that only meant they weren't Zeus or Hypnos.

"You do not want to fight against me," Apollo called, his voice carrying easily through the clearing, though it didn't boom like his father's did. "Leave now and I'll forget you stood against me."

"Can't do that," the man to Dolos's right responded, shaking his head. "Our brother needs us."

Apollo didn't bother trying to convince him, just nodded once. "So be it."

If Chloe had thought things were crazy before, it was nothing compared to now. She'd never been in a fight like this—a battle, really—and felt panic begin to build, threatening to make her useless. There was too much going on. Even just the five gods all using their powers were almost too much. There was so much magic surrounding her it was hard to separate them, hard for her to distinguish magic from her other senses.

Then something rested on her shoulder. A quick glance told her nothing was there, but she recognized this feeling. A ghost was touching her. A ghost that felt like someone she knew. It felt like...Granny.

A sob caught in her throat, but that single touch helped calm her, bolster her, and she lifted her pistol again. Dolos had disappeared again, but his brothers were still visible and she fired at one of them. Another had an arrow protruding from his shoulder, but she continued to fire. She wasn't going to lose her family. She wasn't going to live her life in fear of a god with a grudge.

Things weren't going well for her side, though. Wesley had singed fur and it looked like Diego was getting in more hits than the grizzly was. Phillip had returned and dove right into the fray, but even he looked bloody and battered. Worse, the one god on their side looked like he was beginning to struggle under the combined attacks.

An arm slipped around her waist, another over her mouth. It took her only an instant to realize it was Dolos. Once again, he was dragging her away, but this time her power was firmly under her control, and she didn't hesitate to use it. She wasn't careful, she didn't go slow. No, she latched onto the power inside him and yanked, as hard and fast as she could. If expending power made her feel sluggish and weak, maybe it would affect gods the same way. The only downside was that she wasn't sure she could take enough to bring him to that point without the magic exploding out of her, but she was damn sure going to try.

It took a moment before Dolos seemed to realize what she was doing, but his reaction wasn't one of distress or pain like she had hoped. Instead, it was to pause and ram his knee sharply into her side, just below her ribs. She gasped in pain behind his hand but didn't allow the flow of magic stop. She couldn't, not if she wanted to live.

To her shock, she realized it didn't feel as though power was going to rupture her skin and blast outward. She had taken enough that she should be on the verge of losing control, but she wasn't. Her skin was glowing, brightly, and maybe that was helping to burn off the power as she pulled it into her, or maybe it was the necklace protecting her, but she didn't have time to sit and figure it out.

Dolos kept pulling her away from the others. A few trees now stood between her and her friends, but she realized his pace was slowing. The arm around her waist wasn't holding quite as firmly as before.

Her plan was working.

She hesitated, just for a moment, but was unsure how quickly he'd recover, so she continued to siphon as much as she could from him. She was going to survive this night. She was going to make sure every person in that clearing fighting with her—for her—was going to survive this night.

His knees buckled and he fell, dragging her with him and trapping her body beneath his. Tilting his head back, he screamed, "Mitéra!"

Chloe blinked and her power faltered for a moment in surprise. He was calling for his mom?

That was as far as her thoughts got before all light in the area faded. Her skin went dark, the moon and stars seemed to disappear completely. Even the gleam of her father was fully extinguished. It was impossible to see even a foot in front of her face.

The sounds of the battle gradually disappeared, until there was nothing to see, nothing to hear. It was a bizarre and eerie sensation, but one that felt uncomfortably familiar. Uncertain as to what was happening, Chloe froze, even ceasing the tug on Dolos, in case she needed to act quickly against a new threat. Fortunately, it only lasted for a few seconds, but when the light returned, it seemed diminished. Nothing was quite as bright as it had been before, not even Apollo.

Dolos remained behind her, was still holding onto her, though he was definitely weaker.

Then Chloe realized a woman was standing about ten feet from her. Though she was slender and fairly short, no one could mistake her for fragile. She radiated strength the same way Zeus had radiated power. Her hair was ink black, perfectly straight, and hung past her hips. As dark as her hair was, her skin was equally light, almost skeletal. But it was her clothing that struck Chloe as truly odd. It looked as though the woman was literally clad in a dress made of darkness. It shifted slightly as she stood there, while still seeming to cling to her body.

"I cannot allow you to kill my son, daughter of Apollo." The woman's voice was as unique as her appearance, almost layered and echoing over itself.

"I wasn't killing him," Chloe protested, though she hadn't considered what completely draining a supernatural—or a god—would do to the individual.

"You were," the woman corrected.

Okay, no draining anyone completely, Chloe thought. Killing with a gun had been bad enough. Killing through magic felt as though it would be more…intimate.

Apollo began to approach Nyx, but respect bordering on fear was obvious in his posture. He approached her like she was a dangerous animal, and Chloe remembered what he'd said about Dolos's mother. Nyx, the goddess of darkness. The only other deity that truly scared the king of the gods.

"Nyx, I don't want Dolos dead any more than you do, but I can't let him kill my daughter, either," he called, easing toward them, his steps carrying him along a path that would take him between Chloe and Nyx.

The goddess's eyes, which Chloe realized were solid black, from the iris to the whites, tracked her father. Or she thought they did, but it was hard to tell for certain. "I am sorry, Apollo, but I love my son too much to see him die, even if it is his own doing." She slowly shook her head. "No, the only way for my son to reclaim his…life…is for your daughter to die."

Before Apollo could speak again, darkness began to surround Chloe. It wasn't simply an absence of light. This darkness was an absence of everything. When it covered her mouth, she found it difficult to breathe. When it covered her torso, she could no longer feel Dolos's arm. There was no sensation, just a complete void anywhere the darkness touched her.

No, she wasn't going to die. She wasn't going to allow herself to be sacrificed so a crazy, murderous god could live. She wasn't going to make her brother mourn. She wasn't going to allow her dad to lose the war he'd been fighting for almost three decades.

She wouldn't allow Wesley to lose her.

She. Would. Survive.

Gasping, Chloe lashed out with her power again, but this time her target wasn't the god who had become her enemy. It was Nyx, the most feared goddess in the Greek pantheon. Such an act may well be suicide, was most likely futile, but she had nothing to lose and wasn't giving up.

She wasn't alone, even in that.

Through the shadows trying to smother her, she saw flashes of light, and realized her dad was blasting sunlight at Nyx. It was probably the most effective weapon anyone could wield against a goddess of the dark, but she didn't know if it would be enough.

The battle had begun anew, as well, judging by the sounds she heard, when the darkness briefly left her ears uncovered.

Desperate, running out of air, Chloe dragged as much power from Nyx as she could, but knew she was running out of time. As her body struggled to get enough oxygen, she slumped forward, feeling the cold ground against her cheek, but she didn't stop. She wouldn't stop. Even if the magic exploded out of her, she wasn't going to stop until everyone was safe.

But could she drain enough from such a powerful deity? Enough to make her stop? Or would this be like trying to empty the ocean with a water glass?

A crack of thunder echoed around them and immediately

the shadows withdrew. Chloe sucked in a breath, then another, feeding her starved lungs. Cracking an eye open, she saw Zeus standing beside his son. He was as tall as Apollo, with blue eyes rather than teal, but they had the same blonde hair, though his was longer, almost reaching his shoulders. Where Apollo's jaw was smooth, Zeus's was covered by a beard. And though his stance was proud and powerful, she saw the wariness in the eyes that were so similar to her father's.

He and Nyx stared at each other for a long moment before he waved his arm. The weight behind Chloe disappeared, and she twisted to see Dolos was gone.

Nyx shrieked and took a step toward the king of the gods. "What did you do?" she snarled, as her 'dress' of shadows began to expand. Ghostly limbs began to stretch out, each one reaching for a different person.

"Relax, Nyx. Your son isn't dead," Zeus assured her, which had Chloe pushing herself upright. She wasn't quite up to getting on her feet, but she refused to be fully prone when all hell broke loose. Again.

Those limbs paused but didn't retreat. They were still entirely too close to her friends and family. "Then where is he?" Nyx demanded.

"I've banished him, to Tartarus. He can't leave, but as you are there, I thought that was a fair compromise."

"Why would you do that? We both know you have no love for either me or my son," Nyx asked suspiciously.

"I don't," he admitted flatly, "but I do have love for *my* son, and he loves his daughter." He shook his head. "I'm sorry Dolos lost Cressida, but he cannot continue to blame Apollo for something that wasn't his fault, nor in his power to prevent. And Chloe? She had no part in any of it, yet he targeted her, rather than her father."

Nyx shrugged that off. "The millennia take their toll on a mind, and the worst thing that can happen to a parent is losing their child. While I do not agree with what my son did, I can understand his motivations."

Dismissing Zeus, she turned to Chloe. She said nothing, just stared at her. It might just be Chloe's imagination, but it almost looked as though Nyx looked at her with some sort of respect. For daring to take on such a powerful goddess? For not just rolling over and dying?

Before Chloe could figure it out, Nyx looked to the other gods, the ones who had arrived to help Dolos. "And you all should have known better. Why did none of you think to let me know what he was doing?" she snapped, before the tendrils of darkness shot out toward them. Each of Dolos's brothers were wrapped in the shadows, until they disappeared from sight. When the shadows retreated, the gods—including Nyx—were gone.

Chapter 29

For several long moments, no one moved, then Apollo hurried to her side and helped her to her feet before he wrapped her in a bone-crushing hug. "When Nyx showed up, I thought I had lost you," he murmured.

"Me, too," she admitted, clinging to him as she waited for her body to steady. It surprised her that she still didn't feel about to burst, having drained so much from both Dolos and Nyx, but she couldn't say she felt good. Dolos had bruised her in several places, and the cut along her side had started to ache and burn.

He drew back and cupped her face in one hand, just seeming to need to assure himself that she was alive, if not unharmed.

With the threat over, Chloe had to know everyone was okay. She looked her father over but, while he looked tired, he seemed to be uninjured. Tired she could help with. Resting her hand over his, she pushed some of the stolen power into him and saw his lips curve when he realized what she was doing.

"I'm okay," he assured her.

She smiled tiredly. "Good. Then you can help me heal the others."

"You first." He used some of that power to heal her

injuries, which she appreciated as the cut had begun to throb in time with her heartbeats.

"Thanks." She looked behind him, searching for the others, to make sure everyone was okay. She didn't see Lexi, Phillip, or Reece and wondered where they were, if they were okay. But there was Wesley, still in his grizzly form, standing on all fours, his claws and muzzle damp with what must be blood, but she couldn't tell if he was injured. Diego she saw, lying on the ground beneath Wesley, but it was impossible to tell from this distance if he was breathing or not. Peyton was slumped against the Oak, Mavros standing on her chest, but Chloe couldn't tell her status, either.

"Mavros? She alive?" she called.

The crow's voice was shockingly disappointed when he said, "Yes." He'd never come across as blood-thirsty, despite being a scavenger animal, but she couldn't truly blame him in this situation.

"She's Dolos's daughter," she told her dad and Zeus. "That's going to be a problem."

"No, it isn't," Zeus countered. Another wave of his hand, and Peyton disappeared, which caused Mavros to flap his wings rapidly as his feet were suddenly resting on nothing.

"Did you send her to her dad?" Chloe asked.

"I did," he confirmed with a tiny smile. "I thought it only fitting she spend eternity with her family."

"I appreciate that." She wasn't sure what else to say. No mouthing off to him this time, since she knew who he was and didn't have the excuse of being injured. It was still weird, knowing he was her grandfather.

Zeus inclined his head. "You were lucky. Not many go against Nyx and survive. I don't think she'll come back for you, but as far as Dolos, I've done all I could."

She frowned in confusion. "I thought banishment was permanent?"

Shaking his head, he answered, "Nothing is permanent in

our world, not even death. It's something you should remember, granddaughter." He gave Apollo one last, meaningful look, before he disappeared with his typical boom of thunder.

"I'm not sure how I feel about him calling me granddaughter," she admitted to her father.

Apollo chuckled. "You should feel good. He doesn't often acknowledge grandchildren."

Chloe nodded and walked toward Wesley. She wasn't scared of him in this form, even with the blood on him. Wesley wouldn't hurt her, and it wasn't that long ago that she had ridden on his back. "Are you going to shift back now?" she asked, running her hand over the coarse fur between his ears.

He leaned into her touch before his magic built and his form morphed back to human. One look told her why he'd been putting the transformation off. He always shifted back to human as naked as the day he was born. But he didn't give her a chance to be embarrassed that her dad was seeing her boyfriend nude. As soon as he had human arms again, he gripped her in a hug and buried his face against her neck. Calling it a bear hug was very apt in this situation, as it was tight enough to almost hurt. Since she had almost died, though, she wasn't going to ask him to let go.

"Are you okay?" he asked, voice still gruff.

"Dad healed me. Are you hurt?"

"Few burns, some bruises," he said, unconcerned.

Since her hands were touching skin, she didn't hesitate to focus on healing him. It might be the first time doing it intentionally on this scale, but she wasn't going to let him suffer one second longer than necessary, and her dad was probably checking on the others right now. To her relief, it only took a moment before she felt it work and he sighed as the pain disappeared.

"I should tell you something," he said, not yet loosening

his hold.

Dread tried to build in her belly. "Okay?"

"I kind of killed your ex."

That made the hug kind of creepy, since Wesley had been standing over Diego, and now they were standing beside him. Wrinkling her nose, she stepped back and away from the body, unable to resist looking down at him. There were some claw and bite marks, but the odd angle of his head told her that was probably what had ultimately killed him.

As she stared down at him, she struggled to figure out what she felt about his death. At one point she'd liked him, a lot. She'd slept with him, on multiple occasions, had invited him in her home, her bed. It was enough that it had hurt her when she discovered he'd been cheating on her. And then for her to find out it had all been a ploy to fuck with her and spy on her? It had been a lot. Too much, really.

Then she realized she felt nothing. It probably made her a bad person, but she felt absolutely nothing about him being dead. No relief, no joy, no sadness. It was simply a fact. And since he'd tried to kill her, she couldn't even feel guilt, not this time.

Pulling her gaze from Diego, she nodded at Wesley. "It happens, and he was trying to kill us."

He searched her face, no doubt searching for some sign she was holding something back, but she wasn't, not this time. Accepting that, he nodded. "The others?"

"Peyton's gone. Zeus sent her to Tartarus with the others. I haven't seen the others yet." But she turned to find them now. Phillip was back, and he and Apollo were standing the near the edge of the clearing. "Why don't you find something to put on while I check on them?" she suggested with a glance back to Wesley. "You did take your clothes off before shifting, right?"

"Mostly," he admitted, but he did go to retrieve them.

As Chloe approached her brother and dad, Lexi and

Reece came out of the trees. Reece still looked a little ragged, but Apollo touched him and the injuries disappeared. "Is everyone okay?" she asked.

"We had some injuries, but nothing fatal, of course," Phillip answered her. "Wesley okay?"

"He was hurt, too, but I think I took care of all his injuries. I'd appreciate it if one of you could check when he gets back, though," she said, looking between him and Apollo.

"Gets back?" Lexi asked.

"Yeah. He…ah…well, clothes don't shift with them, you know," Chloe mumbled.

"Damn. And I missed it?"

"Don't you have your own guy now?"

"Doesn't mean I can't enjoy a hot guy," Lexi answered cheerfully. "Is it really over though?"

"It is," Apollo confirmed. "At least for now. Dolos and Peyton were sent to Tartarus. Nyx will probably ensure he doesn't find some way to escape for a little while, but down the road he might pop up again."

"And Diego's dead," Chloe added, unable to force any emotion into the words.

Mavros finally joined them, happily perching on Chloe's shoulder, sending her waves of relief and love.

"You are getting so many treats when we get home," she told him, appreciating the fact that she had such a loyal familiar. She couldn't say he had been her first friend on Salus, but he was one of her best friends, right up there with Lexi.

"Speaking of home, could someone take me to mine?" Reece asked, sounding tired despite the healing.

"That's not a problem. We only brought two vehicles, but I think we can manage to fit everyone," Phillip answered with a smile.

"I'm going to head back to Olympus, so there will be

room enough for everyone." Apollo smiled at Chloe. "But I hope it would be okay if I visited you, now that it won't be putting you at risk?"

"Of course," Chloe answered without hesitation. "I'd love that."

"Good." He gave her one more hug. "And you can, of course, call for me if you need me, or just want to talk. I can't guarantee to show up instantly, but if I can come, I will."

She smiled as she gave him a warm squeeze then stepped back. "Thanks. I will."

"That goes for all of you. If you need me, let me know," he told the others before he disappeared.

"Phillip, can I ride with you and Reece?" Lexi asked. "I have a feeling Chloe and Wesley are going to steal my car, and I desperately want to go see Garrett. I'm all for protecting my family, but right now I just want some downtime. Cuddling with a sweet wolf might be just the ticket."

"Absolutely," Phillip answered.

"I do appreciate you guys helping with this," Chloe told them solemnly as she gave first Phillip, then Lexi a hug. "I know it was a long shot, going up against a couple of gods, especially with Nyx showing up." She paused, focused on the fox. "And I'm so freaking sorry you got wrapped up right in the middle of this and got hurt, Reece."

"It was my choice," Reece answered with a shrug and a smile. "Besides, you helped me when I needed it. This was just me returning the favor. So consider us even."

She gave him a hug, too and shook her head. "More than even. I think I owe you, now."

"Nope. Even."

She could only smile.

Wesley strolled up—clothed from the waist down, fortunately—and though he put his arm around Chloe's waist and pulled her in against him, he looked over the others. "Everyone okay?"

"Yeah, we're good, now," Lexi said, nodding. "Apollo healed us all."

"Speaking of…" Phillip laid a hand on Wesley's shoulder. After a moment he nodded to Chloe. "You did good. Nothing left to heal," he promised with a smile.

"Thanks." She looked the others over as she rested her head against Wesley's shoulder. Then she remembered she wanted to ask something before they dispersed. "Hey, Lex?"

"Yeah?"

"I know you were getting ghosts to help…did you just call any that were in the area, or were you calling specific ones?"

Lexi's normally open face closed down, as close to neutral as she could manage. "Both." She sighed. "And yes, Lydia was there."

"I thought so," she murmured. "I felt her. Just when everything went to hell."

"She insisted on helping as much as she could," Lexi admitted.

"She did. A lot," Chloe assured Lexi, though she didn't want to confess how close she'd been to shutting down before Granny had helped her. "So…thank you. To you and her. Hell, to all the ghosts."

Lexi smiled. "I'll let them know." She hugged Chloe, ignoring the bear attached to her. "I'm heading to Garrett's, but let me know if you need anything, okay?"

"I will," Chloe promised.

"I'll get in touch with Jack, get…that…cleaned up," Phillip told Wesley, nodding to Diego's body.

"Appreciate it," the sheriff told him. "Tell him I cleared it, but need to take care of a few things before I can assist."

"I'll give him the rundown of what happened, too, and contact the remaining councilors."

That wouldn't take him long, since one of the councilors

was dead, and the other banished to the darkest part of the Underworld, but it still needed done. Zane, Colin, and Natalia could handle things.

They split up then. Lexi, Phillip, and Reece all piled into Phillip's SUV, and Chloe climbed in the driver's seat of Lexi's car.

"You're staying at my place tonight," Wesley said, no give in his tone.

Chloe smiled and put the car into gear. "I was planning on it," she assured him, before driving into the night toward his house.

All the while knowing he wasn't as calm as he appeared to be.

Chapter 30

Wesley didn't say a word on the drive to his house. Even Mavros was silent, though he remained on Chloe's shoulder.

She parked next to the cruiser and they got out. The crow nipped her ear then flew off, but it wasn't unusual so Chloe didn't think much of it. Nor did she really think anything was odd when Wesley unlocked his front door and let Lykos out. The wolf took a moment to greet both people, before Mavros cawed and had the pup racing off into the trees to join his feathered friend.

Once the wolf was out of way, Wesley grabbed her hand and hauled her into the house. The moment they were both inside, he kicked the door closed, cupped her face, and gave her the fiercest, most intense kiss of her life.

Chloe felt her back hit the door but barely noticed, not with Wesley kissing her like if he stopped she'd slip away. Her brain went fuzzy, her only thought to kiss him back. To get as close as possible to him. To prove they were both still alive after going against the most feared deity in the Greek pantheon.

While he cradled her face in hands more gently than it looked like he should be capable of, she yanked his shirt upward and got her hands on the hot skin beneath. His muscles leapt beneath her fingers and he growled softly, only to break the kiss so he could pull the shirt up and off, tossing it to the side.

She took the opportunity to get rid of her own shirt before his mouth was on hers again. His fingers undid her bra and slid it down her arms as she kicked her shoes off. Cupping her breasts, he nipped at her bottom lip, even as she arched against his rough hands. When he bent his head, tasting her, teasing her with tongue and teeth, flames lit within her and dragged a moan from her throat.

A hand slid down her body, skimming over her belly, until he could undo the button of her jeans. She expected him to unzip them next, to peel them off her—and god, she wanted him to—but instead he straightened. His hands slid around to her ass, before he boosted her up. Her legs wrapped around his waist and she could feel the hardness pressed firmly against her core. Unable to resist, her arms wound around his neck and she tightened her legs, crushing them together. As she felt him walking, she lowered her lips to his throat, kissing and nibbling at the taut flesh, which made his hands tighten on her.

The next thing she knew, she was trapped between his hard body and the soft bed. Now he did tug her pants off, but when they were flung aside, he only had the patience to undo his own before his tall frame covered her once more. In the next instant, he was inside her, joining them as deeply as possible. Their twin moans mingled as they rocked together in the darkness.

The sex between them had been good—damn good—in the past. It had even been full of emotion. But now, as he stared into her eyes while he moved within her, something more intense, something deeper blossomed in her chest. It wasn't just relief they were both alive, though that was part of it, certainly. Nor was it simple love. This felt like they were joining in a way that went beyond the physical. She'd never believed in soul mates before, and wasn't sure she believed now, but there was nothing else to describe it.

Feeling the pleasure nearing its peak, her hands gripped the back of his head and pulled him down for a kiss. She wanted his lips on hers when she went over that sweet, sharp edge, and he complied easily. One arm slipped under her back while the other slid between their hips, stroking her and adding that last push she needed. Every nerve in her body lit up with pleasure and she cried out against his lips.

He was helpless not to join her, burying his face in the curve of her neck as all the fear, all the stress of the last few days emptied out of them, leaving them with nothing but relief and love.

His pants slipped down some as he moved them until they were fully on the bed, her draped over him, and she laid her head on his chest, listening to his heart beat beneath her ear. Fingers slid up and down along her spine, further relaxing her until she started to drift off.

"I thought Diego was going to kill you before I could get there," he murmured, and she felt the rumble of it.

"I know. I thought I was dead, too," she admitted, her voice equally as soft. "But he didn't."

"No, he didn't. None of them did, but it was still a lot closer than I would have liked." His hand stilled and his arms just wrapped around her, almost too tight for comfort. "I can't believe you fucking went up against Nyx. Don't think I missed that you attacked her, either. I may not be an aether or a witch, but I'm not dumb, either."

"I never thought you were dumb. A pain in my ass sometimes, but not dumb." With some effort, she lifted her head until their eyes met. "I had to attack her, Yogi," she whispered. "That darkness…" She shook her head and tried to figure out how to relay the way it had felt without letting herself dwell on it too much. "It didn't just make things dark. When it was over my eyes, I was blind. When it was over my skin, I couldn't feel. When it was over my mouth and nose…"

"You couldn't breathe," he concluded softly.

She nodded. "Yeah. If I hadn't attacked her, if my dad hadn't attacked her, I don't know if I would have lasted long enough for Zeus to show up." Pausing, she remembered that last look Nyx had given her. "I don't think she blames me for it. I'm not even sure she actually wanted to kill me."

"No?"

"No. I think she sort of respected me for fighting back, even against her. And as for killing me?" She shrugged lightly. "I wasn't—I'm still not—anything to her, not really. She just wanted her son alive. And since I got the impression that draining all his magic would have killed him, she was just protecting her child."

He arched a brow and that lazy brush of his fingers up and down her spine resumed. "It almost sounds like you respect her, too."

"I kind of do," she admitted. "She didn't strike me as crazy. She wasn't acting out of anger or some warped sense of vengeance or justice like Dolos was. She was just protecting her kid, despite the fact that he was so fucking crazy you could almost smell it. I can't blame someone for protecting their kid. If I had one, I like to think I'd be the same way."

His hand stilled. "Do you want a kid? Someday, I mean?"

Like his hand, she froze. Part of her wanted to analyze that question, but she was honestly too tired for that. No, she went with simple honesty. "Someday, sure." She smiled faintly and laid her head on his chest once more. "It's not like I don't have time to figure out being a demigod aether before I worry about learning how to change diapers and make a bottle."

He smiled faintly. "True."

For several minutes they simply enjoyed the closeness,

the quiet. The utter serenity that came from knowing no one was currently gunning for her. That maybe she could have some peace, to truly figure out her new life. To enjoy being in a relationship with Wesley, to learn about her brother and father, and to spend time with her best friend.

He broke the silence again. It was almost like he had some sense of when she was about to fall asleep. "What will it take to convince you to move in here with me?"

She cracked an eye open but felt her lips curve. Hopefully he couldn't see the smile in the dark. "Why should I move in here? Maybe you should move in with me. It is a family place, after all. Dad even told me I was born there."

"Yeah, but your backyard is full of trees. I've got the lake and the view."

Damn. She couldn't argue that. He did have a better backyard than she did. Not to mention his house was bigger.

He wasn't done, though. "Lykos seems to like the yard, too. And when it warms up, I'll bet he'll be playing in the lake."

"That's not necessarily a good thing," she said dryly. "Don't wet wolves stink?"

"No more than wet bears."

"I've never smelled you when you were both a bear and wet," she pointed out.

"Hell, Boo-Boo. I'll go outside, shift, and let you spray me with the fucking hose if it means you'll say yes," he drawled before his fingers teased along her side until he found a ticklish spot and made her squirm.

She swatted at his hand until he subsided, then waited until she was sure opening her mouth wasn't going to result in a laugh. "I'll say yes under two conditions."

His eyes narrowed with amused suspicion. "What two conditions?"

"First, you tell me you love me."

He chuckled. "That one's easy enough. I love you. More

than I thought I'd love an annoying PI who started causing trouble her first twenty-four hours on the island."

Now her eyes turned to slits. "I'm not sure if that's an acceptable 'I love you'."

He only laughed harder. "Fine. I love you, Chloe Chadwick." He paused. "Better?"

"I suppose."

"What's condition two?"

For this one she looked up at him, wanting to watch his reaction. "Sometime in the next year, I want you to make an honest woman out of me."

His lips curved into a slow smile. "Is that it?"

What kind of reaction was that? He was amused by it? What exactly did that mean? "Yeah, that's it," she replied, knowing her voice was a little snappish.

"That's easy enough then." He rolled her off him and toward the center of the bed. Unencumbered, he swung in the other direction, turned on the lamp, and pulled open the drawer of his nightstand. After grabbing something, he rolled back to her, holding it up for her to see.

Even in the dim light, she could make out the shape of a ring box. She didn't move, only stared at it for a long moment before looking to him. "Wesley?" she asked, voice quiet and not quite certain.

"This was my grandmother's. She gave it to me when I was thirty or so but held onto it. Told me to let her know when I found someone I loved as much as she loved my grandfather, and she'd send it to me." He opened the box, letting her see the ring inside. The band was white gold, with tiny, intricate swirls and lines, and had a single solitaire. Her breath caught when she realized the stone was a teal sapphire.

A hunch had her asking, "When did you ask her to send it to you?"

He drew in a deep breath, smiled faintly, and said, "Do

you remember the first time I kissed you?"

"In the office? Of course." She wasn't likely to forget.

"A couple days after that."

She blinked. "But…" She shook her head. "Not only was I was with that rat bastard then, but there's no way you could have loved me back then! You barely knew me. And most of that time you suspected me of murder."

"No," he said firmly as he shook his head. "I never actually suspected you. I had to go through the process, but I knew you weren't a murderer."

"Okay, but you still barely knew me," she insisted.

"No, I didn't know you well," he agreed, "but some part of me knew. Maybe it was because the ring matches your eyes, maybe it's an animalistic thing, maybe it was something else entirely. But I *knew* this ring was meant for you."

She believed him. It was a little crazy, but she believed he meant every word. "Now I feel bad for the time I spent with him and not you," she admitted. "But I realized, after I caught him with Peyton, that I was only with him because he was…safe."

His brow furrowed. "You don't think I'm safe? You know I'd never—"

"Emotionally safe," she cut in. "I could like him, could care about him, but I couldn't love him and wasn't likely to actually be hurt by him. With everything else that had changed, I subconsciously opted for the guy who couldn't actually touch me."

He grinned. "Does that mean you're going to accept the ring, then?"

"Depends." She twisted until she could free her left hand, wiggle her fingers. "You going to put it on me?"

He pulled the ring from the box and gently slid it onto her finger. "So?" he prompted as he ran the tip of a finger along the back of her hand. "Will you marry me?"

"I suppose I have to, now, because you're not getting this

ring off my finger."

The box got tossed over his shoulder before he pulled her into him and kissed her again.

When Chloe had first been told the truth about herself and her family, she thought she'd never catch her breath, never get her feet beneath her again.

Now, she knew she wouldn't, but she fully intended to enjoy every moment of the wild ride, with Wesley and her family, right by her side.

MEG M. ROBINSON

Epilogue

Two weeks later...

"What happened to you not having a lot of stuff?" Lexi asked as she lifted a box from the trunk of Chloe's car.

"I don't," Chloe said with a grin as she dodged the happy wolf who was running like a maniac around the people moving like ants between Chloe's car, Phillip's SUV, and the cabin on the lake. "My stuff was all moved in three days ago," she explained as she grabbed a chest from the back seat.

"Then what is all this?"

"Granny's stuff. Phillip and I made a quick trip to Boston to clear out the rest of her things from her house."

"That makes more sense," Lexi said after a moment before she carried the box inside.

"I'm just wondering what Wesley thinks about his house being overtaken by your stuff," Phillip said as he grabbed the last box out of his vehicle and closed the door with his hip.

"That I have an attic and your sister's been a pain in my ass since the day I met her," the man in question said, but when Chloe shot him a glare, he was grinning. Even the shoulder bump Phillip gave him didn't diminish it.

She strode over to him and dumped the trunk in his arms.

"You love every minute of it," she told him before kissing him lightly.

"Eh, I'd say every other minute."

Laughing, Chloe went back to her car, grabbing the last box as Zane peeked around her. "What can I grab?" he asked.

"Just my bag." She pointed with her elbow. "This is the last of the boxes."

Going inside, Zane and Lykos following after her, she carried it to the guest room that had temporarily been turned into a storage room. Only until she could sort things out, she'd promised Wesley. But they both knew the bulk of it would end up in his attic.

She took the bag Zane held out to her and dropped it on the dresser in the bedroom she now shared with Wesley. "You hungry?"

He grinned and adjusted his glasses. "I know I look like I never eat, but I'm pretty much always hungry."

"Think Cole and Wesley have the grill going, yet?"

"Probably."

"What is Cole, anyway?" she asked in a low voice as they made their way toward the back deck. Despite the snow on the ground, Wesley and Chloe had decided to repay the help people had given by doing dinner. Since neither of them could cook all that well, nor did they want to just order pizza or take out from Banquet, they'd gone for Wesley's one major culinary skill. Grilling steaks.

"You don't know?" Zane asked, surprised.

She shook her head. "He's never used any magic around me, so there was nothing for me to sense."

A smile curved his lips. "I think there probably was, actually. Active magic or not, we still have that magic within us. I'll bet if you focused, you could sense it and identify what a person was."

Her feet just stopped and she stared at him. After a

moment, she laughed. "I guess I haven't graduated beyond needing mentors, huh? Elemental or the whole," she wiggled her fingers mysteriously, "demigod crap."

Zane chuckled. "No one ever learns everything, so everyone needs a teacher their entire life, even if that teacher is them. He's a metal elemental, though."

Handy, for a mechanic. She wondered if his powers had inspired his job, even. "That kind of makes sense," she decided with a nod as they headed through the kitchen and onto the back deck.

Wesley and Cole were indeed standing in front of the grill, the latter just placing potatoes on the grates. Phillip sat in a chair, Mavros perched on his knee, both watching as Lykos raced around the yard, chasing something only he could see. Garrett was leaning against the railing, one arm loosely wrapped around Lexi's waist as she leaned against him, a beer in his other hand.

When Zane crossed to Cole, running his hand down the other man's arm, Chloe just stopped and took in the sight, unable to prevent a smile from claiming her lips. With the exception of her dad, all of her favorite people in one place. Even better, everything was quiet, peaceful. Oh sure, there had been plenty for her and Wesley to do at work since Dolos had been sent to Tartarus, but nothing major.

As if she'd summoned him—and maybe she had—there was a flash of light that heralded her father's appearance. Everyone stopped, but as soon as it registered that it was friend, not foe, they relaxed once more. Garrett looked a bit awestruck, and Chloe realized this might be the first time he'd ever met the sun god. He hadn't been around when they were chasing Dolos.

"Hi, Dad," Phillip said, grinning at the god. "I was wondering if you were going to show up."

Chloe wasn't as restrained. She hurried across the deck and hugged Apollo tight. "I was wondering *when* you were going to show up," she admitted as he gave her a warm squeeze.

"Of course. Didn't I tell you I was going to be popping in?" Apollo asked when he drew back, only so he could crouch down to rub an ecstatic Lykos.

"Yeah, but that was two weeks ago," she pointed out.

He glanced up and smiled. "You've been busy."

Her eyes narrowed. "Have you been spying on me?"

His gaze flicked to Phillip, to Lexi, then back to Chloe before he grinned. "Not a bit."

Oh, she didn't miss that. "Have you two been *reporting* on me?" she accused her brother and best friend.

"I haven't seen him since that night," Lexi promised, though she couldn't quite meet Chloe's gaze.

Phillip didn't hedge, but nodded and said, simply, "Yes."

Chloe folded her arms over her chest and gave them both the look they deserved. "You do realize that he can ask me himself how I'm doing, right? And I'm not a kid."

"You're his kid," Phillip said with a shrug, picking up his beer and taking a drink.

Wesley made the mistake of chuckling and earned a glare of his own. "Don't blame me. I didn't give him daily updates." He crossed the deck to wrap an arm around her shoulder and kissed the top of her head.

Chloe was both resigned and delighted when Apollo focused his attention on Wesley. Specially, the arm that was currently wrapped around her shoulders, not quite possessively, but like it simply belonged there.

"Maybe you should have," Apollo said, his voice deceptively calm. It didn't fool Chloe, not even for a second. Judging by the slight tension in Wesley's arm, it didn't fool him either.

"Why is that?" Wesley asked, keeping his words just as even.

"Because then you could have also told me exactly what

you're planning to do with my daughter."

Yep, all the amusement faded. "Dad," she groaned. "Can we not do the what are your intentions with my daughter thing?"

"I missed out on your childhood, Chloe, even your teenage years. I think I'm entitled to act like a dad now and again."

"It's fine," Wesley said, glancing to Phillip. "You didn't tell him?"

Oh, Chloe wanted to punch her brother the moment the shit-eating grin appeared on his lips. "I didn't think it was my place," he answered.

Wesley only sighed and used his free hand to reach for Chloe's left, lifting it so the ring on her finger glinted in the fading sunlight. "I'm planning to marry her, love her, and give you lots of grandbabies."

Chloe's eyes went wide and she felt her face go pale. "G-grandbabies?" she sputtered. They'd talked about babies—once—and she wanted them at some point, but she wasn't quite ready yet to be a mom. Maybe in a decade or two, but not now.

Everyone there, her father included, devolved into laughter at her reaction. Apollo was the first to recover, though, and smiled at her. "Hopefully not too soon. I want to spend time with you before my attention is taken away by other adorable little demigods."

"Definitely not too soon," she said quickly. "We just moved in together!"

"That's okay. We have lots of time, and the longer we wait..." Wesley trailed off, considered, then bent his head to whisper in her ear, "The longer we wait, the more we can practice how to make babies."

While she thoroughly approved of lots of practice, she wasn't going to say so with her dad standing just a few feet away. Deciding to change the subject, she cleared her throat and focused on her father. "There's something I've been wondering. Two somethings, actually. Didn't get the chance before, since we had bigger priorities."

Apollo's head cocked. "What's that?"

"First, do you know how I can speak Greek without ever studying it?"

"Oh, I can answer that," Phillip chimed in.

"Then why didn't you tell her before?" Lexi asked as she bent her head back to rest against Garrett's shoulder.

"I didn't know it was bothering her." But he did give Chloe an apologetic look. "It's not something all demigods get, but from what I've heard, the closer you are to the Olympians, genetically, the more likely you are to have it sort of written into your DNA."

"Really?" Zane asked, his inner-geek intrigued. "Is it the same dialect for all demigods, or does it differ? Are there different levels of fluency?"

Apollo studied Zane curiously for a moment. "The same dialect, and if they have the ability, they all seem to be able to speak it like a native speaker. You're the one who helped Chloe learn to use her aether abilities, aren't you?"

Realizing the god was focused on him, the tips of Zane's ears went pink and Cole chuckled. Chuckled! Chloe hadn't known that was possible. "I am..."

"I told the others that if they ever needed me to call for me and I'd be there if I could. I'd like to extend that to you as well. You helped her survive, and that's not something I can ever repay."

The redness spread from Zane's ears to his cheeks. "No need to repay me. I—"

"You helped my daughter survive," Apollo repeated, voice measured, serious.

Helplessly, Zane glanced from Chloe, to Cole, then back to Chloe.

"Don't look at me. I'm with him on this one," Chloe told

him with a smile.

"I...thank you," he finally said.

"You said there were two things, though?" Apollo asked when he turned his attention back to Chloe.

"Yeah." She'd worn the necklace she'd found since the night they'd confronted Dolos. The spell had been depleted, but she'd kept it on for some reason. Now she tugged it from beneath her sweater so he could see it. "Do you know anything about this? I found it in a false compartment in one of Granny's trunks. It had a note with it that said it was for protection, but no signature. I also didn't sense any magic on it, so I'm not sure how it could protect anyone."

He stepped closer, letting the pendant rest on his fingertip. A smile teased at his lips. "This is the necklace you tied that spell to, isn't it? The one to protect against god powers?"

She nodded. "It is."

"So it was for protection?"

"Well, yeah, but only after I made it that way."

He let the necklace drop and arched a brow. "But it was still for protection?" he pressed.

Something in his tone tickled her subconscious. "Did you give it to her?"

His lips curved fully, now. "No, I didn't. But I know who did."

"Who?" Lexi asked, unable to keep quiet, but Apollo's eyes remained on Chloe's.

"Your grandfather."

Chloe frowned. "Zeus gave my grandmother a necklace?" she asked skeptically. It didn't sound like his style.

Wesley snorted, while both Apollo and Phillip chuckled. "No," her dad answered, "not him. Your other grandfather. Your mother's father."

"Lachlan?" He nodded. "I don't get it. Wasn't he a fire elemental?"

"He was, but as you were told months ago, sometimes even elementals get visions."

"You?" Wesley asked.

"Me," he confirmed.

"If you knew, why didn't you stop it sooner?"

The amusement disappeared from Apollo's face. "Even for the gods, it doesn't always work like that. True, my prophecies tend to be clearer than most, but having another god involved can obscure things. I knew that necklace would be instrumental in protecting someone I cared about, that it needed to get to Lydia, but nothing else, not then."

Chloe drew away from Wesley and wrapped her arms around her dad. "It's okay. We did stop Dolos, and I still ended up on Salus. Still found my family," she told him as he held her tight.

"You did," he agreed, his voice rough, "but I wish you hadn't had to suffer so much to get to this point."

"Same here." She really wished she had gotten a chance to know her mom, and to know the true Granny, but did her best not to wallow in those thoughts. "We can't change the past, though, and we won, finally. Let's focus on that."

Apollo kissed the top of her head before he leaned back and smiled at her. "Of course."

A quick, whispered conversation between Zane and Cole had Chloe, then everyone else, looking in the direction of the two elementals. "What's up?" Lexi asked them.

They realized they had the attention of everyone present and went quiet, Zane blushing lightly again. But it wasn't the sweet, nerdy one who spoke, but the taciturn Cole. "You want to focus on the good, right?" he asked, directing the question to Chloe.

"Sure," she answered slowly, curious as to what was going on in his grumpy brain.

He nodded sharply, straightened, and slid his arm around Zane's, pulling the taller man in snug against him. "We're also getting married."

For several seconds there was no reaction but for Zane's ears going bright red. It took that long for everyone else to process the unexpected words.

Lexi let out a squeal and rushed them, throwing her arms not just around Zane, but Cole as well. The latter didn't look particularly pleased to be included but accepted the excited embrace. His scowl only deepened when Chloe did the same thing the moment Lexi released them. Even the congratulations from the other men didn't dampen his innate surliness.

"When did this happen?" Lexi asked, beaming at the couple.

"I don't care about the when, I'm just so happy for you two," Chloe said when she stepped back, grinning. Happy and more than a little pleased. Months ago, she'd given them the tiniest of nudges, just wanting Zane to have a chance with the man he clearly had a thing for. She had no idea how successful that nudge would be.

Maybe she actually had a knack for this matchmaking thing.

"It's new," Zane assured Lexi, giving her a shy smile, though it did nothing to hide the elation in his eyes.

Lexi's smile was sly and she glanced from Zane to Chloe. "Maybe you two could have a double wedding."

Cole shook his head, giving the eye to Phillip and Apollo. "Don't think so."

Zane cleared his throat. "What he means is, we want something small, just with close friends and family, and your wedding is, well, you've got a lot more family, so it would be bigger," he clarified diplomatically.

Chloe grinned. "I may have more family, but I haven't met them all," she pointed out.

He leaned toward her and dropped his voice, but it didn't actually hide the words from anyone. "Yeah, but your family is full of *gods*."

She smothered a laugh but nodded. "True enough."

Apollo sniffed and leaned against the railing. "Not all of us are high maintenance," he pointed out.

Phillip burst out laughing. "Yeah, but her step-grandmother is the goddess of marriage. She might not like how her husband sleeps around, but she does like Apollo, and loves weddings."

"Holy shit," Chloe burst out, realizing just who he was talking about. It was yet another familial relationship she hadn't put together before that moment. "Are you seriously saying Hera might come to the wedding?"

Wesley looked a little ill. "Do you think we could elope?"

Waving a warning finger at him, Lexi shook her head. "Nuh uh. No way am I missing her wedding!"

"Neither am I," Phillip said firmly.

Apollo simply folded his arms over his chest and smiled, showing perfect white teeth. Clearly, he wasn't going to miss the wedding either.

Wesley groaned and dropped his forehead to Chloe's hair. "See what I mean, Boo-Boo? Constant pain in my ass."

Since she felt a little like he looked, she couldn't protest this time. It was one thing to think of her dad coming to her wedding, god or not. It was another thing to think of other Olympians showing up. "How likely is it there will be a lot of gods at the wedding?" she asked weakly.

"A lot?" Apollo shook his head. "Not likely. A handful of them?" He shrugged. "You should probably count on it. Myself, my stepmother, and my sister for sure. Artemis is excited to meet you. Zeus doesn't really do weddings, but Hypnos might show up."

Chloe sighed and leaned her head against Wesley's shoulder before she smiled, resigned. "Then yeah, no double wedding. I wouldn't do that to you, Zane."

"Thank you," he said with utter sincerity—and a slight

green tinge to his face.

"Oh come on, it's not that bad," Lexi protested. "And it's not right now, either. Let's eat and relax and just be happy that we survived!"

Cole and Wesley went back to the grill, while Chloe leaned against the railing, her dad on one side, Lexi on the other. And despite the gods she would probably be meeting at her wedding, she could only smile. She'd gone from having absolutely no one, to this growing group of friends and family. As crazy as they might all make her, she wouldn't trade them in for anything.

She watched Cole and Wesley bicker about the proper way to grill steaks. Saw Phillip absently petting Mavros while Lykos curled up literally on Apollo's feet. Listened to Lexi and Zane discussing wedding ideas. All she could thing was, Now, I'm really home.

About the Author

Meg is a fantasy author who lives in north Georgia with her husband of eighteen years, teenage son, and a zoo full of critters. She's unapologetically goofy, which amuses her family to no end.

Her favorite hobbies do revolve around writing, as she reads more than she cares to admit. When she's not working on her next story, or enjoying someone else's, she enjoys playing video games, camping with her family, or being crafty, in a very literal sense. Fortunately, she currently has a job which allows her to plot and write at work, which gives her plenty of time to work on the next story.

She's loved Greek mythology and any story of the supernatural (with the exception of pure supernatural horror) since she was a child, and tries to incorporate the myths she's heard into her stories. It was actually the mystery surrounding Stonehenge that led her back to writing and helped her finish her first novel-length story. She's always on the lookout for a new myth or mysterious artifact to help spark her creativity. Her catch phrase when it comes to writing is "What if?", as it opens up so many possibilities.

You can find more about Meg M. Robinson and her upcoming novels here:

https://megmrobinson.com/
https://www.facebook.com/megmrobinson

CPSIA information can be obtained
at www.ICGtesting.com
Printed in the USA
LVHW032156080922
727900LV00004B/57

9 798985 016437